STONE GROOVE

ERIK CARTER

For Mom and Dad,
who both, in their own ways, inspired my love of story.

CHAPTER ONE

Washington, D.C.
The 1970s

HE'D BEEN TOLD to maintain his position, but Dale Conley had never let something like a set of orders get in his way.

His target had suddenly mobilized, heading right toward the Memorial. And Dale could see the shape of a rifle under the man's bulky field jacket.

Dale was going to follow the target.

To hell with his orders.

He was among a crowd of tourists outside the Jefferson Memorial, by the water's edge. The people around him were all smiles, chatting, the pleasant hum of vacationers happily taking in world-famous sights. It was still morning, but the air was very warm, almost hot were it not for the strong breeze. The sky was bright blue with billowy clouds. Gentle waves in the Tidal Basin lapped against the curved retaining wall.

To this point, Dale had been looking out to the water and the Washington Monument beyond, remaining as inconspicuous as possible as he occasionally shifted his attention to someone standing nearer to the massive rotunda behind him: Willard Ledford, the guy Dale had been trailing for the last three weeks. He was a monster of a man in a long, olive green military field jacket. Six-foot-three with lengthy arms. His skin needed a good washing, his cheeks were covered with a mangle of dark scruff, and his eyes had that same wild look that all the crazies had.

For the last ten minutes, Ledford had been staring toward the massive marble structure. It had a portico entrance, capped with a decorated pediment, that led to the main rotunda—one hundred sixty-five feet in diameter with a colonnade of twenty-six Ionic columns, perched high atop an expansive plane of terraced steps. The design was open-air with a shallow dome as the roof, and inside, towering over flocks of onlookers snapping photographs, was the celebrated nineteen-foot bronze sculpture of Thomas Jefferson—one of the nation's Founding Fathers, primary penman of the United States Declaration of Independence, and the country's third president.

Standing in the shadow of Jefferson was the person whom Ledford had been observing from a distance: Frank Ayers, a nineteen-year-old Senate intern. He was tall and gangly, his suit fitting loosely over his bony frame. Acne peppered his cheeks. His hair was parted in so perfect a way as to make a statement. A declaration, if you will. This was a young man with ambitions.

For several minutes, Ayers had stood alone. And during this time, his eyes had bounced quickly, nervously over the crowd until his contact arrived—a middle-aged man with big cheeks and a big stomach. Like Ayers, the man wore a suit, though his looked cheaper, less deliberate. The pair struck an urgent conversation, both of them periodically stealing glances at the crowd around them.

It was the moment at which the second man arrived that

Ledford made his move. Ayers had no idea that the big man had been watching him, that Ledford was now moving in on him like an apex predator. But Ledford, similarly, had been ignorant to Dale's surveillance.

And to the fact that he was now being followed.

Dale slipped into the crowd, moving quickly enough to begin closing the gap but not so quickly as to draw a reaction from the people around him and alert Ledford. The guy was easy for Dale to track, as the peak of his head—with its greasy, unkempt hair—towered over the others while he wormed his way closer to the Memorial.

A scratchy voice came from the small device in Dale's right ear.

"Conley, what the hell are you doing?"

Dale knew that there would be an immediate response to his change of position. He angled his face slightly lower, toward the microphone clipped to the collar of his leather jacket. "Taking action. Ledford's on the move."

"*Stand down.* Do you want to blow this whole operation for us?"

"I thought you were ready for this assignment to be over, Agent Mather? That you were sick and tired of this 'smartass agent' the powers-that-be brought in to lend you a hand?"

And, right on cue, Dale felt a smartass grin come to the corners of his lips.

The response that sounded in Dale's earpiece was more of an animalistic growl than human language. "Damn you..."

Dale looked up, briefly taking his attention away from Ledford's massive frame as it split the crowd in front of him, climbing the steps. At the far end of the Memorial, leaning against one of the gigantic marble pillars, was Colton Mather, Dale's partner for this assignment. Colt was in his early forties, black, slightly short and with an average build. Mustache and sideburns. He wore a dark brown corduroy suit with flared legs, a pale yellow shirt, plaid tie. He held a tourist pamphlet to his face, pretending to read it, and he looked over its top edge, directly at Dale. Even from a distance, and even with most of Colt's face covered, Dale could see the anger flowing out of him.

Dale pulled off his sunglasses, put them in the pocket of his jacket, and locked eyes with Colt as he responded. He needed to make direct eye contact with him; Colt needed to see just how serious Dale was being.

"Three weeks we've been watching them," Dale said. "I follow Ledford; you follow Ayers. This is the sixth time Ayers has met here with his contact, and every other time, Ledford's kept his distance from the kid, always stayed outside the Memorial watching the other two. Ledford's planning something."

And whatever that "something" was, Dale could sense that it was going to be big. He felt a sense of foreboding sizzling across the warm morning breeze.

Colt's reply was even more perturbed than his last one. "We still don't fully know what Ayers and his contact have been meeting about, whether Ayers is doing this on the Senator's behalf or behind his back. We're *this close* to figuring it out, and if you blow our cover, we may never know. What makes you so sure Ledford's up to something?"

"Call it gut instinct."

There were a thousand tangible factors in Dale's line of work, but at the end of the day, he put most of his faith in his intuition. And it rarely let him down.

"Your *gut instinct?* Conley, my SAC gave us a strict order to observe only. I was working this case for two months before you came on. The AG is keeping tabs on this, for God's sake. Don't screw this up for me. I repeat, stand down. When we—"

"He has a gun, Colt."

A slight pause.

"What?"

"Ledford has a rifle."

A longer pause. Then a quiet reply.

"You'd better be right about this, Conley." The speaker in Dale's ear hissed as Colt let out a sigh. "I'll head that direction. We can close in on him."

"No, you stick with Ayers. If something goes down, the kid's gonna be scared shitless. He's already a nervous wreck. When he sees that a six-foot-three, homeless Grim Reaper is out to get him, you'll have him singing like a sparrow."

Dale ascended another one of the terraced steps leading to the portico. He'd nearly closed the gap—Ledford was only about twenty feet away, halfway up to the building. Above, Ayers still stood with his contact by the bronze sculpture, heads lowered, nodding, an important conversation.

Ledford then stopped, got down on one knee, and threw off his jacket.

And there was the rifle.

It was a precision piece of craftsmanship and spotless. A long scope rested on top. The stock was stained a deep brown, the sun glinting off its highly-polished finish. All of it was clean and oiled and maintained and pristine—exactly the opposite of Ledford himself. And as Ledford cradled the gun expertly in his hands and got into position, the poise with which he did so made Dale wonder if he'd been a sniper in Vietnam.

There was only a half second before the crowd perceived the danger. A couple solitary screams echoed through the marble followed quickly by an all-encompassing pandemonium. A surge of energy rushed through the crowd, and everyone changed direction, heading away from the Memorial. They bashed into Dale as they funneled around him on either side.

Dale drew his Smith & Wesson. He glanced up for a fraction of a second, just long enough to see Ayers and his contact drop to the floor, taking cover, and Colt sprinting toward them. His attention returned to Ledford.

The man's broad chest raised as he took in a long, deep breath. A sniper's breathing technique. This guy was trained.

And he was going to shoot.

Dale planted one foot on the step ahead of him, getting a solid position, and aimed his revolver at Ledford. More screams, panicked eyes, people clearing out of his way. Before he could fire, though, Ledford quickly pulled his face away from his rifle's scope. There had been a shout.

Someone in uniform was flying down the steps toward Ledford, much closer than Dale, almost upon him—a Park Police officer, pudgy and short. He shouted.

"*Hey!*"

Ledford swung the rifle away from the rotunda and fired.

There was a spray of red mist from the backside of the cop's shoulder. A scream, an anguished face, and he hit the stone steps hard, knocking himself unconscious.

Ledford quickly pivoted the rifle back toward the rotunda. Unlike the precision tactics of a few moments earlier, Ledford was now going the brute force method. There was no preparatory breathing technique. He just immediately began to squeeze the rifle's trigger.

Dale didn't have a moment to spare. He fired.

The shot *cracked* across the stone surroundings.

Ledford roared.

Like the Park Police officer's wound, the round struck Ledford in the shoulder. But Ledford didn't grab the wound. Nor did he writhe in agony.

He just stood up.

And faced Dale.

Dale was running toward him, up the steps, within feet of

him. He leveled his revolver again, but Ledford swung one of his loping arms, the fist cracking right into Dale's weapon.

Since a gunshot had been but a nuisance to Ledford, it wasn't a surprise to Dale that punching a hard piece of metal didn't faze the man. The gun flew from Dale's hands and clattered on the stone steps, sliding several feet away, well out of reach.

Dale flew at Ledford and got both hands on the rifle just as Ledford was about to aim it toward Dale. The two of them struggled for possession of the gun. Dale gritted his teeth, putting everything he had against the big man's brawn, but he quickly felt the power struggle shift in Ledford's direction. Dale kept himself in great shape, but this guy had natural strength. Beast strength.

Dale felt the metal barrel quiver in his left hand as it began to move down and toward Dale's face. Ledford's grimace became flavored by a bit of a smile. He intended on blowing Dales brains out point-blank. And he was going to enjoy it.

Dale wasn't going to be able to outwrestle an oversized demon. He'd have to use a bit more finesse. One leg behind Ledford's, hooking the knee. He clenched his hands tighter on the rifle and gave it a solid tug.

Then Ledford fell. Right toward Dale.

The solid wall of human mass that was Willard Ledford crashed down upon Dale, and Dale's leather jacket provided little cushioning as both men landed hard against the marble. There was a quick, sharp pain as the stone steps dug into his back.

The rifle flew away, bouncing erratically, loudly, heading toward the Tidal Basin. Like Dale's gun, it was now well out of reach for both men.

Dale's cheek smashed into cold marble. He felt his lip split, tasted blood. He stole a glance to the rotunda. Ayers sprinted out of the columns, down the terraced steps. Colt followed in hot pursuit, shouting. In the distance was the sound of approaching police sirens.

Dale felt big arms and legs clambering all over him. He tried to pry his legs through Ledford's to gain some leverage, but the creep quickly wrapped one of his arms around Dale's neck and squeezed hard. A bulging bicep crushed Dale's throat, and he coughed.

"Who the hell are you?" Ledford said. He sounded as crazy as he looked. And he stank.

Dale grunted, fighting for breath as he spoke. "Call me an admirer of sorts, Willie. I've been following your work for the last few weeks."

"I was just about to take one of the conspirators off the planet before you interrupted, goddamn you! I keep a careful eye on the Memorial. I come here every day, knowing that *someday* I'd catch one of them. And then I finally found one. That kid. He's been holding secret meetings here for the last couple months."

"And why have you taken it upon yourself to be the Memorial's guardian angel?"

"Because the Jefferson Memorial has been a meeting place for Freemasons for thirty years."

Dale would have rolled his eyes if they weren't about to pop out of his head. The work Dale did for his agency frequently brought him into direct contact with weirdos just like this—those who think the whole world's in on some master plan, and they've figured it all out.

"Somebody's seen one too many episodes of *Outer Limits*."

Dale's neck was in a vice. He stuck his fingers beneath Ledford's forearm and pulled up with all he had. It didn't budge.

"It's a modern version of the pagan Pantheon." Ledford spoke quickly with short, choppy breaths. He pulled his face around to Dale's, inches apart, keeping Dale's neck hooked in his elbow. "Masons use Pantheon structures as allusions to the Temple of Solomon. The Dome of the Rock. The Knights Templar knew the truth, that the Dome was the site of Solomon's Temple. And that's why Masons continue to use Pantheon domes in their buildings. This one here in the world's capital is the perfect meeting place."

"You're blending your history, Willard. Stirring up your myths. Individually, the things you're referencing are real. Thrown together, they make no sense whatsoever." Dale pulled at Ledford's arm, and the grip tightened even further. "You see, I work for a special group within the Department of Justice, using my expertise in history. And I've been watching you. When a homeless man starts trailing a Senate intern while at the same time making multiple trips to the Library of Congress to research Freemasonry, it throws up a few red flags. Go in without a fight and make this as easy on yourself as you can."

Ledford tugged at Dale's neck. "I don't think you're in any position to make demands."

"Sure I am. And you know why? Apple pie."

Dale felt the grip around his neck lighten ever so slightly. The bizarreness of his last comment had truly perplexed Ledford—which had been the intent.

"Apple pie?" Ledford said in that unsettling, cracking voice of his.

"That's right. Rich's Diner. Ever been? Best pie in the city."

It really was. The apple pie had even been voted so by area residents, having made it onto the *Best of D.C.: Desserts* list three years in a row. The rest of the food at Rich's was fairly pedestrian, but the pies were heavenly.

And for some reason, as he wrestled with Ledford on the cold, hard steps outside the Jefferson Memorial, the thought of Rich's apple pie had entered Dale's mind. The taste of it. Dale savored the little things in life. They were what made grappling with the likes of Willard Ledford worthwhile.

"I'm about to put you away, Willard. And while you're sitting in a jail cell awaiting your fate, I'm gonna go and enjoy a slice of the world's best pie. Plus there's this cute new waitress there I've been meaning to talk to."

"I'm not going anywhere," Ledford hissed. He paused, tilting his head to listen to the approaching sirens, which were louder now, echoing through the columns at the rotunda above. "I'll never let myself be taken by a corrupt and wicked bureaucracy. I'm going to snuff out your life then I'll take my own. Two men on opposite sides of tyrannical government control, bowing out together. Yin and yang. Very poetic."

Ledford tightened his grip even more. Dale gagged, and his eyes watered.

"Never been into poetry myself," Dale said. "I'm more of a rock and roll kind of guy."

Visualization. It's what athletes used to win games; it's what businessmen did before the negotiation. Dale thought about himself in the gym—pumping out pushups, lifting heavy weights—and with a surge of energy, he flipped Ledford over his chest.

Dale's body rolled down several steps with heavy, painful thuds. He scrambled to his feet, drew his fists, and looked up just in time to see Ledford rushing toward him with a roundhouse swing. Dale stepped back, feeling the breeze from the big fist as it missed his face by an inch.

Ledford snarled. He took a couple more swings, a left then a right. Dale avoided the first blow, but the second connected with his stomach, clipping his lowest rib. Dale staggered back, and Ledford rushed toward him again.

Dale's feet weren't set, and the swing he threw was puny and off-target. Ledford smacked Dale's hand out of the way and landed another solid blow, this time on Dale's shoulder. The impact tremor shook Dale's whole body.

There was a glint in Ledford's eye and a slight curl on his lips, a look that said, *I'm going to finish this. Now.* He pulled back for a massive swing, giving Dale time to react. Dale ducked, and the death hammer that was Ledford's right arm went sailing over his head. From his crouched position, Dale sprang up with an uppercut that landed right where he wanted it, squarely under the man's jaw.

He felt Ledford's stubble against his knuckles, the oil and sweat of his face. Ledford's lower teeth cracked into the upper row. His head snapped back, and the momentum from his missed blow spun his body around ninety degrees before he began to tip over.

Slowly, like an old oak tree that wasn't quite ready to be felled, Ledford's body pitched forward. Dale sidestepped just as Ledford came crashing down to the marble steps.

———

A couple hours later.

There was still some apple pie on the small porcelain plate in front of Dale. Two or three bites' worth. He was saving it, savoring the experience, because the pie had tasted just as exquisite as he'd imagined it would during his scuffle with Ledford. Huge chunks of apple. Just enough tanginess. Big grains of sugar caramelized on top.

Plus he was in mid conversation with a beautiful woman. The last couple of bites could wait a moment.

"You sure don't look like a special agent."

The waitress eyeballed him. There was a small, skeptical grin on her face. It was a nice smile. Pretty. Not the kind of smile that tells a story but one that gives a thousand little hints. Lots of sparkle. And a bit of mischief.

She wore a light red, almost pink, dress with white trim around the edges, snug in all the right places. She was the new waitress. Her name tag read *Julia*.

Dale was angling for her phone number, but the window of opportunity was small. The lunchtime crowd around them was thick, and Julia had several other tables. Though Rich's Diner was a greasy spoon, the clientele's greasiness level varied widely—everyone from government employees to construction workers to cops to teachers. The smell of toasted bread mingled with that of raw, midday humanity. There was the rumble of voices and the clatter of silverware. A steady flow of people moved behind Julia as she looked down at Dale with that smile on her lips and a hand on her hip.

Dale flashed a smile in return. "What do you mean I don't look like an agent?"

"Just look at you."

Dale glanced over himself. He was wearing his usual—a T-shirt and 501s. His tan leather jacket was on the seat beside him. "What? Because I'm not wearing a suit?"

"You're a mess. Your lip is bleeding!"

Dale checked his reflection in the window. She was right. The corner of his mouth was indeed split, blood already black and crusty in his two-day beard. He remembered the burst of pain a couple hours earlier when his face had struck the marble step at the Memorial.

In addition to the wound, his appearance was generally disheveled. Patches of sweat still showed through his pale blue shirt. His thick brown hair and sideburns were tussled. After the events at the Memorial, he hadn't wasted any time procuring his slice of apple pie. Once he'd completed his paperwork—that most detectable of tasks—he'd headed straight to Rich's, not even stopping at a restroom.

He took a paper napkin from the holder on the table,

dipped it into his water then wiped at his lip. He looked at Julia and gave her a little shrug.

"Occupational hazard."

Julia motioned toward the window where, in the distance, you could just make out the Washington Monument.

"You work out there, huh?"

She bit her lip. It was clearly all she could do to keep from laughing.

Dale played right along. "Indeed I do."

"Do you protect the p resident?"

"That's the Secret Service."

"So you spy on the Russians, stuff like that?"

"That's the CIA."

"Aren't all those agencies basically the same?"

Dale smiled. "Not quite."

Julia gathered a couple of Dale's used napkins and glanced back at her other tables. "If you were a special agent, wouldn't you have a badge or something?"

"Yep." Dale fished in his pocket and tossed his badge on the table.

Julia picked it up. Her expression became more serious. "This looks real..."

"Nah. I had it made just to impress you."

Julia scrutinized the badge.

"Department of Justice," she read. "So that means you're an FBI agent."

"Not the FBI. I'm part of a small group of agents with knowledge in specialized fields. But I'm afraid that's all I'm permitted to tell you."

He couldn't tell her that he was an agent of the Bureau of Esoteric Investigation, a tiny, covert group within the DOJ.

Julia studied the badge, running a finger along its engravings. "Hmm. So, this is, like, top secret?"

Dale leaned forward and lowered his voice. "You won't tell anyone, will you, Julia?"

She smiled and handed him his badge. By the change in her expression, she seemed more convinced—but not completely.

"Far out..." she said. "So what's your name, Agent?"

"The name's Dale."

But it hadn't always been. Dale Conley was the name they'd given him when he joined the BEI. He hadn't liked it at first, preferring the name he'd developed—Max Iron. Naturally, this less-than-mature name choice had been shot down by the higher-ups. But he'd grown to love the name Dale Conley, and now he fully and deeply identified with it. He was Dale, and Dale was he.

"I'm Julia." She offered her hand and Dale shook it. "So you foiled a shooting, got the crap beat out of you, and caught the bad guy. And yet you came to a place like Rich's Diner to recover? That's the part I find hard to believe."

He pointed to the plate in front of him. "Apple pie. Duh."

Julia laughed. "Good point."

There was a certain sparkle to Julia's eyes now. Her smile, which had been bemused and skeptical, was now easy and genuine. It was time to close the deal. "When's your shift over, Julia? I know this great place down the road. You and I ought to—"

Just as he was about to submit a dosage of irresistible charm, a deep voice bellowed from the other side of the diner.

"*Agent Conley.*"

All the customers turned to look. But Dale didn't. He knew who was behind him. There was no mistaking that voice.

CHAPTER TWO

DALE HEARD the jingling of the bell on the front door as it closed followed by the *tap* of approaching dress shoes.

Julia looked to the entrance, raised an eyebrow, and began to step away. "I'd better get back to my other tables."

She left.

A man stepped around to the other side of Dale's booth and sat down across from him.

It was Walter Taft, Special Agent in Charge of the Bureau of Esoteric Investigation. He looked angry. He was always angry.

Taft had a sizable paunch and thin hair that was once red but was now not so much salt-and-pepper as it was salt-and-paprika. His eyes were close-set, and his skin was always shiny, something Dale attributed to constant stress-induced sweating rather than an oily complexion.

The BEI was a clandestine group within the Department of Justice, but the powers that be thought it prudent to have a more "traditional" man at the helm. Thus, an FBI agent was called upon to head the operation. How they decided upon Taft, Dale would never know. Managing the whacky personalities in the BEI required a level of patience few could manage —and Walter Taft was the type of man who got frustrated at his wife's cat for being "too damn incompetent."

Dale leaned around Taft and watched as Julia tended to one of her other tables. He sighed. "Now look what you did, sir. I was really making some progress."

"I don't give a damn about your romantic conquests, Conley. I've got a job for you."

Dale pointed to his busted lip. "The blood's barely dried from the last job. You're welcome, by the way, for stopping a deranged lunatic with historical conspiracy delusions who was about to assassinate a Senate staffer before we could find out what classified intel said staffer was leaking."

"Mather has the kid?"

"Being processed as we speak, but the weasel's already spilling the beans. Apparently he was leaking tidbits of info from Intelligence Committee memos, selling to the highest bidder. Quite the little entrepreneur."

"Then you've done your part. Time for your next assignment."

Taft slapped a manila folder on the table.

Dale grabbed the folder but hesitated before opening it. He'd worked for three weeks straight without a break on the Willard Ledford case, and he was tired.

He leaned past Taft again and looked at Julia.

"Open the damn folder, Conley."

"You're testy today, sir. Need a smoke?"

Taft grumbled. He reached into his pocket and brought out a small bag. He dumped some pistachios into his hand and cracked one open.

"Peggy?" Dale said.

Taft's wife Peggy was always trying to get him to stop smoking with alternative habits. She'd tried, unsuccessfully, to get him hooked on lollipops, cheese crackers, and one silly notion of celery sticks.

"Open!" Taft said and tossed a pistachio into his mouth.

Dale grinned and opened the folder. There was the usual single-page memorandum on DOJ stationary. He read for a moment—and the grin quickly dropped from his face.

The message was brief.

BUREAU OF ESOTERIC INVESTIGATION   DEPARTMENT OF JUSTICE

Memorandum

```
TO      :  Dale Conley          DATE:   August 18, 197
           Special Agent
           Bureau of Esoteric
           Investigation

FROM    :  Walter Taft
           Special Agent in Charge
           Bureau of Esoteric
           Investigation

SUBJECT:  Marshall Village Disappearance

        1. Members of the Marshall Village (utopian commu-
           nity; Staunton, Virginia) disappeared. All 147
           members accounted for on Monday, 16 August. By
           Wednesday, 18 August all missing. 84 males (16
           youth); 63 females (12 youth).

        2. Rendezvous with SA Cody Wilson, FBI, for further
           information and assignment details.
```

Dale's mouth hung wide open by the time he'd read the short message.

"Mass disappearance," Taft said, his voice quivering with the rage he always had toward faceless scumbags. "Discovered last night."

Dale kept looking at the numbers. *One hundred forty-seven people. Twenty-eight of them children.* He'd never heard of so many people disappearing at once.

"These people. They're just ... gone?"

"One day they're there. By a couple days later, they're all gone. Every last one of them." Taft squeezed a pistachio shell between his fingers.

"But how?"

"That's what you're gonna find out, pretty boy."

Taft always called him "pretty boy." Dale wasn't going to argue about being good-looking, but he thought of himself as more of a Clint Eastwood, Steve McQueen type than a "pretty boy."

He scanned the note again. "What does this have to do with the BEI?"

"Agent Wilson will fill you in on the way."

Each BEI case began with a "liaison" agent from another federal agency. NSA, DEA, the Marshals—but most often the FBI. Until the BEI agent determined that the case was appropriate for the Bureau, the liaison was in charge.

Dale had worked with FBI Special Agent Cody Wilson once before, his very first assignment. And it hadn't been peachy keen.

"So I'll be headed to Staunton, Virginia, sir?" Dale said as he turned over the memo and found the form he needed to sign to release himself from the assignment with Colton Mather. He reached toward Taft, who handed him a pen.

"That's right. None of your usual antics with this one,

Conley. You hear me? And try shaving, for Christ's sake. You're a federal agent."

Dale returned the pen and ran a hand over his stubble. "I thought it looked cool."

In the same way that mathematicians working in the DOD were given slack with their eccentricities, so too were BEI agents. This leniency bothered Taft to no end. Even though Dale was by far one of the most normal agents, Taft still hated his T-shirt-and-jeans approach to life. And Dale enjoyed pushing the man's buttons.

Dale slid his ticket toward Taft. "Since you blew it for me with Miss Julia there, you could at least pick up the bill."

Taft growled again.

"Fine," he said and snatched the ticket. "But the moment Wilson gets here, I want your ass out that door and on your way to Staunton."

"And when will he be arriving?"

The bell on the front door jingled again. Dale turned around.

Agent Wilson stood in the doorway. "Let's roll, Conley."

CHAPTER THREE

DALE SAT in the passenger seat of an Oldsmobile Custom Cruiser as he and Wilson barreled south down I-81.

"Wilson, geez..." Dale said and ran a hand over the vinyl of the door panel. "Don't you have to be married with kids to buy a station wagon?"

"It suits me. Lots of storage."

That was an understatement. It was a nineteen-foot, 5,000-pound beast with a 127-inch wheelbase. Ahead of and behind them were the blaring sirens and flashing lights of a Virginia State Police escort, four cars in all.

"How old are you anyway?" Dale said.

"Thirty-three."

Dale shook his head. Wilson would have walked right past Olds 442s at the dealership to buy this hunk of metal.

Dale had begged Taft to let them take his glorious car, Arancia, but his wailing was ineffective. Wilson was told to drive, and Dale was to spend the two-and-a-half-hour trip reviewing the information that had been gathered as of the previous night. Dale had taken a cab to follow Willard Ledford to the Jefferson Memorial, which meant that Arancia was still parked safely in the BEI garage. This gave him some solace.

A folder of photographs was on Dale's lap.

"The owner of the local farmer's market discovered the disappearance," Wilson said. "He stopped by on Monday, and everything was fine. When he went by to pick up their crops on Wednesday, they were all gone."

Wilson sat tall and straight, both hands on the wheel. He was a large man with an athletic build and round, pinkish, Midwestern cheeks that belied his polished image. There was an afterthought of a mustache on his upper lip, small and well groomed. He wore a dark suit and sunglasses—the government-approved, uniform-compatible type.

Dale's shades, which were folded up on his lap next to the folder, were wireframes and had been bent out of and back into shape several dozen times.

The photos in the folder were black-and-white 8.5x11s. The picture on top showed a small village, antiquated, looking straight out of the eighteenth century.

"Tell me more about the group," Dale said

"The Marshall Village. Utopian community led by Camden Marshall. In the country outside Staunton, between there and Dayton."

"Dayton?" Dale said as he studied the village in the photograph. "So they're Mennonites?" Having lived in the Shenandoah Valley for much of his life, he knew that there was a large Mennonite population in the area near Dayton and Harrisonburg.

"No. They adopted some of the Mennonite lifestyle, but the Marshallites—that's what they call themselves—they're not a religious group."

"Philosophically-based," Dale said. "A traditional utopian community." There was probably a copy of Edward Bellamy's *Looking Backward* on every Marshallite's nightstand.

Dale flipped through the photos. A young girl sitting on the front steps of a wooden home. A smiling couple standing next to a mound of corncobs. All the people had old-fashioned, rural-type clothes. The women wore dresses and bonnets. The men wore buttoned shirts and trousers with suspenders.

There was a yellowed newspaper article stuck between the photos. Dale unfolded it. Its headline read:

THE CURIOUS MARSHALL VILLAGE: AN EXERCISE IN TEMPERANCE

The photograph at the top of the article showed two young girls with a wheelbarrow in front of the village. Dale skimmed over the article's content. *...believes in a complete absence of monetary gain ... all revenue is immediately liquidated into physical goods for the village ... Camden Marshall first taught his concept of a resource-based economy at Virginia Tech University...*

"And now they're all gone," Dale said.

"Every man, woman, and child."

Dale scrutinized one of the photos, this one of a man tending to a plow in a field surrounded by rolling, wooded hills. He didn't know what to make of this whole thing. A lot of times these fringe communities practiced utopian socialism wherein the participants shared community resources equally. This certainly seemed to be the case with the Marshall Village, but it also had the added element of the antiquated buildings, clothes, and tools. What was the point of all this? Was it some sort of ideological aim, a belief that "times were better" a couple hundred years ago?

Dale looked back at the newspaper article again. *...Marshall believes that his village can serve as an inspiration for small town government...*

"The leader, Camden Marshall," Dale said. "What's his story?"

"Keep flipping. You'll find a picture of him."

Dale turned over a couple more pictures of people in rural clothing and found a color, head-and-shoulders shot of a man in a contemporary suit and tie. Mid-fifties. His dark hair had streaks of gray, and his face was wide and handsome.

"He's a professor," Wilson said. "He taught at Virginia Tech until he started the village. Economics. One of those '60s radicals. Remember that student protest over national tuition rates? He was one of the leaders. Teaches a resource-based economy."

"Resource-based economy? Me no gets. Please to be explaining."

"An alternative to a monetary economy. It advocates sharing all the world's resources equally."

"Socialism."

"Kind of," Wilson said. "You could say it's the ultimate product of socialism. Marx's endgame. Resource-based economy calls for the complete elimination of money. Machines would do the bulk of the manual labor, and people would be free to think and innovate."

Dale and Wilson exchanged a look.

"Camden Marshall's giving the general population way too much credit," Dale said. "If they were free from work and money, people wouldn't be writing symphonies and creating new technologies. They'd be getting drunk and having day-long porn marathons."

Dale shook his head.

"Of course, he's our prime suspect now," Wilson said, "since he led all these people out into the middle of the woods in the first place."

The thought had already crossed Dale's mind. When a woman turns up dead, the first person who goes under the magnifying glass is the husband. This assumption is often wrong, but it's often right too. The same thing held true for Camden Marshall. The man could have been abducted right along with the rest of them, it's true, but for now he was Dale's primary person of interest.

"How did Marshall convince a hundred and fifty people to follow him?" Dale said.

"Charisma. Persuasion. Sheer force of personality, it would seem."

Dale nodded. As much as society liked to celebrate the power of the individual, especially these days, people had an unsettling tendency to follow the leader. Folks with a bit more charm, a few more brain cells, and, most importantly, the ability to see through the world's bullcrap could easily persuade the swarms of dull-minded stooges surrounding them to do just about anything they wanted. Dale had seen it before. This was another reason to suspect Camden Marshall.

He flipped the photo of Marshall over. The next photo was a wide shot showing the whole village, which was composed of little white houses, all one-story in height and very plain.

"It's an odd case, no doubt," Dale said, looking at the pastoral scene in the photo, "but I don't understand why you've called the BEI."

"There's one more detail. They found a stone in the back of the village. It had a word carved into it. *Roanoke.*"

Dale whipped around. "Roanoke. The Lost Colony..."

Wilson nodded. "Now you see why you guys were brought in?"

Dale's brain began firing at a mile a minute. Roanoke. America's greatest mystery. It was England's first attempt to colonize the New World. Four hundred years ago. Before Jamestown. Before the Pilgrims.

And it ended when all 117 of the colonists vanished.

Dale stammered. "Whatever happened to the Marshallites ... Whoever did this ... They're trying to make a connection to the Lost Colony."

"Exactly."

"And the stone."

Wilson turned to him for a moment before quickly returning his attention to the road. "What about the stone?"

"It's sort of like the Dare Stones."

"The what?"

"The Dare Stones. They were found back in the '30s. A bunch of stones with messages carved in them, supposedly a record of what actually happened to the Lost Colonists."

A hiker stumbled upon the first Dare Stone in the summer of 1937. In the following months, dozens more stones showed up from North Carolina to Georgia, outlining the fate of the people who disappeared from Roanoke Island. Most experts had since concluded that the stones were forgeries.

"What are you saying, Conley? That the rock from the Marshall Village is one of those stones?"

"No," Dale said. "But whoever carved *Roanoke* on that stone dang well knew about the Dare Stones. It's yet another copycat."

The BEI recruited Dale for his genius-level knowledge of history and his aptitude toward puzzles. As such, he was handed a lot of copycat cases. When these whackos couldn't find enough adventure in their modern lives, they emulated the calamities of the past. For three dark weeks last year he'd chased down a man who worshipped Jack the Ripper. Just a month ago he'd caught a guy who wanted to be a modern-day cattle rustler. Dale found him behind a pile of manure deep in Texas cattle country.

Dale rubbed his hands together in anticipation and

watched the thick woods of the Shenandoah Valley fly past as they continued to zoom along. "How much longer?"

"Another hour. Just hold tight." Wilson shook his head. "It's fun to watch you BEI guys work. There's quite a brain in that head of yours. Ought to work on your bearing, though. You could at least shave."

Cripes. Two demands to shave in less than an hour.

CHAPTER FOUR

DALE ALWAYS THOUGHT it a shame that people didn't know their history—and this wasn't just because it had been his major back in college. Everyone needed a solid understanding. If people didn't know where they came from, how would they know where they were going?

It was no surprise that the Marshall Village disappearance was imitating the Lost Colony. Death, war, disappearances—the story had it all. The colony was cursed from the very beginning when the initial founder of the operation, Humphrey Gilbert, drowned. His half-brother, Sir Walter Raleigh, gained the charter, and, after failed initial attempts, another group of colonists ventured to the New World under the leadership of Raleigh's friend, John White. Very soon this group also fell into despair.

White returned to England to seek aid. The Atlantic was treacherous, and he barely made it alive. When he arrived, he was greeted with even more grim news. The Spanish Armada, the invincible naval force, was bearing down on England. All able ships, including White's, were commandeered for the fight. He was marooned in his homeland, leaving his family and the rest of the colonists stranded halfway across the world.

It was three long years before White was able to return to Roanoke Island. When he did, there was not a soul in the village. The colonists had simply vanished. And they were never heard from again. That is, until the first Dare Stone was found in 1937, allegedly left by Roanoke survivors.

Dale thought about this now as he stared out into the empty Marshall Village. Someone had been very familiar with the details of the Lost Colony and the Dare Stones to choose to carve *Roanoke* in the wake of the Marshallites' disappearance.

He stood with Wilson, a rotund sheriff, and half a dozen deputies at the edge of the village. It was a group of about thirty homes and barns surrounding an open area in the center. The wooden buildings were rustic and sat in mottled shade from the tall trees looming above on all sides. In the immediate center was a stone well. Yellow police tape circled the village.

Dale had seen villages similar to this before. Amish and Mennonite communities. Living history villages. But nothing quite like this. The village was deep in the woods, a good mile or two from the nearest home. The houses were arranged in a circle. There were no paths, no sidewalks, just the large grassy area in the center worn down by footsteps. The gravel road that led to the village was a hundred feet away from the buildings, and the area between—where they'd just parked— was simply a cleared section of the woods with a pair of tire ruts.

Dale had left his jacket in the Custom Cruiser. The sun was so hot he wished he'd left his shirt too. He took a step ahead of the other men and dropped his sunglasses to the end of his nose. He shaded his eyes with his hand and scanned the village.

Aside from the flapping of the yellow police tape barrier and the movement of branches in the slight breeze, it was completely still. A ghost town. The only sound was the noisy droning of the cicadas in the trees.

Dale wiped the sweat from his brow and pushed his sunglasses back up. He turned around to the other men.

The sheriff's arms were crossed and resting on his gut. Carl Brown was a bowl of a man. He stood about six feet tall with a big, jowly face and mitts full of thick fingers. Augusta County was small and rural, but Dale thought about how much larger Brown's responsibility would have been in the 1700s. At one time, Augusta was an enormous swath of land covering nearly all of modern-day Virginia as well as Kentucky and the Great Lakes states. The western edge went all the way to the Mississippi River.

When Dale and Wilson first arrived, Brown shook both their hands vigorously despite the sideways look he gave Dale. Brown looked ready to detonate when Dale requested a few minutes alone with the village, but Wilson quickly stepped in to quell any anger, assuring the sheriff that this dude in a sweaty T-shirt and jeans was indeed a federal agent.

Wilson was good at giving these local types a look that said *Don't worry about this guy—he's with me*. He'd used that look on more than one occasion on Dale's first assignment. By now Dale figured Wilson wouldn't talk about him to fellow law enforcers like he was his goofy kid brother. After all, that first assignment was a major success for Dale, despite Wilson's persistent belief that Dale had been reckless.

"Where's the stone?" Dale called out to the sheriff, who stood about twenty feet behind him. The sheriff muttered, and Dale fought the urge to lash out. Brown needed to get over his consternation—and quick. This was a federal crime scene now.

"All the way in the back," Brown yelled. Behind him, his deputies looked ready to jump on Dale like a pack of hyenas.

Wilson and Dale ducked under the police tape. There was a hollow, empty resonance floating in the village. Dale carefully scrutinized the buildings as they passed. They were of simple construction with wood siding, black-shingled roofs, and square windows. Whitewashed and well maintained. There was a small porch on each building, and most had a chair or two on this porch.

"Didn't the Roanoke colonists leave some sort of clue behind?" Wilson said.

"You're right, Wilson," Dale said. He thought he noticed a hint of a proud smile form on Wilson's face. "The only clue John White found in the empty village was the word *Croatoan* carved into a fence post. Someone had also carved *C-R-O-A* into a tree, like they didn't even have the time to finish a second message."

"What's *Croatoan?*"

"The name of a nearby island and also one of the Indian tribes. Some think the colonists fled to the island. Others think that they were absorbed into one of the tribes. Or that one of the tribes killed 'em."

"Whoever carved *Roanoke* on the stone could be emulating the carvings on the fence and tree."

"Maybe. But look around. Plenty of tree trunks he could have carved up. No, our copycat is making a double nod—to both the *Croatoan* carvings and the Dare Stones."

They reached the backside of the circular arrangement of buildings where there was a row of outhouses.

"Supposed to be down here," Wilson said and led Dale to the end of this row. There were foot-tall weeds surrounding it, and, at first, Dale overlooked it.

It was a round stone about two feet across. Lines of blood zigzagged over its surface, like chocolate syrup drizzled on a dessert. The blood had dried into thick black goo. Rivulets ran down the sides to the ground. A half dozen flies buzzed about. *ROANOKE* was scratched into it in large, capital letters. The scratches looked fresh, the carved parts bright and clean looking against the dark color of the stone.

ROANOKE

The two men knelt down. Dale pointed toward the dirt where the rock entered the ground. "The stone's been here a while," he said.

The earth met completely flush with the edge of the stone. The grass grew longer around the stone where the Marshallites had missed it when trimming. Dale pushed on the stone, and it moved slightly, some of the moist earth sticking to the surface of the stone.

Wilson nodded his agreement. "We got a soil sample to the lab. They tell us the rock's been here for at least three years."

"But the letters are fresh," Dale said. "Any prints?"

Wilson shook his head.

Dale held out a hand as he continued to look at the stone. "Gloves."

Wilson scowled.

Dale turned his attention to him. "Gloves ... please?"

"I'm not your lackey, Agent Conley," Wilson said. He reached into his suit jacket and handed Dale a pair of latex gloves.

"Thanks." Dale put on the gloves and ran a finger along the scratches. "Not very deep. Definitely not done with a chisel or anything like that. Pocketknife, maybe." He fished into his jeans and retrieved his own pocketknife. He stuck the blade in the scratches. Definite possibility.

"Even a car key could have made those scratches," Wilson said.

Dale touched the blood on the rock with a finger. His glove stuck to its tackiness as he pulled away. "Had the blood tested?"

"Results came back just before we left D.C."

"Not human, is it?"

"Well ... no. But how do you—"

"Elementary, my dear Wilson," Dale said. "There's not another drop of blood in the rest of the village, none in the grass surrounding the stone. Just on the stone itself."

"Meaning?"

"Meaning no one was hurt. The blood was put here on purpose. It's just theatrics. Someone got some cow's blood from a butcher shop and splattered it on this rock. They're trying to scare us."

Dale stood up, and Wilson followed his lead. They headed back toward the buildings.

When Dale tried to understand the type of person who would leave a bloody mess as a visual scare tactic, his mind kept flashing on one word. *Immaturity*. Chances were this rock was a prank from some damn punk teenagers who'd been learning about the Lost Colony in their American history class. Maybe the teacher decided to make the lesson flashier by mentioning the titillating mystery of the Dare Stones. Something happened to the folks in the village, of course, but the rock and the blood could very well have no connection.

"What's with the grin?" Wilson said. "Know something I don't?"

"Just a hunch."

There was a glint of light from the other side of the village, and Dale turned to look. A car was driving slowly along the solitary gravel road to the east of the village. He could just see it through the trees, little flashes of it appearing now and then.

"What's wrong?" Wilson said.

The car was positively creeping by, and this sent Dale's internal alarms into hysterics. If it went any slower, it would have stopped. It was some sort of late-model coupe. Light in color, probably white.

"Does a lot of traffic come through here?" Dale said.

"Brown said there's about a dozen homes within a mile radius. It's probably just a local getting an eyeful. They're not used to crime scenes out here in the boonies."

The car drove past a small clearing in the woods, and for a moment Dale could just make out a figure in the driver seat— a man wearing dark clothing who seemed to be watching them as he inched by.

"I suppose," Dale said.

CHAPTER FIVE

THE MAN PEERED at the police through the trees as he crept along the gravel road. A handful of the ignorant local sheriff's deputies were standing behind the police tape. Walking from the back of the village was a different pair of men—one in a suit and one wearing a blue T-shirt and jeans. The latter would be the BEI agent.

Presently the two men stopped and looked in his direction. He knew that they couldn't see him through the trees, but he still cinched up the hood on the black jacket he was wearing.

He continued at his slow pace, and soon the village grew fainter and was replaced by nothing but a tangle of green leaves. A single house down a long dirt driveway passed by on the right, and then the road began to curve to the west. When the road reached a dead end, he pulled the car over.

Tall trees surrounded him, sunshine poking through the leaves. All was quiet except for the cicadas and other chattering insects. It was the kind of place a hillbilly would go to dump a broken refrigerator.

The man looked out his window to the left. He knew that

the village was straight through those trees, due south, about a quarter mile. This made him smile.

He turned to the young girl sitting in the passenger seat. She stared straight ahead, right over the top of the dash. Her face was blank, and she hadn't said a word during the whole trip. Of course she hadn't. He hadn't told her to. She did only what he asked. Whatever he asked.

The man put his hand on her hair. It was silky and smooth. Young things always felt so fresh, so new. Children, saplings, baby animals. They were as clean as they were pure. He twirled one of the girl's golden curls through his fingers. She continued to stare forward. Not budging. The nightgown she wore was pretty and white.

She would do whatever he said. It was a power that thrilled him, and he never tired of it. But he knew that he could never use this power the way that Father had used it with him. That was where Father had faltered. He hadn't respected the power.

The man let the strand of the girl's hair slide out of his fingers.

"Look at me," he said.

The girl turned and looked at him now, the first time during the whole excursion. Her eyes were large and blue, her skin satiny. She remained expressionless.

"Are you ready for your task?" the man said and smiled.

CHAPTER SIX

DALE AND WILSON walked up to one of the houses and stepped onto the porch. The boards squeaked beneath their feet. Dale approached the front door and looked at the doorframe. He ran his hand along it. The wood was smooth, the paint fresh.

"Sheriff's Office found no signs of forced entry," Wilson said.

"And all the buildings have been checked?" Dale said as he looked at the hinges.

"All of them. Every building is just like this. Not a single object out of place. It's like they vanished into thin air."

When John White returned to the Roanoke Colony in 1590, there were no signs of a struggle. The colonists were simply gone. As Dale looked from the porch out into the pristine, empty village beyond, he wondered how someone in the 1970s could make such a large group of people disappear without a trace. There was a three-year gap between White's departure and his return to find his family and companions missing. The Marshall Village, on the other hand, was seen on Monday and had entirely disappeared by Wednesday.

At the beginning of a BEI investigation, the investigating agent had to decide if the case fit the BEI's mission. Dale was trying to determine whether or not someone had actually been imitating the Lost Colony. His gut told him that it was just some prankster who put the carving on the rock. But the similarities between the two disappearances certainly gave him pause. Both groups had roughly 150 people. Both lived in the woods. Both vanished without a trace.

They walked inside and into a kitchen, stark and plain. Like the outside, the walls were painted white. The cabinets, tables, and other furnishings were bare wood. No refrigerator, no running water. A wood-burning stove sat in the corner.

The heat was even more oppressive within the walls of the house. Dale rubbed a finger along the countertop. His fingertip came up clean, not a speck of dust. There wasn't a dirty dish or soiled rag in sight. The kitchen was spotless.

They walked toward the rear of the house, where there were two other rooms, a smaller room to the left, and a larger room in the back. Neither doorway had doors, just a frame. They headed for the larger room.

"What do you think, Wilson?" Dale said.

"I'm at a loss."

"That makes two of us."

If every building was just like this, Dale didn't know what to make of it. Every part of him was saying that if something terrible had happened to these people there would be some sort of sign. Wrecked furniture. Kicked-in doors. Misplaced rifles. But this house was pristine. Could they have all been killed? Some sort of poisoning? If so, could someone have gotten 147 bodies out without any of the locals noticing?

They stepped into the back room. There was a bed, a dresser, and a small table with two chairs in the corner. Like the kitchen, all the furnishings were old-fashioned and made of unfinished wood. The mattress looked to be stuffed. Dale walked over to the dresser and pulled out one of the drawers. Inside were neatly folded, agrarian clothes of the type he'd seen in the photographs. He closed the drawer, and they moved to the next room.

"I do wonder, though," Wilson said, "about a connection to modern-day Roanoke. Maybe it has nothing to do with the colony at all. Maybe *Roanoke* on the stone is referring to Roanoke, Virginia."

"Too many coincidences for there to be no connection," Dale said. "Whoever wrote *Roanoke* on that rock knew damn well about the Dare Stones. Of all the town names in all the world to carve on a rock, they chose *Roanoke*? And why the hell would they decide to carve *anything* on a rock in the first place? Sorry, Wilson, I'm not buying it."

"No offense taken. You're the braniac." There was blatant insincerity in his tone.

They stepped into the second room. It was a child's bedroom. There was a small bed and dresser, scaled-down versions of those they'd seen in the last room. Dale went over to the dresser and pulled out one of the drawers. Inside were more neatly folded clothes.

He picked up one of the dresses in the top drawer and let it fall open. It was small, the right size for a girl of maybe six years or so. The cloth had an unmistakably handmade feel. Holding the dress suddenly felt eerie to Dale. Whoever this little girl was, she'd been here in this room only three days prior. And now she was gone. They were all gone.

It's funny how the smallest of things can have weight. The tiny dress in Dale's hands felt very heavy now. He put it back in the drawer.

———

They stepped out onto the porch and continued into the

main grounds of the village again. The heat that had felt oppressive a few minutes earlier was a relief after being in the stuffy house. Dale pushed his bangs from his forehead. His sideburns were making his face feel even hotter. He'd considered shaving them before, but they looked too damn cool.

"You had all the alone time you need?" Wilson asked as he looked across the village to the sheriff and his men beyond the police tape barrier.

Dale had forgotten about the other men waiting for them. If they'd seemed perturbed when Dale and Wilson left them, they looked positively fuming now.

"Yeah," Dale said. "I wouldn't want anyone to blow a gasket."

They stepped off the porch and into the main grassy area again. Wilson stepped aside, faced the other men, and waved his arms in the air.

The deputies made their way under the police tape and into the village.

Wilson sighed and took off his jacket. "Stinkin' hot," he said and gazed out over the empty village. "Does this place bring back a lot of bad memories?"

Dale flinched.

Wilson had a way of dredging up things that were best left unsaid. His detached objectivity was clearly an asset to his work as an agent, but it made him unable to realize when he was stepping on toes. He meant nothing personal by his obliviousness, but it was frustrating all the same.

The truth was, the instant Dale saw the Marshall Village, the memories came flooding back to him. But he'd forced them from his mind to focus on his duty at hand. Leave it to Wilson to pull them right back into the spotlight.

"Been trying not to think about it, Wilson," Dale said.

"You figure that's why you were assigned this case?" Wilson said. "Because of your past?"

And there he went again. Wilson could be more than a little oblivious. He had the tact of a dockworker.

"I wouldn't presume to guess why I'm given any assignment," Dale said, though he knew Wilson was right. He'd been assigned this case because of his past.

The sheriff and his men spread through the village around them, taking photographs and writing notes.

"So, did the Roanoke Colony kidnappers strike again?" Wilson said. "Is this a BEI case?"

Dale peeled off his rubber gloves. He inhaled and tried to calculate his response. "The verdict's still out. But I don't think so."

He had an inkling that his time with this case was almost through. And he was thankful for that. He was still worn out from the Willard Ledford case and the literal beating he'd received at its conclusion. Taft and Wilson had not only interrupted his celebratory pie at Rich's Diner, but they also derailed his flirtation with fair Julia. He was anxious to get back to town for another chance.

There was a loud snap of a branch from the woods. Dale, Wilson, and the sheriff's men all turned and looked.

There were a lot of deer in this area. Black bears, too. Not long after moving to Virginia at the age of ten, Dale encountered his first bear while hiking a trail. The best response his prepubescent self could muster was to simply freeze in his tracks. This had, unwittingly, been a much better alternative to running, which would have only increased the chances of aggression from the bear.

He watched the trees for a moment. And saw nothing. Just the movement of a few branches in the breeze.

But then there was another noise, and he looked back again. Another noise. And another. Snapping branches, crunching leaves. Something was moving, and it was coming toward them.

The men chattered. A couple of them joked about a venison dinner.

The noises drew closer, and within moments a figure was visible. But it wasn't a deer or a bear. It was a person.

And the person was headed their way.

CHAPTER SEVEN

DALE'S SENSES BLISTERED, and he felt the reassuring weight of his Smith & Wesson Model 36 against his lower back, tucked into his jeans. His mind flashed to the car that had crept by moments earlier. He'd sensed that there was something not right about that vehicle, and now he had a strong feeling that his apprehension was warranted.

Whoever was approaching was wearing white clothing, which made the individual readily visible, though the person was off in the distance. The woods obscured Dale's view, but it was clear that the figure was drawing nearer.

Sheriff Brown stepped up beside Dale and Wilson to get a better look. He cupped his hand over his mouth.

"This is a crime scene," the sheriff yelled out. "Stop where you are."

The person continued toward them.

Brown kept on yelling. "This is Sheriff Carl Brown of the Augusta County Sheriff's Office. Stop where you are immediately!"

The figure still didn't respond. The crunching footsteps drew closer.

"I said *halt!*"

The person continued toward them.

Brown motioned toward his men, and they all drew weapons. Dale pulled his gun from its holster. Wilson did the same.

The person was closer yet. Long blonde hair was visible. And feminine features.

It looked like ... a woman. But as the figure drew nearer, Dale realized that he was wrong again. It wasn't a woman at all.

It was a little girl.

She was wearing something long and white—a nightgown or dress. She was barefoot.

"It's a child!" Dale yelled to the others. "We've got a child!"

Brown waved his hands at his men. "Hold! *Hold!* Lower your guns!"

The girl was now a hundred feet from the edge of the village. She was small, no more than eight years old. Her arms were outstretched, a vacant look in her eyes. She was screaming something. Dale couldn't make out the words. Her voice was shrill, piercing, with a quality that sounded less like a girl's and more like a woman's. Or a witch's. It sent a chill over Dale's flesh.

She seemed not to notice the men, just continued moving forward. Dale could now see painful-looking cuts and scrapes covering her arms and legs. Her feet were bloodied. She wore a nightgown that had been white at one time but was now a dingy brown. It was old-fashioned, in the style of the Marshallite clothing.

She was one of the missing people.

As she got closer, her screaming became clear. "Virginia! Virginia Dare! Virginia Dare!" She repeated this over and over.

For the second time, Dale felt a chill. His brain could hardly register what he had just heard from that little girl, the name she had said ...

Wilson dropped his sunglasses and looked at Dale. "Dare? As in the Dare Stones?"

Dale nodded slowly. "Virginia Dare was the first English child born in the New World. John White's granddaughter. She was quite possibly killed as a little girl. The first Dare Stone was supposedly written by her mother as a memorial to Virginia and the girl's father, who was also killed."

He watched as the small, screaming girl got closer and closer to them.

Dale wasn't a superstitious man, but seeing this spectral-looking child in antique clothing lurching through the forest screaming the name "Virginia Dare" gave him the heebie-jeebies. In the last 400 years, there was great speculation as to how and why Virginia Dare—and the rest of the Roanoke Colony—had completely vanished from the earth.

He shook his head. It was just a little girl. This was the 1970s, not the 1590s, and something or someone was compelling her to trek through the forest toward them.

She needed help.

Dale holstered his gun. He stepped out from behind the house and jogged over to the woods.

Brown yelled out behind him. "Agent Conley, what the hell do you think you're doing?"

"Conley!" Wilson said.

Dale stopped within a few feet of the edge of the woods. He could see the girl clearly now. She continued to scream.

"Dare! Dare! Virginia Dare!"

She was a cute girl. Her eyes were clear blue. Freckles on her cheeks.

Dale dropped to a knee.

She was within fifty feet of him. There was a glazed-over

look in those blue eyes. He'd seen it before, years ago—that dead, vacant stare. He'd hoped to never see it again. But here it was, on the face of this mystery girl creeping out of the forest. It made Dale's heart thump in his chest.

"Virginia Dare! Virginia Dare!"

The girl was very close now. Only a couple yards away.

"Hi sweetheart," Dale said. "You doing okay?"

She stopped walking, stopped screaming. Silence rang in Dale's ear. The girl was an arm's length from him. Her head turned slightly toward him, but her blue eyes looked past him, through him. She remained perfectly still, her little arms at her sides. Crosshatched red scratches covered her skin. A drop of blood rolled down her left hand.

The girl's face was lifeless. Some sort of hell had happened to this child. If Dale could look at her just right, if she could see that he wasn't going to hurt her, he could get through to her. He opened his eyes wide, put a small smile on his face.

The girl's eyes focused. She was looking right at him now. She saw him.

He smiled bigger and slowly reached out a hand, like one would to a scared dog. Slowly, slowly.

The girl didn't notice his hand. She continued to look into his eyes.

Dale eased his right knee forward. His fingers were inches from her shoulder.

The girl opened her mouth. And screamed. A guttural, penetrating shriek. She sprang forward, knocking Dale over and latching onto his arm. Steely fingers dug into Dale's shoulder, and small, sharp teeth bit down hard through his T-shirt.

Dale howled.

He thought again of the bear that he encountered when he first came to Virginia. If the bear had actually gotten a hold of him, he imagined its bite would have felt something like this girl's. Her teeth dug into his flesh with unrelenting force. His eyes watered, and he pulled at the girl's back.

One of the deputies rushed over and grabbed the girl. Still clinging to Dale, she flailed out wildly at the man. Her long, sharp nails caught him across his eye and cheek, flinging blood into the grass. The deputy screamed.

Three more men grabbed the girl's arms and legs and pulled her from Dale. The girl writhed about viciously, thrashing in their arms like a violent cat being hauled to the vet.

Dale grabbed his arm. The pain pulsed into his hand.

As the men fought to control the girl, Dale noticed something—a note safety-pinned to her back. The deputies were a swarming mass of arms and legs and swear words, but for a brief moment when the girl's back was facing him, he was able to read what the note said. It was written in permanent marker with big, scratchy letters—the same style of markings that had been on the stone.

don't forget to upend every flag

Dale's BEI mind went to work immediately. Upend the flags ... Turn the flags over? What flags? He looked around the village. There were no flags.

Wilson came up to him. "You okay?"

Dale nodded.

Sheriff Brown strode over to his men as they fought with the girl, who was screeching loudly. He yanked the note from the girl's back and looked at it quizzically. He turned to Dale. "What the hell is this about?"

The girl broke free from them and bolted back toward the trees. She cut to the left, but the sheriff lunged forward and tackled her. She bit Brown's hand and took off again. He caught the back of her dress.

"Smith! Maynard! Pullman!" he yelled. "Get over here. She's one little girl."

The deputies wrestled the girl from the sheriff.

"Now put her in one of the cars and get her to the damn hospital."

The men pulled the girl toward the far end of the village, stopping to grapple with the deranged child every few feet. They yelled out as the girl continued to bite and scratch with animal-like brawn.

Brown looked at the note in his hand and shook his head. "Christ," he muttered. "Miller!"

A young deputy—who had been standing by the vehicles and watching the chaos with unnerved awe—ran over to Brown.

"Yes, Sheriff?"

The sheriff handed Miller the note. "Bag this."

A loud shriek blasted out from the opposite side of the village. The deputies were manhandling the girl into the back of one of the sheriff's cars. She twisted in their arms and kicked one of the men in the ribs.

There was a creak of a branch in the forest. Dale looked. The tree limbs slowly rocked in the breeze. The cicadas continued their racket. He thought about the dozens of other missing people. If one girl had wandered back into the village …

"Sheriff Brown," Dale said. "There are one hundred forty-six other people. They could all be out there."

Brown turned and looked at the trees. "You might be right." He cupped his hands over his mouth. "Miller!"

Miller was on the other side of the village putting the note into a plastic bag. He jogged over again.

"Yes, Sheriff?" he said, out of breath.

"We're gonna run a sweep," Brown said, "and search the woods for any other survivors. Now, you get those other boys over here, and we'll fan out in one big circle, fifty yards apart. Me and the fed boys will head north. You space the rest of them around us."

"Yes, sir," Miller said.

"And give me that," Brown said, pointing to the note that had been pinned to the girl's back, which was now in a plastic bag.

"Conley," Wilson said and stepped toward Dale. "What about that car that passed by? You sure were keeping an eye on it."

Dale thought about it. The car had crept by slowly, deliberately. Minutes before the girl appeared.

"Sheriff," Dale said. "The gravel road over there. Where does it go?"

"Along the east side of this property, going north. Then curves west. Dead ends a quarter mile from here."

Dale figured as much. With the shape of the hill to the east, there wasn't anywhere else for it to go. That meant that the road would end up due north of the village—exactly the direction from which the little girl appeared.

"A car drove by a few minutes ago," Dale said. "That little girl might have been dropped off."

"*Dropped off?*" Brown tipped his hat back and dried his forehead. He looked to the north and sighed. "Son of a bitch. Okay, Conley. We'll check it out. Hold this." He shoved the note at Dale and turned to Wilson. "You stay here and help with the sweep."

Wilson opened his mouth as though to protest and looked at Dale.

"Come on, boy," Brown said to Dale before Wilson had a chance to respond. "Let's move."

Brown smacked Dale on the ass and bounced off toward his car.

CHAPTER EIGHT

SHERIFF BROWN SLAMMED on the brakes, and Dale flew into the dash. Moments earlier, Dale hadn't been able to locate the seatbelt in the split second between when he got in the sheriff's Ford Custom 500 and when Brown spun the big boat of a car onto the gravel road.

There was a fork in the road. Brown studied it.

"This way." He spun the tires, taking the left side of the fork.

Dale crashed into his seatback. "How far is it to 81?"

"Five miles."

The engine revved louder as the sheriff accelerated. They followed a paved country road that wound along the little dips and undulations of the countryside. Dairy farms and open pastures zipped by.

Even in a tense moment like this, one couldn't help but appreciate the idyllic beauty of the Valley. The lush green grass, the blue mountains in the distance, the clusters of cows watching the speeding car with mild curiosity. Dale was lucky enough to spend much of his formative years in this region, and he was thankful for any chance to return. Even if he was riding in a Hell-bound death machine.

The sheriff took a sharp curve fast, and Dale slid to his left on the vinyl seat, smashing into the sheriff's side. He sank into Brown's big, sweaty arm. Dale repositioned himself and resumed his search for a seatbelt. Instead he found a metal peg where the seatbelt once existed.

"Sorry about that," the sheriff said. "Been meaning to have that replaced." He chortled.

Dale gripped his seat with both hands.

They came over a rise, and the landscape opened up before them. Ahead of them was a white car—like the one Dale saw through the trees earlier. It was a Plymouth Duster.

"That's it, Sheriff."

"Okay, here we go."

Brown punched the gas even harder, throwing Dale back, then flipped on the lights and siren, which came to life with a blare.

Dale put his sunglasses on and leaned forward. Though he didn't want to believe that this person had actually dropped off the little girl, deep down part of him wanted the Duster to bolt so they could chase it.

They were about a quarter mile away from the other car now.

"Write this down, Fed," Brown said. He read off the license plate number. "Alpha-Delta-1-3-2-8."

Dale sifted through the burger wrappers and empty packs of Marlboros sliding around the floor and found a piece of paper and a pen. The pen was sticky. He wrote down the number.

Dale grinned. His heart pounded, and his fingers tingled. This was one of the greatest perks of the job—the thrill of the chase. "Looks like a standard Duster to me, but by the way that thing took off, I think we might have a sleeper 360. Can this girl catch 'im, Sheriff?"

He smacked the dashboard.

Brown scoffed. "Cat got an ass?"

They barreled over a hill and lifted off on the other side. The Custom 500 sailed through the air, and Dale saw the horizon line drop. They were floating. Dale's stomach rose up first, followed by his whole body. For a moment he was levitating above the seat. His head touched the roof.

With a thud and some loud squeaking from the 500's springs they came back to earth. Dale somehow landed backwards in his seat, twisted into a contorted ball. His face smashed into the headrest.

The sheriff was laughing again, a constant *he-he-he* kind of laugh like he was chasing a grandchild around the backyard.

Dale turned himself back around. Ahead, the Duster had gained some distance from them. It took a curve and disappeared from sight.

Brown followed the curve, and when they got around it, the Duster was gone. Horizon to horizon there was nothing.

"Dammit," Brown said. He gunned it.

"Where we going now?"

"There's only one road that goes out to 81." He pointed to a crossroad about a quarter mile away. "That'n there."

Gravel spat from the tires of the Custom 500 and clattered against its underside. They came up to a corner, and the sheriff slowed down just enough to get them around it. The car fishtailed as they pulled through the other side. With a surge of gas, Brown pushed them down the road. On either side of them were open, hilly fields. But ahead the road plunged into a forest.

They drove into the darkness of the trees, and after a few hundred feet, they exited into the sunlight again. An interstate overpass was in front of them. They skidded to a stop by the on-ramp where a cloud of the Duster's dust lingered.

The highway was accommodating a decent flow of afternoon traffic—plenty of cars and tractor-trailers. Dale scanned the vehicles. His eyes bounced about to the different white cars passing by, but the Duster was nowhere to be seen.

"Dammit," Brown said. "We lost him." He smacked the steering wheel and cursed under his breath.

The radio on the underside of the dash came to life. "Sheriff?" a man's voice said.

Brown snatched the receiver out of its cradle. "What?" His lips were so close to the receiver he sprayed it with spit.

"That girl from the village. They got her in a bed at the hospital. They want to talk to you."

"Fine, Miller," he said. "We'll be there."

Brown slapped the receiver back into place then goosed the engine—whipping the car around 180 degrees—and headed toward the northbound on-ramp for the interstate.

Dale resumed his position, clinging to the seat for dear life.

CHAPTER NINE

DALE HATED the smell of hospitals. The sweet, warm, putrid odor always made him queasy. Once as a young teenager, he puked all over his aunt in a hospital when he came to visit her. One wouldn't believe how quickly a sick woman could jump out of her bed.

Now Dale felt that same queasiness as he stood with Sheriff Brown by the little girl's bed. The fact that his stomach had just been tossed about the cab of the sheriff's car for the last half hour wasn't helping matters. The room felt warm and light. There was a thin layer of perspiration on his forehead. He put one hand on the bed rail and looked at the girl to remind himself of why he was there.

The bed engulfed the girl's tiny frame. Her eyes were closed, and she breathed slowly and heavily. They had her in a gown. The sheets were pulled up to her chest. There was a tube taped to her right arm that traced up to an IV.

A doctor—in a lab coat over a paisley shirt and corduroys —had been talking since Dale and Sheriff Brown entered the room. He told them that the girl was panicked but fine. No serious injuries, no signs of sexual assault. He was short and stocky with a mop of thinning, sweaty, curly hair. A furrowed brow sat above his jowly face, and his skin was as oily as SAC Taft's. The man was a troll.

The nurse standing quietly next to him, though, was a goddess. She stood about five-foot-seven with straight brown hair pulled into a ponytail. She also wore a lab coat, which covered her button-up blouse and loose-fitting, flared slacks. Her face had just a dusting of makeup, and her expression was serious—so serious that she seemed unapproachable.

The doctor was refusing to let Dale and the sheriff talk to the girl, and this had made Brown spitting mad.

"What do you mean we can't talk to her?" he said.

Unlike the deputies back at the village, the doctor wasn't intimidated at all by Sheriff Brown's loud tone and overbearing demeanor. In fact, the little man had been downright rude to them from the moment they'd walked in.

"The girl's asleep. I think you can understand that. And keep your voice down, Officer."

"That's *Sheriff*," Brown said through his teeth.

"You drugged her?" Dale said.

"Chemical restraint," the doctor said. "She was attacking people. I understand you were one of those attacked."

"Can you revive her?" Dale said. "It's really damn important that we talk to her, Doctor."

"Doctor? I'm not the doctor here. She is."

He pointed to the gorgeous woman standing beside him.

"So who are you?" Dale said to the man.

"I'm the nurse."

Dale looked back and forth between them. The man had been doing all the talking since he and Brown arrived.

Dale turned to the woman.

"I'm Dr. Susan Anderson."

Dale glanced at the white lab coat she wore over her blouse. Her name was embroidered on it.

SUSAN
ANDERSON

The nurse's lab coat was also embroidered.

BRIAN
ANDERSON

Dale had already noticed that both of their coats had "Anderson" on them but assumed that it was the name of the pediatric unit.

"Anderson," Dale said. "So are you two—"

"He's my nurse and my brother," Susan said.

"I guess you're who I should be talking to, then. We must speak to this girl. There's a whole lot riding on it."

"Please explain," she said.

"What's to explain?" Brown said, his hands clenched in big, round fists. "This girl is our witness. Now, you listen here—"

"No, *you* listen. I'm the doctor here, and until you give me a good reason to revive this girl, she's staying just like she is."

Brown's teeth bared, but Dale stepped in before he could spit out some obscenity. He put his hand on the large man's chest and eased him back, giving him a *calm down* look.

He turned to Susan.

"Please understand, we have a hundred and fifty missing people. This girl is our only witness, the only person who might know what happened to them. It's vital that we talk to her."

Susan cleared her throat. She looked at the girl in the bed, paused, and then nodded.

"I'll take her off the IV. When she comes around, we'll let you know."

Her brother turned to her.

"Susan," he said, utter disbelief twisting his face. "You're really going to listen to these hayseeds?"

Susan looked from the girl to Dale to her brother.

"I ... I think it's for the best, Brian." She spoke quietly, not looking him in the eye.

The nurse threw his hands up and stormed out.

The room was filled with a heavy awkwardness. Dale slowly turned to Susan.

"Thanks."

He nodded at Brown, and they left.

As they reached the door, Dale looked back at Susan and gave her a quick smile. She quickly looked away.

So much for first impressions.

———

Dale had always found the humidity in the Valley to be quite comfortable. On a day like today, though, low humidity didn't make a bit of difference. Harrisonburg, Virginia's Rockingham Memorial Hospital sat on the side of a steep hill and was serviced by a busy road. The cars piled up at the traffic light revved their engines and honked, not quite living up to Harrisonburg's moniker of "The Friendly City." But, then, only a precious few of the cars had air conditioning. As Dale stood among waves of shimmering heat rising from the blacktop of the hospital parking lot, he looked at the big box that was the sheriff's Custom 500 and knew their pain. Pretty soon he'd be sealed in that sauna again.

Sheriff Brown rested on the trunk of his car scrutinizing the note that had been on the girl's back as well as a picture of the blood-splattered stone. He cursed and used a handkerchief to sop up the sweat from his armpits and face.

Dale leaned on the car beside him. The hot metal of the trunk burned his arm, and he jumped. He looked at the photo

—the carved letters of *ROANOKE* and the trickles of blood —then turned to the note. The scratchy, erratic style of the handwriting, he could tell, was deliberate. Perfectly imperfect. Like the blood on the stone, the creepy text was a scare tactic.

"What do you figure it means?" Brown said and touched the note with his finger.

Dale looked at the writing.

don't forget to upend every flag

"I'm not sure," he said after a long moment.

"That slippery son of a gun in the Duster wrote it, ya know?"

"That'd be my guess too."

Brown pointed at the note. "And what flags is he talking about? Weren't no flags at the village."

"It's a riddle, Sheriff. He's talking in code. Are there any signs or banners in the village? Anything else that's similar to a flag?"

Brown scrunched his lips and looked to the side. "Nope."

Damn. Dale tried to think of anything he saw in the village that could be substituted for *flag*. He thought of the clothes he had seen folded neatly in the dresser. The blankets, too, had been neatly folded. There wasn't a misplaced stitch of cloth in the whole place.

Brown grunted and leaned up off the car. "I suspect you're going to want a ride. They got you boys some rooms down there in Staunton."

Dale glanced at his watch. It was later than he thought— pushing six o'clock. "That'd be great..." he said, trailing off as he looked at the note again. He wasn't ready to give up on this. Not yet. He pointed at the note. "May I take this with me, Sheriff?"

CHAPTER TEN

THE STONEWALL JACKSON HOTEL in Staunton, Virginia, was built in 1924 and was the most desirable accommodations in town. It was designed by H.L. Stevens in Colonial Revivalist style and featured marble floors, chandeliers, the Colonnade Ballroom, and a Wurlitzer Organ. It sat atop a hill in downtown with a large sign on the roof that lit up bright red at night. Dale had been in the lobby several times when he was younger, but he'd always hoped for the opportunity to stay in one of the rooms.

He wasn't going to get that opportunity during this assignment.

Special Agent in Charge Walter Taft was a notoriously cheap bastard. As head of the Bureau of Esoteric Investigation, he followed a policy of "second cheapest." Taft's thinking was that if a guy purchased the second cheapest available option, he wasn't getting the worst product available, but at the same time he was still saving money. Therefore, his agents received the second cheapest kind of ink pens and the second cheapest brand of briefcase. And when they traveled, his agents stayed at the second cheapest available lodging.

In Staunton, that meant the Ashbury Motel. The city's second most reasonable accommodations sat just off the exit to the interstate highway and right next to a filling station. The rooms had small wall-unit air conditioners and televisions—black-and-white as they were—which were both proudly advertised on the motel's sign. The gal at the front desk was a sweet old thing who greeted Dale and Wilson with a warm smile and the promise of fresh-baked cookies each day of their stay. Her name, conveniently, was Mrs. Baker.

It was dusk, and Dale was sitting on a folding chair outside the door to his room. He gazed forward across the parking lot toward the filling station. Beyond the gas pumps were the mountains, bluish violet framed above by a pale orange sky. Above this was a thick layer of clouds, their borders crisp and bright from the sunlight they concealed, and further above, the sky still retained its earlier blue. The sunsets were always gorgeous in the mountains, and it was one of the reasons Dale returned as often as he could. Though he was only a couple hours away, this was an entirely different world than the crowds and crime of D.C.

He was glad to be back in Staunton, even if the visit would be in the hectic, strained manner of a BEI investigation. Dale knew the place well, as he'd lived for a while in Harrisonburg, about a half hour away. Staunton was a quirky, unique city of about twenty-five thousand people. Even the name was a curiosity, being pronounced *Stan-ton* rather than *Stawn-ton*, as one would think.

He took a sip of water from the coffee mug he'd brought out from his room and turned his attention to the note on his lap. "Upend ... flag..." he mumbled.

He'd hated Wilson earlier for callously bringing up his past. But now, as he tried to figure out the message on the note, he realized that it could be helpful to think back. As uncomfortable as that might be.

The camp he had been at was quite different than the Marshall Village. It was more utilitarian, with cinder block buildings and pole barns in the back. Dale tried to remember if there was anything that might have resembled a flag. Something the Marshallites might have had at the village as well. He thought hard for a few moments—and drew a blank.

He strummed his fingers then set the note on the small wrought iron table next to his chair. The phone from his room was sitting on the table as well. It had a long cord, and he'd brought it out with him when he sat down. He'd been procrastinating on the phone call he needed to make. Sometimes it's hardest to call the people you care the most about. Especially your parents.

Dropping his birth name when he joined the BEI hadn't been nearly as hard on Dale as it had been on his mother. *I gave you the name,* she would say. *I should damn well get to call you by it.* Mom hadn't understood how he could give up everything he'd once been to go around chasing "murderers" and "perv-o's." She was especially flabbergasted that he chose to do so *after* he made his fortune. Timing, she contended, was never Dale's strong suit.

To make matters worse, the nature of his work with the Bureau meant that he often had to change their plans at the last minute. Dale met his mother for breakfast once a week, but he'd had to cancel on her that morning, as he'd been following Willard Ledford to the Jefferson Memorial. Mom had been less than happy when he'd broken the news, but he hung up with the promise that he would give her another call as soon as possible.

He dialed. "Hey, Mom."

"About time I heard from you." Her voice had the character of a pile of wet leaves. "You chasing some crazy clown again?"

She didn't say *clown* metaphorically. Last year he'd tracked down a deviant who thought he was the world's latest messiah and showed it by driving around the Southwest in a clown suit, exposing himself to women and senior citizens.

"Not this time, Mom."

"So what are you doing?"

"I'm afraid that's classified."

"Can't tell your own mother. What a world. I hope this job is worth it to you, Waddy."

"Don't call me Waddy." It was her nickname for him. It was based on his birth name, and he couldn't let her use it. He'd always hated it anyway.

"Fine." She sighed loudly, deliberately into his ear.

Dale rolled his eyes. "Did you have a good day, Mom?"

"Oh, it was wonderful. The neighbor walked her dog twice today, not once." Her sarcasm came in thick, measured doses.

He should have known how asinine it was to ask a seventy-six-year-old shut-in how her day had been. "I need to get going. Duty calls. Always a pleasure."

"Fine. I love you, Waddy."

Waddy again. There were donkeys less stubborn than his mother.

"Love you too."

He hung up.

A noise came from the opposite side of the parking lot. Wilson was walking down the small hill that led up to the filling station. He'd left a few minutes earlier saying he needed to grab something. In his hand was a six-pack of beer. He struggled to keep his balance on the sloped grass in his dress shoes.

Dale watched as Wilson crossed the parking lot. Earlier at

Rich's Diner was the first time he had seen Wilson since they were partnered together for his first assignment. While the rest of the Department of Justice, including SAC Taft, hailed Dale as a new prodigy after his success with the case, Wilson was the lone holdout. Dale's answer to the riddle posed by the perpetrator had been incorrect, and Wilson felt that Dale's steadfast belief in his answer had been arrogant. When Dale solved the case with a bullet rather than his brain, Wilson had said he was reckless.

Wilson popped one of the cans of beer off the plastic six-pack holder as he approached. He extended it to Dale, who took it.

"You know I don't drink," Dale said and tapped his mug of water with the beer can.

Wilson gave him a look. "One beer won't kill you."

"I suppose not."

He'd never been a drinker, though he often found himself in situations where drinking was a de-facto necessity. At a disco, for instance, he always ended up with a beer. Somehow a nice glass of iced tea just doesn't fit in that environment. Still, in situations like the one with Wilson that was currently presenting itself, Dale did his best to refuse drinking. If a guy thought you'd have one beer with him, he would then think you'd be willing to have multiple beers with him. And Dale didn't like full-on drinking. It clashed with his passion for physical fitness, and alcohol had a tendency to make a perfectly fine person look like an ass. Dale could handle that one just fine on his own, thank you very much.

But Dale conceded. He smiled, pulled the tab on the beer, and took a drink. He grimaced but tried to hide it. He'd never liked the taste of beer, even in college. While others quarreled about the flavor of domestic versus imported beer, Dale thought it all tasted like cat piss.

He smacked his lips and tried to clear the taste from his mouth. "A preemptive peace offering?"

Wilson sat down in the other lawn chair. "Just call it a nice gesture."

Dale was encouraged by Wilson's deed, but he wasn't naïve. Word had it from some of Dale's FBI acquaintances that Wilson referred to Dale as "the BEI Fluke." One beer wasn't going to drop Dale's guard.

They were quiet for a moment, each sipping their beers and looking out across the parking lot. There was a steady noise of cars from the highway.

Despite knowing that he shouldn't drop his guard, Dale also knew that he should try to thaw the ice. Wilson had indeed made a nice gesture with the beer. He could return the favor.

"How are things in the ol' Cody Wilson love life?" Dale had to pause slightly before he said "Cody." He could never remember the guy's first name. It was always "Wilson" or "Agent Wilson." That was it.

Dale on the other hand preferred to go by his first name, much to the chagrin of Wilson and SAC Taft and others like them. When the Bureau had given him the name "Dale Conley" and expunged his Prior Identity, or PI, one of the first things Dale did to take ownership of his new moniker was to fully adopt the first name.

"My love life? Awfully personal, don't you think, Conley?"

"Not like I asked your favorite position," Dale said. "Just chit-chat."

"I don't have time for a love life. I'm in a committed relationship with the FBI."

"Wonderful. I bet you're a blast at parties. But, then, you don't have time for parties."

"No." Wilson looked at the note on Dale's lap. "May I see that?"

Dale handed it to him.

Wilson frowned as he looked it over. "What do you make of it?"

"Not sure. With messages like this, the guy's usually messing with you. There're double meanings all over the place."

Dale was always getting cases with riddles. Occasionally, he would get a guy who really knew what he was doing. A guy like that would use ciphers or ancient languages. But most of the time, the riddles were basic word-replacement. The suspects always thought they were cleverer than the police, teasing them with clues that they believed were brilliant. The problem was, a lot of the time these riddles were challenging not because the clues were brilliant but because they *weren't* nearly as brilliant as the suspect thought, making the connection between the words flimsy at best.

"What do you think the double meanings are in this one?" Wilson said.

Dale took the note back from him. "A word that sticks out to me is *upend*. Too formal. That's key to this. But to upend a flag..." That's how Dale always began examining riddles, by looking for the words that stood out.

"Maybe he means flying a flag upside down," Wilson said. "To desecrate it."

"That's not the only reason one flies a flag upside down."

"No?"

"Flying a flag upside down is a sign of distress." American flags had historically been flown upside down in times of trouble, on sinking boats or besieged outposts. "You know, Wilson, you might be onto something."

"What about *flag*?" Wilson said. "Maybe there's a double meaning there."

Dale had been focusing so much on *upend* that he hadn't considered alternative meanings for the word *flag*.

"Banner, pennant..." Wilson said.

"Ensign, standard ... Streamer. The colors. Stars and Stripes."

"Old Glory, Union Jack."

"Jolly Roger."

The two of them were quiet for a moment as they thought.

"Any of those lighting a bulb?" Wilson said.

Dale thought about it.

"Heck no," he said with a chuckle and put the note on the table.

"So what do you think?" Wilson said. "Is this a BEI case?"

Dale shook his head. "Nope."

Wilson gave him a confused look. "But it has all the requirements. A word chiseled into a piece of rock, a connection with a centuries-old mystery, a note with a riddle..."

"All true, but here's what I think. Those folks are in a world of hurt, and you got to find them as soon as possible. The note on the girl is clearly from the kidnapper. But as far as the word *Roanoke* being scratched on the rock, I think that some piece-of-crap high school student read about the colony in history class, heard about the abduction, and decided to play a little prank. You've got a real sicko on your hands, but not the kind that the BEI deals with."

The parameters on what constituted a BEI case were quite stringent. Since there were so few BEI agents—currently seven—the use of the Bureau's limited resources was carefully allocated. It was the responsibility of the agent to make the determination, and if Dale continued on with this case knowing that it wasn't fit for the Bureau, SAC Taft would pop a seal. Dale once tried to smudge the definitions so that he could continue on with an assignment in Hawaii. Taft's wrath upon his return to D.C. had been immeasurable.

Besides, Dale was ready to get home. He was ready for

some rest. He was ready to see Arancia. And, if he played his cards right, he was hoping for a date with Julia from Rich's Diner.

Wilson took a sip of his beer. "So what do you suggest we do?"

Dale pointed at the note. "I suggest you get a good cryptographer."

CHAPTER ELEVEN

THE NOTE from the Marshall Village sat on dirty, matted carpet. It drew closer to Dale's face, then farther away, over and over. He'd placed it on the floor between his arms, in line with his face, as he did pushups, sweating out the poisonous alcohol he'd consumed. Since he'd determined this wasn't a BEI case, he had only until the morning to contribute. And he'd be damned if he was going to let the riddle beat him.

The only light in the room was from the lamp on the nightstand, which put out a warm, golden glow in the darkness. A drop of sweat fell from the tip of his nose and landed on the plastic bag covering the note. He read the words repeatedly, obsessively. If he tried long enough, he'd have his moment of clarity when everything would click. At least that was the plan.

don't forget to upend every flag

He upped the speed of his pushups, propelling himself faster and faster. The riddle sitting before his face was simple.

Six words. So why the hell couldn't he figure it out? He refused to believe he was too stupid to figure out this simple riddle.

His pecs burned, and his arms began to shake. This was his final set, and he gave it his all before the last repetition, letting himself drop. Lying on the floor, his chest heaving, he stared at the note.

"Think."

Flags? What the hell could they have meant by *flags*? The word danced around his brain, touching every corner but leading him nowhere. He didn't have a damn clue.

He stood up and slung the note in the direction of the bed. It fluttered to the ground.

After a shower, Dale stood by the air conditioning unit in a fresh pair of briefs. The cool breeze felt good on his moist skin. He caught his reflection in the mirror. His chest and arms still had a nice pump from the pushups. He nodded his approval. A woman he dated once said he was the vainest man she'd ever met. He was comfortable with that.

He climbed into bed and slid the note under his gun, which sat holstered on the nightstand. It was a Smith & Wesson Model 36 Chiefs Special revolver. Five-shot, chambered in .38 Special. Nickel-plated. Round butt with original S&W wood grips. A tiny but powerful weapon. The small holster fit under the waistband of his jeans or even in his pocket—it was just as inconspicuous as Dale himself needed to be.

He stared up toward the ceiling, his hands behind his head. Wilson's words echoed in his mind. *"You figure that's why you were assigned this case? Because of your past?"*

Dale had always done his best *not* to think about his past, particularly the part Wilson was referencing. But there were times like today, with Wilson's help, when he had no choice but to remember.

The images came upon him in quick flashes. For a moment, he was back there again. There was the noise all around him, so loud and chaotic that it made his ears hurt. People shouting, screaming. And the bell, clanging loudly, incessantly, outside.

He was on the bed, his arms and legs lashed to all four corners. The rope was made of hemp, coarse, and it dug into his wrists. He was naked. They'd stripped him.

Selfish. He was being selfish. He wasn't the only one suffering. Dale turned his head to the side, and he saw Spencer on the other bed. He too was naked, tied down. Spencer was crying.

Dale yelled out to him, screamed his name at the top of his lungs. This angered the people looming over him. A large woman moved into his line of sight and slapped him across the jaw, hard enough to snap his head back to the other side.

He looked now at the people standing above him. They were shouting, and their faces were stoic, but a couple of them were stifling jeering grins.

The bell continued to ring. The damn bell.

Dale thought of the POWs in Vietnam and how much they were enduring. He tried to use this as strength. Mind over matter. If he could just focus on some other detail. He turned his face from the people and tried to concentrate on the ground. The floor was dirt with a spattering of stepping-stones. Grass grew in the spaces between.

One of the men spat upon him. Three more of them did the same. The shouting was so loud, so chaotic that he could not understand what they were saying. He only caught the occasional word.

Coward.

Righteous.

God.

Punishment.

Presently the chaos of the voices began to clear, and the shouting synchronized. They were chanting.

"You shall not leave! Ours is the way, and we cannot diverge!"

They shouted this in unison. Over and over. The voices got louder yet. The volume was oppressive, melding with the clanging of the bell. Dale could feel the sound on his face.

One of the men stepped forward holding a bullwhip. He loomed over Dale.

Darnell Fowler. His ugly face was contorted in rage. Short, red, coarse hair. Flushed skin. Lips curled back over a line of spear-like teeth.

"Ours is the way!"

———

Dale jumped out of bed. He breathed heavily and put his hand to his forehead.

He grabbed the coffee mug from the nightstand, filled it at the sink, and gulped down the water. His 501s were laid across the chair in the corner. He threw them on, buttoned the fly, and then opened the door.

He leaned against the doorway. The temperature had dropped quite a bit since the heat of the day. He took a few deep breaths. It had been a long time since he'd thought about all that.

A line of paving stones led up to his doorway. They were red and weathered. Most of them were cracked. His mind flashed to the stones from his memories, the stones on the floor, the ones he'd tried to concentrate on during the ordeal.

And then something clicked in his mind. It was the *eureka* moment after all.

The stones.

He ran inside and grabbed the note off the nightstand. He squinted his eyes, focused on the word *flag*. That was it. Sometimes all it takes is a traumatic memory to jog a guy's creative juices.

He ran to Wilson's room and pounded on the door. Wilson opened the door, rubbing the sleep out of his eyes.

"What the hell, Conley?"

Wilson rarely cursed, so even saying "hell" meant that Dale was really pushing his luck.

"I've figured it out. We gotta go," Dale said.

"Figured what out?" Wilson said, still rubbing his eyes.

"The note. Hurry."

"Wait a sec. How did you figure it out?"

"*Upend every flag.* Double meanings. We were focusing on the wrong word—*upend*. We should have been looking at *flag*."

"We did. Banner, pennant, ensign, standard. Remember?"

"Yes, but we were thinking too literally. Flag. Flag*stone*. Stone! Upend every stone. *Leave no stone unturned.* The Dare Stones."

It was the moment of clarity Dale had been looking for. Often with these riddles the whack jobs writing them tried to use the most obscure synonyms possible in a dull attempt to conceal their own lack of creativity. The thesaurus had become Dale's best friend. A more obscure name for a *stepping-stone* is *flagstone*. Since someone was emulating the Dare Stones, the connection between *flag* and *flagstone* could not be a coincidence. They wanted Dale to go back to the village and *upend* the rock with *ROANOKE* carved onto it.

Dale knew it had been wise to not give up on the riddle. As he always said, everything works out if you give it time.

Wilson began to nod. It was clear that a light bulb had gone off in his head. "The stone at the Marshall Village..."

"That's right. The first Dare Stone had the obituary information for Virginia Dare and her father on the top. But when the hiker who found the stone turned it over, there was more written on the other side."

"And you're thinking that—"

"That there's more information on the back of that stone in the village."

CHAPTER TWELVE

THE VILLAGE WAS PITCH BLACK. The stars were out, but the moon was hiding in the clouds. Wilson left the Custom Cruiser's headlights on, and the light went about halfway into the village, nearly to the well.

Dale and Wilson stepped under the police tape. They each carried a large Kel-Lite. The wind was blowing.

"I hope you're right about this," Wilson said. "Something doesn't feel right about coming out at one in the morning to the spot where a hundred and fifty people just disappeared."

"You scared of the dark, Agent Wilson?"

"No, I just don't want to end up as part of somebody's living doll collection."

Wilson had a point. For all they knew, the creep—or creeps—behind all this could be hiding out in the trees somewhere. Hell, there could be someone in the village itself, waiting behind the supposedly empty doors of the buildings to snatch the agents.

As they continued across the village, the light from Wilson's station wagon began to fade. Their path was lit only by the bouncing spheres of yellowish light from their flashlights.

"Be a heck of a time to see a bear, wouldn't it?" Dale said.

Wilson grumbled. "So what was written on the other side of the Dare Stone?"

"I'm not sure. Remember, the Dare Stones were discredited a long time ago. But it outlined what happened to the colonists, why they weren't at the fort when John White returned."

"So our stone might just tell us what happened to the Marshallites."

"Bingo."

They slowed down as they reached the far side of the village. Dale scanned the area with his flashlight until he found the *ROANOKE* stone.

He walked over to it and crouched down. He stuck his fingers around the edge and tried to move it. It barely budged.

"Yeah, I'd say this thing has been here for a while," Dale said. He stood up and gave the rock a good kick with the heel of his boot to loosen its hold in the ground.

Wilson put a hand to his forehead. "You mind being a little more careful with the evidence, Agent Conley?"

Dale knelt down again and began to pull back on the rock. "Give me a hand, would ya?"

Wilson crouched beside Dale, and the two of them pulled their combined weight against it. The rock teetered in place for a moment then tumbled from its resting spot, rolling onto its side.

The bottom of the rock was covered with an inch of moist earth. An earthworm struggled in the dirt. Dale plucked it out and put it in the hole where the rock had been.

"There you go, fella," he said.

Wilson rolled his eyes.

Dale began to brush the dirt from the bottom of the rock. Soon carved letters appeared. He grinned. "Yes, yes, I knew it."

Most of the dirt had been removed, and it was clear that there was quite a bit of writing on the rock. But the dirt filling the etchings made the words illegible.

Beginning at the upper left-hand corner, Dale quickly flicked the dirt out of each letter with his finger. A message appeared.

you'll find them where the others were but not quite.
names can be deceiving.
in line with a form not quite to have, at the caravan-makers.

"*Where the others were but not quite*," Dale read. "Another riddle."

Then he thought about something, a seemingly small detail—the word *Roanoke* carved onto the top of the stone.

And he felt the hairs on his arms begin to rise.

"Oh my god..."

Wilson stepped up to him. "Conley, what's up?"

Dale's mouth opened. At first he could hardly speak. "Someone carved *Roanoke* on top of this stone within the last few days. The markings are fresh."

Wilson nodded. "Right. What's your point?"

"The soil expert said this stone hasn't been moved in years." He pointed to the rock, to the long, dirt-covered lines of text on its bottom side. "Someone carved that message and planted it here with full knowledge that it wouldn't be seen for a very long time." He looked Wilson square in the eye. "*Someone's been planning this abduction for years.*"

CHAPTER THIRTEEN

DALE JUMPED UP IN BED. The phone was ringing. He answered.

"Hello..."

"Conley?" It was Sheriff Brown.

"Yes?"

"Get your ass to the hospital. The girl's awake."

———

Dale and Wilson walked into the hospital room. Dr. Susan Anderson, her brother the nurse, and Sheriff Brown stood over the girl's bed. Brian Anderson was kneeling over, looking directly at the girl.

She was sitting up, a couple of pillows propped behind her back. There were dark circles under her eyes. She looked past everyone with that same absent look that she had worn in the village.

Seeing the look on her face again, Dale's mind flashed back to other empty stares, dead eyes.

"Conley?" Wilson said.

Dale had stopped by the door.

"Sorry," he said and joined the others at the bed.

Susan momentarily made eye contact with him. He grinned at her. She pretended she didn't notice.

Brian was speaking to the girl.

"How about your family?" he said. "Can you tell us about them?"

The girl gazed forward blankly, not looking at Brian or anyone else.

"Father," she said.

Again the girl gave Dale pause. She hadn't said "Father" like she was calling out to her daddy. She'd said it like a title.

"Who is your father?" Brian said.

"Father. Father and the Man in Black."

The nurse stood up and approached the two agents.

"That's all she'll say. 'Father' and 'the Man in Black.'"

"What's her name?" Dale said.

"Now, how would we know that? Unless her name's 'the Man in Black.'"

His eyes flicked up and down, as if scanning Dale to find the precise cause of his stupidity.

Susan walked over, looked quickly at her brother and then turned to Dale.

"There's no way of knowing anything about her yet."

Dale nodded.

At least she'd acknowledged his existence.

"And the Man in Black?" Wilson said.

The sheriff cut in.

"Don't know that either. We've been trying this for twenty minutes, and neither of these two," he said, motioning toward Brian and Susan, "can get a damn straight answer out of the kid."

Susan put her hands out in a mediating manner.

"Sheriff Brown, please, try to understand. What we're attempting to do here is—"

"Susan, for Christ's sake," Brian said. "Can you be the doctor here and take command of this damn situation?" He looked at Brown and Dale. "Gentlemen, this girl has been through incredible trauma. Trauma we don't yet understand."

Dale looked at the girl.

"Man in Black," she said. "Father and the Man in Black."

"Johnny Cash?" Dale offered.

Susan whipped around to him, looking aghast and angry. A little joke never hurt anyone, but it appeared to have offended the hell out of Susan.

"What methods have you tried?" Dale said to her.

Brian answered for her. "We've attempted gentle, non-intrusive, oral communication."

"In other words, you've tried talking to her," Dale said.

Brian scowled ... but said nothing.

Dale stepped toward the bed. The girl breathed slowly, her gown rising and lowering at a steady, even pace. Dale waved a hand in front of her face.

"Father," she uttered.

Dale leaned down, put his face in her line of vision.

"Hi, sweetheart. How are you?"

"Man in Black. Father and the Man in Black."

"Bet you've been going through some real rough times lately, huh?"

He put his hand on the bed, about ten inches from her arm, and eased it toward her.

What Brian was doing wrong was that he was keeping his distance from her. If Dale could make contact with the girl, he reasoned he had a good chance of getting through. The power of touch and all that.

"Father," the girl said.

"Why don't you tell us what happened to all your friends and family. Everyone here, we all want to help them."

He guided his hand closer to her arm. Three inches away.

"Father and the Man in Black."

"You want us to help your friends and family, right?"

His fingers touched her skin. The girl closed her mouth, quieting for the first time. Dale gazed deeply into the girl's eyes.

In his peripheral vision, Dale saw Susan nod appreciatively.

The girl's lips began to part...

...and she shrieked wildly, lunging at Dale. She swiped at him, clawing at his face. Her nails raked across his cheek, tiny razors.

"Only Father and the Man in Black!" she screamed, her small face pink and twisted with violent rage. "Only they may know, only they may speak!"

Dale staggered back, holding his cheek. "Son of a gun!"

He put pressure on his face and wondered how clean that girl's nails were—especially after spending an indeterminate amount of time in the woods. There was blood on his fingers.

Brian and Susan rushed over to restrain the girl as she thrashed about wildly.

Brian yelled out. "Susan, we need more diazepam!" He turned to the sheriff and the agents. "You three, out. You've brought enough chaos."

"We ain't going anywhere until the doctor tells us to," Brown said.

"Susan," Brian implored. "*Come on!*"

"Yes. Go," Susan said. Her gaze rested on Dale for just a moment. "Out. *Now*."

"Come on, boys," the sheriff said to Dale and Wilson.

The three exited the room.

———

They strode briskly away from the room. Dale dabbed at his injury. There were what felt like three or four scratches going diagonally down his cheek, nearly meeting up with the wound on his lip from Willard Ledford.

Dale looked at Wilson. "That girl's been brainwashed. I saw it in her eyes. I know the look."

Wilson tilted his head and frowned.

"Come on now, Conley."

"I'm positive."

Brown gave them a look. "You two mind letting me in on what you're talking about?"

"Agent Conley spent some time at the hands of ... a cult," Wilson said.

Dale could always count on Wilson to provide blunt truth when needed.

After college, Dale struggled in the wide world, barely keeping his head above water. Just before things reached a cataclysm, his friend Vance came along and bailed him out. He offered Dale a position as a reporter at his startup newspaper, *The Worldwide Weekly Report*, whose goal was to explore the eccentric types of news stories that traditional papers wouldn't cover—conspiracies, paranormal activity, government cover-ups.

Toward the end of Dale's second year on the job, the *WWR* got a scoop about a strange group of people calling themselves the Collective Agricultural Experiment. They were a socialist Christian community in rural Virginia, at the mouth of the Chesapeake Bay. Their leader was a man named Glenn Downey. Certainly the community was bizarre, but that alone was not titillating enough for the *WWR*. It was only when there were rumors of disciplinary beatings and armed guards that Vance decided to investigate, sending Dale and a young intern photographer named Spencer Goad in undercover.

The problem was, their covers were quickly blown. And the repercussions had been terrible.

"I was at the Collective Agricultural Experiment," Dale said to Brown, "and I saw people acting just like that girl in there. That same glazed-over, crazy look."

Brown stopped abruptly. "You were one of the CAE survivors?"

His mouth hung open.

Dale nodded.

"So you think the Marshall Village was a cult too?"

"I didn't at first. But now ... yes."

The idea had been bouncing around his head since he first crossed under the police tape at the village. He'd tried to keep the thought away, but the girl's maniacal behavior showed that his initial intuition was right. Her chant-like repetition of *Father* particularly bothered him. At the Collective Agricultural Experiment, Glenn Downey had his followers call him Father.

"This is your investigation now, Mr. BEI," Wilson said. "What do you need from me?"

"I need you to be my research assistant."

"Come again?"

"The clue on the stone. We need to—"

There was yelling from the opposite end of the hallway.

"*Hey!*"

It was Susan. And she was pissed. She rushed toward them from the girl's room and walked right up to Dale.

"What the hell was that in there?"

"I beg your pardon?"

"In her room. Johnny Cash? Really? Are you that insensitive?"

"You mean, what I said?"

Dale had to think for a second before he realized what she was talking about. He'd made a little quip about Johnny Cash when the girl said "Man in Black." It had seemed an appropriate time to cut the razor-sharp tension—and to give a nod to a living legend. Dale wasn't a particular fan, but who didn't love "Ring of Fire"?

"Yes, what you said," Susan said. "You're awfully cavalier for someone investigating a mass kidnapping."

Wilson took a step toward her. "Dr. Anderson, if I may, I assure you Agent Conley might seem like a real rogue, but I know he has nothing but the safety and well-being of the missing people on his mind."

Dale bit his lip, fought back some fake tears. "Wilson..." he said and put his hand on the other agent's shoulder. "That's the sweetest thing you've ever said about me."

"You see?" Susan said. "Why don't you try growing up, Mr. Conley?"

"Well, although I'd like to stay here and have you show me the errors of my wicked ways, Agent Wilson and I are investigating a mass disappearance. So, if you please." He gave Susan a deep bow then turned back to Wilson. "Come on. We don't have much time."

Dale, Wilson, and Brown walked briskly to the exit.

As they pushed through the doors, Dale looked back down the hall. Susan stood where they had been. Her arms were crossed with one leg kicked out to the side.

Dale waved at her.

She turned on her heel and stomped back toward the girl's room.

Dale watched her leave then pushed through the exit door.

If only he wasn't embroiled in this assignment, he would have been chasing her with unhinged zest. Susan Anderson was smack-yourself-across-the-face attractive. And Dale could also see intelligence, resolve—and deep kindness.

But he had to stay razor-sharp, understanding now that the Marshall Village was the same breed as the Collective Agricultural Experiment. If things ended at all like they had for the CAE, the missing Marshallites were in even more trouble than he had thought.

He hated thinking of the CAE. And he hated that he was now going to have to reflect on his experiences there to help him solve this case. It had been years. But he could still hear that damn bell.

CHAPTER FOURTEEN

THE BELL RANG INCESSANTLY. It was a sharp noise, the kind that feels like it's stabbing through your skull.

Dale sat at a chair facing the desk. On the other side was a cracked leather office chair, turned away from him. He could see only the top of Glenn Downey's head. They'd been like this for the last two minutes since Dale came in and was told to take a seat.

Dale had wanted to resist. He wasn't one to take orders, particularly from captors. But the odds were stacked heavily against him. There was a man standing in the corner with a gun, and Dale had a feeling he knew what this impromptu meeting was about. The only thing it could be about. They'd discovered who he was and why he had come to the Collective Agricultural Experiment. They found out that he wasn't a true believer. That he was, in fact, a reporter.

This was two days before his first attempted escape. With Spencer. Through the woods. When they were caught and beaten.

The clock on the wood-paneled wall ticked between

the *clangs* of the bell. Glenn's chair remained unnervingly still. Darnell Fowler stood in the corner holding an AK-47 across his chest, one of the many gifts the CAE received from Soviet sympathizers. He sneered at Dale, his eyes never looking away from him the entire time Dale was there. He was about five-foot-six and muscular for his small frame. His hair was short and red with the texture of a Brillo pad.

When Dale and Spencer had first arrived, they were quickly introduced to Darnell and his Blue Guard. Darnell was like Covey, the infamous slave-breaker in Frederick Douglass's autobiography. He was everywhere at once, a specter, appearing at random throughout the camp. Behind buildings, popping out from bushes. Always with a club or his whip. And though Darnell certainly wasn't a Rhodes Scholar, Dale imagined he had been quite bright back in the real world. The owner of a successful lawn care business, something like that.

The bell finally stopped ringing.

The chair squeaked and turned, and then there was Glenn Downey, his eyes registering stifled anger from behind his tinted glasses. He threw a wallet across the desk. It was Dale's. He and Spencer had been forced to surrender any personal items when they first entered the camp. This blew Dale's original idea of using pseudonyms.

"I knew your name sounded familiar," Glenn said. His voice had a heaping helping of Texas in it. He held up a newspaper—a copy of the *Worldwide Weekly Report*. "Didn't you think anyone would catch on?"

He dropped the paper on the desk.

And here Dale was thinking no one read the *WWR*.

There was an article by Dale's Prior Identity on the front page. A small, smiling picture of him was next to the byline.

Dale wasn't one to back down, but at the moment he was

more scared for his life than he had ever been. "We'll leave. We'll leave right now, and you'll never hear from us again."

"Really?" Glenn placed his fingers together in a bridge under his nose. "I have your word on that?"

"Yes. My word of honor."

"Your word of honor."

Glenn smiled and looked at Darnell, who chuckled.

He stood up. He was short, only an inch or two taller than Darnell, and thin as a rail. His thick brown hair was a helmet hairsprayed firmly to his skull. The mustache on his sunken face made him look like a macabre cowboy, and his tan shirt and brown suit pants drooped off his frame.

"Somehow I don't trust that honor of yours," Glenn said. "After all, didn't you lie about your intentions when you came here?"

"Let us go, please. Spencer's just a kid. He's our college intern."

"There are infants in this camp. I think a college kid can fend for himself. And you too. No, I won't be letting you leave. You've been here for a week now." He pointed at the leering man in the corner. "As you've seen, Darnell and the Blue Guard have all means of escape well guarded. Not that it's entirely needed. Up until you boys came here, everyone who joined the CAE did so of their own free will. Only a couple of escape attempts. And those who have tried have been very disappointed afterwards."

Darnell took a step forward, hoisting the gun up higher across his chest. He smiled wider. His skin shined in the light coming through the blinds.

"I think we are really going to learn to love each other," Glenn continued. "You'll be my greatest challenge yet. Can I convert two nonbelievers? I'm willing to bet I can."

Dale had known all his life that few people around him

could match his will and his independence, but this place had taken one hell of a toll on him after only one week. As Glenn and Darnell stared down upon him, he wondered if Glenn might be right. Maybe he wasn't strong enough.

CHAPTER FIFTEEN

IT WAS QUIET, and it smelled like books.

Dale sat at a table in the library of Madison College. There were the usual sounds—books opening and shutting, pencil scratches, a door quietly closing in the distance. The very atmosphere of a library was conducive to mental expansion.

Madison was Dale's alma mater. It was a fitting place for his interest in history, having been named for James Madison, the fourth President of the United States and principle draftsman of both the Constitution and the Bill of Rights. It was a small school and was mostly sheltered from the turbulent '60s. Dale hadn't been one for partying or joining silly groups with well-meaning causes and goofy names. But he did pick up one good friend, his potluck freshman year roommate, Vance.

Sitting on the table in front of him was the stone from the village. He'd put it on a plastic garbage bag to protect the table. The college students gave sideways glances as they walked by. The words scratched into the bottom were much deeper than those spelling *ROANOKE* on the top. The carver had obviously wanted them to stand the test of time since the message was to be buried in the ground for years. Dale touched the letters. They were a good eighth of an inch deep and must have taken a long time to carve.

He shut the book he'd been reading and rubbed his eyes, stretched his back. He had just a cursory knowledge of the Dare Stones, and he and Wilson had only found one text with any information. Fortunately it was a good one.

The story of the Dare Stones was almost as fascinating as that of the Lost Colony itself. A tourist from California named Louis Hammond discovered the first Dare Stone while looking for hickory nuts off U.S. Highway 17. This was 1937, a year which just so happened to be the exact 350th anniversary of the Roanoke Colony. *The Lost Colony* musical was also opening that year to commemorate the anniversary. This improbably perfect timing of the stone's discovery was one of the main reasons that it was deemed a fake.

The stone's message was allegedly the work of John White's daughter, Eleanor, and described an Indian attack that wiped out most of the colony, including Eleanor's husband, Ananias Dare, and their daughter, Virginia. Though the stone could have easily been lost to time as nothing more than an elaborate hoax, it found a supporter in history professor Haywood Pearce, Jr. Despite the inconceivable timing, Pearce held that the stone was authentic.

In 1939, a stone-hauler named Bill Eberhardt discovered the long-sought second Dare Stone. Over the next three years, forty-seven more Dare Stones were discovered all over the South, mostly by Eberhardt. Professor Pearce endorsed these stones as well. A journalist accused Eberhardt of using acid to forge the stones' inscriptions, and when acid was subsequently found at Eberhardt's workshop, even Pearce had to admit that the new stones were frauds. But he still maintained that the first stone was authentic. Even when no one else did.

Dale found himself identifying with Professor Pearce. Like Pearce, Dale had been ostracized to the periphery of society because he based his actions on convictions, beliefs, what he perceived to be right. The road to hell that's paved in good intentions? It's a freeway. Six lanes wide.

A stack of books landed on the table. Wilson stood in front of him. "Here are the other ones." He plopped into a chair.

Dale put a finger to his lips. "Quiet, Wilson. This is a library."

Wilson groaned. "Any luck?"

"Look at this." Dale pointed to the book.

On the left page were two images of the original Dare Stone—the top side of the stone and the bottom—each covered with small, scratchy letters. On the opposite page were transcriptions. The top side said:

ANANIAS DARE &
VIRGINIA WENT HENCE
VNTO HEAVEN 1591

ANYE ENGLISHMAN SHEW
JOHN WHITE GOVR VIA

And the bottom read:

FATHER SOON AFTER YOV
GOE FOR ENGLANDE WEE CAM
HITHER ONLIE MISARIE & WARRE
TOW YEERE ABOVE HALFE DEADE ERE TOW
YEERE MORE FROM SICKNES BEINE FOVRE & TWENTIE
SALVAGE WITH MESSAGE OF SHIPP VNTO US SMAL
SPACE OF TIME THEY AFFRITE OF REVENGE RANN
AL AWAYE WEE BLEEVE YT NOTT YOV SOONE AFTER
YE SALVAGES FAINE SPIRTS ANGRIE SVDDIANE
MVRTHER AL SAVE SEAVEN MINE CHILDE
ANNANIAS TO SLAINE WTH MVCH MISARIE
BVRIE AL NEERE FOVRE MYLES EASTE THIS RIVER
VPPON SMAL HIL NAMES WRIT AL THER
ON ROCKE PVTT THIS THER ALSOE SALVAGE
SHEW THIS VNTO YOV & HITHER WEE
PROMISE YOV TO GIVE GREATE
PLENTIE PRESENTS
EWD

"Is that English?" Wilson looked at the words like they'd just spat on his mother.

"Elizabethan English," Dale said. "Early Modern."

"Great. Care to translate?"

Not long ago, Dale would have gone cross-eyed looking at all the strange spellings and oddly placed *V*s. But last year he had a strange case in which his suspect believed there were anarchist messages hidden in the original texts of Shakespeare. As such, Dale had a rudimentary knowledge of Early Modern English.

"The top side says, 'Ananias Dare and Virginia went hence unto Heaven, 1591. Any Englishman show John White, Governor of Virginia.'"

"John White," Wilson said. "The man who went back to England?"

"Right. The leader of the colony. It's asking any

Englishman who found the stone to show it to Governor White."

"And the back side?"

Dale scanned over the text. "'Father, soon after you went to England we came here' … 'Misery and war' … 'Half dead' … There were twenty-four people left. The Indians brought them a message about an English ship, but they didn't believe it was White. Then the Indians suddenly turned on them, killing all but seven. Virginia, her child, was 'slain with much misery.'"

Wilson looked at the words carved into the Marshall Village stone. "That doesn't connect at all." He sighed and crossed his arms.

Dale read the riddle.

> *you'll find them where the others were but not quite.*
> *names can be deceiving.*
> *in line with a form not quite to have, at the caravan-makers.*

He looked from the Dare Stone's message to the riddle. There were a couple of parallels—the use of the word *heaven* and the idea of explaining the fate of a group of lost people. But the parallels were thin, and there was certainly no direct correlation. The creep wasn't going to make it that easy on him.

The *others* in the first line was clearly a reference to the original Roanoke colonists. So the writer was saying that the missing Marshallites could be found where those colonists had been … but not quite. The colonists had been at Roanoke Island. But what would be *not quite* Roanoke Island? Another place nearby?

Dale grabbed one of the books Wilson brought, an atlas, and found a map of the area. Roanoke Island lay between the North

Carolina mainland and the barrier islands of the Outer Banks. Perhaps one of the other islands? Directly east of Roanoke Island was Bodie Island, which was actually a peninsula. South of Bodie was Hatteras Island. Each island had several towns, and Dale cringed a little at the number of potential candidates.

Wilson leaned in closer.

Dale pointed to the map. "I'm thinking the place that the clue is referring to is somewhere near Roanoke Island, somewhere in the Outer Banks."

Wilson looked at the stone from the Marshall Village. "Would any of those places have anything that's a *form not quite to heaven?*"

"Not that I—Yes, of course!"

A student who was sitting a couple tables away shushed him.

"Sorry," Dale whispered then turned the atlas to face Wilson. He pointed to a town only about fifteen to twenty miles from Roanoke Island.

Kitty Hawk.

"*A form not quite to heaven*—an airplane," Dale said. "The world's first manned flight took place not twenty miles from the Roanoke Colony. At Kitty Hawk." Two incredibly important places in American and world history were right down the road from each other. History does quirky things like that.

Wilson nodded. "I'll be danged," he said. "You've done it again, smarty pants."

Dale nodded. It did seem to fit perfectly.

Maybe too perfectly?

The second line of the riddle was giving him pause. *Names can be deceiving.*

"What's wrong?" Wilson said.

"Suddenly I'm not so sure."

"What do you mean? *A form not quite to heaven.* An airplane. It doesn't get much more clear-cut than that."

"That's why I'm suspicious."

These riddles weren't always technically complex, but every word counted. And there was too much here that didn't fall into place. Yes, the airplane connection was obvious, but what was there about Kitty Hawk that would be connected to *caravan makers?*

Wilson scowled at the note. "*Names can be deceiving.* So what deceiving name could he be talking about?"

That was the question. Kitty Hawk ... Cat Eagle? Feline Raptor? There was nothing about the name Kitty Hawk that seemed deceiving. So maybe he was extending his search too far. Maybe he needed to look back to the original stone, back to ...

Roanoke.

There was the Roanoke Colony of the 1500s that existed on Roanoke Island. But these days there was also the city of Roanoke, Virginia. A city famous for its railroad industry.

The caravan makers.

"That's it! You said it yourself, Wilson. Back at the village. Roanoke, *Virginia.*" Dale pulled another book from the stack, this one a tourism book of the Southeast. He quickly flipped to the section about Roanoke. "*Where the others were but not quite.* The original colonists were from Roanoke Island. Today we have the city of Roanoke—two completely different places with the same name but not quite. And look at this. 'Roanoke is perhaps most famous for being the home of Norfolk and Western Railways.' Trains, Wilson. *Caravans.*"

Wilson nodded slowly, hesitantly.

Dale looked at the book in front of him again and clapped. "I knew we'd find it. Everything works—"

"Everything works out if you give it time, I know." Wilson waved it off. "But what about *the form not quite to heaven?*"

That troubled Dale too. It was the vaguest part of the riddle. As such, it was likely the most important part as well.

"I don't know," Dale said. "But I know this much—we need to get to Roanoke, Virginia."

"You're sure about that?" Wilson raised an eyebrow. "Roanoke, Virginia, is hundreds of miles from Roanoke Island. It'd be a heck of a misjudgment."

Of course it would be. Wilson's calculated trepidation was one of his strongest attributes as an agent, but it got in the way when Dale needed to make a firm decision and see it through. During their first assignment, Dale took a snap shot that shattered the kidnapper's femur and saved a young girl's life. Wilson thought that Dale had been reckless. Dale's Model 36, with its 1 7/8-inch barrel, wasn't known for its accuracy, and neither, particularly, was Dale. But in the end, the girl was alive, and the creep was in prison.

Wilson's hesitance was more annoying than helpful. Dale knew when to follow his intuition. And he was right about this. "Roanoke, Virginia. That's where they are."

CHAPTER SIXTEEN

DALE STOOD in the shadow of the massive Norfolk and Western corporate headquarters in downtown Roanoke. If there was anywhere in the country that could be considered a *caravan maker*, this was it.

During the drive there, Dale read up on the building in the books from Madison College. Of course, neither Dale nor Wilson were Madison students, so the urgency of the situation required them to creatively "borrow" the books— shoving them into Wilson's briefcase.

The building was a 150,000-square-foot art deco behemoth located in the heart of downtown. It was built in 1931 as an eight-story, 138-foot corporate castle that could withstand almost anything. The impetus behind creating such a sturdy building was the loss of the original headquarters to a fire in 1896. Not ones to tempt fate, Norfolk and Western made this building to last. Not only was it fireproof, but it was built on a foundation of solid rock with steel foundation columns that sank to a depth of ten feet below the surface of the basement, which itself was seventy-two feet deep. The construction included one million bricks, two million pounds of structural steel, and 5,000 cubic yards of concrete.

In short, the building was imposing.

Norfolk and Western was the *caravan maker*, and Roanoke was the location that was *the same but not quite*. Dale was certain. But what he didn't know was where precisely the riddle wanted him to go. He had considered going to the nearby Roanoke Shops, which was Norfolk and Western's storied manufacturing and maintenance facility where they famously made their own engines. Dale thought that this was a long shot. After all, how would the kidnapper be able to hide a hundred forty-seven people in a busy plant full of steel and machinery? Still, it was worth considering, so he'd sent Wilson to check it out.

The more logical location was the company's corporate headquarters, so that's where Dale had gone. The final piece of the puzzle remained—*in line with a form not quite to heaven*. He didn't doubt that solving the kidnapper's riddle would lead him to the kidnapped people. These crazies always made their puzzles challenging but solvable. After all, if the puzzles weren't solvable, no one would ever see their genius.

The problem was that once Dale found the people, they were just as likely to be dead as alive.

Heaven could mean one of two things—some representation of a blissful hereafter, or a reference to the sky. As Dale wasn't quite sure how to get to the afterworld in the middle of downtown Roanoke, his first instinct was to look upwards.

He cupped his hand over his eyes and peered toward the tops of the buildings. Nothing out of the ordinary. A plane passed overhead, and for a split second he thought that maybe this was the work of the kidnapper. It was a jetliner and was several thousand feet away. Dale felt absurd. Sometimes working among the delusional gave him a tendency toward paranoia himself.

In the distance were the Blue Ridge Mountains. Something caught Dale's eye, something on the side of one of the peaks. It looked like some sort of communications tower at first, but as he looked at it for a moment, he realized it was not a tower at all. It was a star. Not a point of light, but a geometric star. A giant, five-pointed star, like a sticker on a grade schooler's paper.

A star. A form that was supposed to be in the heavens, but was rather stuck on the side of the mountain. *A form not quite to heaven.*

Why the hell would someone put a huge star on the side of a mountain? He pushed his sunglasses back onto his nose and looked around for someone to ask. Across the road was a coffee shop. He jogged over.

It was a small place with raggedy booths and raggedy patrons. The air was thick with smoke, and there was a cooler of pies on the front counter. It was the kind of place Dale would like.

He went to the counter where a large, older woman was reading a newspaper. She looked up from her paper and gave him a big smile as he approached.

"Help you, sugar?"

"I'm wanting to know what that star is on the mountain out there."

She just looked at him for a moment. "Not from around here, are you?"

"No."

"It's the Roanoke Star up there on Mill Mountain. It's the city symbol." She leaned around the cash register and thumbed through the various brochures that were displayed there. She grabbed a red one and handed it to Dale. "Here."

It read:

Roanoke: The Star City of the South

Dale thanked her and headed toward the exit.

"Not gonna get nothin'?" she called after him.

On the front of the brochure was a picture of the star he had seen. It was composed of a series of five concentric neon stars held up by a metal scaffolding structure set among the mountaintop trees. Next to the picture was a brief paragraph.

The Roanoke Star gives the Star City its nickname. Constructed in 1949, it sits over 1,000 feet above the city and can be seen for miles. The star is 88 ½ feet tall and weighs 5 tons. Soon, to celebrate the nation's bicentennial, the star's colors will be changed from all white to RED, WHITE and BLUE!

Dale stuffed the pamphlet into his back pocket and pushed through the glass door of the coffee shop.

Adrenaline surged through him. This star was his *form not quite to heaven,* and the Norfolk and Western headquarters was his *caravan makers.* Now he just had to figure out how the two were *in line.*

He looked back at the building. The best he could figure, the southeast corner of the building would logically be the most inline with the star—the corner of Centre Avenue and Jefferson Street. He ran over.

The corner was nothing of note. Just brick walls and a decorative tree in the sidewalk. He looked all around him. Cars and other buildings.

He leaned against the tree and looked back out to the star, hoping that somehow inspiration would strike. This had to be the place.

But he sure as hell was at a standstill.

Dale stuck his hands in his pockets and dropped his chin to his chest. That was when he saw it.

A rock about one foot across. It was in the square of earth surrounding the tree he was leaning against. Like the *ROANOKE* stone back at the Marshall Village, this stone was buried in the dirt.

Also, like the stone at the Marshall Village, there were letters scratched upon the surface.

CHAPTER SEVENTEEN

THE MAN'S heart was still racing. Conley had walked right past him. Who would have thought that he would choose to come into the coffee shop? Of all fluke decisions, why in the world had Conley decided to come in here? It was a good thing the man always prepared himself for every contingency.

He was dressed like a working-class man—at least how he imagined a working-class man to dress. He wore a big, red flannel shirt and a pair of greasy jeans. To help further disguise himself, he wore a pair of sunglasses and sported a two-week beard, which he'd been growing out for the occasion.

And Conley hadn't noticed him at all.

He just walked up to the front counter, asked the old hag about the Star, and left with a brochure. Twice he'd walked right past him, once on the way in, once on the way out. Within a foot of him. So close that he felt his breeze. He could smell him.

When he first came to Roanoke to stake out the logistics, the man had decided upon the coffee shop because of the large glass windows. They faced Centre Avenue and looked upon the Norfolk and Western building. The perfect vantage point. From here he could witness everything, and he wouldn't have to sit in a parked car or stand suspiciously on the street corner. There were even counters with barstools right up against the windows on either side of the door. He couldn't believe his luck when he first found the place. It was another sign that this was all meant to be.

His excitement was at a rapid boil, not just from seeing Conley so close, but because he could see Conley putting everything together. He'd watched him find the building, search for a *form not quite to heaven*, succumb to frustration, and finally he saw him look out to Mill Mountain and discover the Star. It was thrilling to see his plan come together so wonderfully, and it made him bulge in his pants. The ache was fantastic.

He'd known that Conley would be able to put together all the pieces. He was the puzzle man, after all. Now there was only one more piece left for him to discover.

Conley had done so well thus far, as a matter of fact, that he'd given the man a fright. Back in Staunton he hadn't anticipated that Conley would actually chase after him. When he drove by the village the second time and saw all the idiot police trying to handle the girl, he figured he was home free. Several minutes later, he was beyond surprised to see a sheriff's car flying down the road behind him with its lights on. Of course, whatever the hillbilly had put into that Custom 500 hadn't stood a chance against the 360 he had in his Duster.

The man had handled that minor hiccup perfectly. He easily lost Conley and the fool sheriff. And since then everything had gone exactly as planned. As predicted, Conley figured out the initial clue that he pinned onto the girl's back. That led him to the second clue under the rock in the village. Ever since he buried the stone several years ago, it had always nagged at him that maybe he had made the riddle too obscure, that Conley wouldn't be able to decipher it.

But here he was in Roanoke, Virginia, sitting back comfortably, drinking coffee and watching Conley as he did indeed put the finishing touches on the riddle.

Conley was about fifty yards away. He wore a tan leather jacket and jeans and was leaning against the tree. Just then he noticed the stone and bent over to read what was scratched on its surface.

It was time.

The man grabbed the walkie-talkie that was sitting on the counter in front of him and pushed the button. "Proceed."

He smiled and took a sip of his coffee.

Conley was about to get a big surprise.

CHAPTER EIGHTEEN

DALE LEANED TOWARD THE ROCK. There were tiny letters scratched in the corner, so small he couldn't read them.

He knelt down, getting closer. The letters were about half an inch tall. They read:

look up ↑

Dale's stomach sank. This couldn't be good.

He stepped away from the tree, tore off his sunglasses and looked upward. The brick wall of the building loomed over him. It was dizzying. He squinted in the sunlight and shaded his eyes with his hands. At first he saw nothing.

Then he noticed something. Small shapes on the top of the building, peeking just over the edge. Barely visible. He narrowed his eyes but couldn't make out what they were.

He ran into the road. A pickup truck honked at him, and he skidded to a stop as it veered to miss him. The driver spat some colorful words as he regained speed. Dale went to the opposite sidewalk and looked to the top of the building again.

Now he could tell what it was he'd seen. Feet. The feet of four people wearing Marshall Village attire. They were standing on the very tip of the building, their toes over the edge.

"Oh my god."

Dale instantly went into a full sprint and crossed the road once more. He ran down the Jefferson Street sidewalk and burst through the front door of the building into a busy lobby. People in dress clothes crisscrossed the marble floor, going about their business. Several of them stopped what they were doing and looked at him in frightened confusion.

Dale came to an abrupt halt, his boots squeaking. He scanned the lobby. At the far end of the room was a single set of elevator doors with a large group of people waiting. That wouldn't do. He needed a staircase. There were some office doors, a set of restrooms, and a front desk with a reception- ist, who stared at him suspiciously. Then he saw a door for a stairwell in the corner of the lobby.

He bolted toward it.

On the opposite side of the room, Dale saw someone moving toward him. It was a security guard. He was a tall black fella with muscles bulging through his dark, police-style shirt. Dale also noticed a set of killer sideburns that ran all the way down to the man's jaw line. He was momentarily jealous.

The guard threw himself in Dale's path just as he was about to make it to the door. "Sir, is there something I can—"

Dale pulled out his badge and pushed the guard down in one continuous motion. "Federal agent."

He threw open the door and rushed to the stairs.

The security guard barked behind him. "*Hey.*"

Dale bounded up the steps two at a time. His footsteps echoed loudly up and down the stairwell. As he made it to the second-floor landing, there was a banging of a door below him. He glanced down.

The security guard had entered the stairwell. He looked up at Dale. "*Stop!*"

Dale continued to race up the stairs. He was quickly to the third floor. Then the fourth.

Below him, the security guard was still pursuing, a determined grimace on his sweat-covered face.

By the fifth floor, Dale was winded. But he reminded himself of his purpose—the people on the roof. He was nearing the top. The door to the rooftop entrance was within view.

He grabbed onto the handrail and pulled himself up. Just as he reached the door, he was suddenly yanked backwards.

A strong hand grabbed him by his shirt and threw him against the wall. A jolt of pain ran through Dale's back.

The guard stuck a forearm against Dale's throat.

"What exactly do you think you're—"

"I'm a federal agent," Dale said. "You have people standing on the edge of your roof."

"Let's see some I.D."

"There's no time." Dale moved for the door, but the guard yanked him back.

"Get it out."

Dale frantically dug his badge out of his pocket, fumbling with it in his anxiousness.

The security guard looked at it. His eyes lit with recognition. "Department of Justice," he said before his voice turned suspicious. "But what the hell is the Bureau of Esoteric Investigation?"

The guard lessened his grip on Dale.

Dale snatched the badge back.

"Will you just unlock the goddamn door? There are people out there."

The security guard looked uncertain for a moment before conceding. He turned around to face the door and grabbed a six-inch key ring from his belt—then stopped abruptly.

"Uh-oh."

"What's wrong?" Dale said.

"I have the key to the door lock, but I don't have a key to that." The guard pointed to a chain and padlock wrapped around the push bar. "We didn't put that there."

Goddammit, it was another little ploy from the kidnapper. These creeps always liked to make their situations as elaborate as possible.

For about two seconds, Dale was at a loss for what to do next. Then he pushed the security guard behind him. "Stand back."

Dale pulled his Model 36 from its holster, aimed at the door...

"No!"

...and fired. There was a terrific roar from the shot. Both men ducked instinctively to avoid a ricochet.

The security guard opened and closed his jaw, trying to pop his ears.

Dale looked at the chain. The bullet had shorn a shiny groove into one of the links. Nearly severed but not quite. A tiny bridge of metal, less than a sixteenth of an inch thick, held the link together.

"Let me see the door key."

The security guard searched through the keys on his key ring and found the right one. He handed it to Dale. The ring was still attached to the guard's belt via a retractable cord, and the guard stumbled as Dale pulled toward the door.

Dale unlocked the door and disengaged the push bar so that the chain was the only thing holding the door shut. He took a step back and gave the door a strong kick. A jolt of vibration went through the sole of his boot and all the way up his leg.

But the door didn't open.

He looked at the guard. "Little help?"

The guard stepped beside him.

"Okay," Dale said. "Three ... two ... *one.*"

They both kicked, and the door flew open with a crash, smacking loudly against the wall outside. Their momentum carried them forward, and they stumbled out onto the gravel of the building's roof.

The bright sunshine was jarring, making Dale squint. Then he saw them. They were on the opposite end of the building, four people wearing Marshall Village clothing and standing on the very edge of the roof.

CHAPTER NINETEEN

THE SECURITY GUARD stepped next to Dale.

Two men and two women. Their backs were facing Dale as they stood on the parapet surrounding the roof, perfectly still with their arms at their sides. Up this high, the light breeze had become a wind. The woman on the end had waist-length hair, and it tossed around her violently, a light brown cocoon wrapping her small frame.

Aside from the sound of the wind, Dale detected other noises coming from the ground below. Shouts, fearful screams. A crowd. The Marshallites had drawn gawkers.

He slowly walked toward the people, about thirty feet away, trying to make as little noise as possible on the gravel covering the roof's surface. He holstered his revolver.

"Folks?" he said.

The woman with the long hair turned around. Her feet wobbled for a moment as she moved. Dale grimaced and reached out feebly with his hand. His heart thumped in his chest.

The other Marshallites remained motionless, looking out to the distance.

The woman was in her mid-thirties. She looked through Dale with a blank, mile-long stare. Her arms remained at her side. As the hair whipped around her face, her blue eyes appeared for brief moments.

"He told us someone would be coming," she said. Her voice was flat.

Dale continued to inch toward her. Slowly. He didn't want to spook her. She and the other three had been brainwashed. Just like the girl back in the hospital, this woman's mind was in someone else's pocket.

"Who told you this?" he said as he took another slow step toward her.

"The Man in Black."

The girl from the village had said the same thing. Over and over. *The Man in Black. Father and the Man in Black.* She had said that they were the only two who could speak. Back at the Collective Agricultural Experiment, Glenn Downey, the one who called himself Father, was the only one who was allowed to speak. The Marshallites, however, were under the influence of two men. Somehow that seemed even more sinister.

Dale watched the woman's face. It remained completely still, like the rest of her. She had the look of a waitress on the eighth hour of a nine-hour shift, but there was still strength to her face, though, a sort of resilient beauty.

There was the wail of police sirens from below.

"Why are you doing this?" Dale said.

"He told us we must."

Dale was getting closer and closer. "I'm here to help you down."

"He told us you would say that."

Dale was within feet of her now. He reached out toward the woman. "Why don't you just step down, okay? Take my han—"

"STOP!" the woman screamed in a tone that rang in Dale's ears. "You can come no further. The Man in Black wants you no closer than a yard from us."

Dale glanced back at the security guard, who looked just as confused as Dale was. He shrugged his big shoulders.

"Why?" Dale said to the woman. "What did the Man in Black tell you to do?"

"If you wish to stop our descent from the building, he wants you to decipher this." She slowly raised her arm. In her hand was an index card.

Somehow Dale knew there were going to be another riddle. As he took the card from her, it caught in the wind, nearly blowing away. He gasped.

A single word was written on the card in black marker, the same scratchy handwriting that had been on the stone and note back at the village:

ORCA

"You are to decipher that note," the woman said. "If your answer is incorrect, we shall take the final descent."

"Decipher? I don't understand."

The woman didn't respond. She simply turned back around and faced the same direction as the other three people.

From behind, the security guard yelled out. "Enough of this."

Dale looked back just in time to see the guard rush toward the people.

Without turning around to look, the woman again shrieked. "STOP!" She stuck one leg out over the edge of the building.

There was screaming from the crowd on the street below.

Dale grabbed the guard by the arm as he ran by and yanked him back. The large man's momentum nearly pulled both of them down. Dale gave him a vicious look.

"Wait," Dale said to the woman as he pushed the guard behind him. "Wait. Just please put both feet back on the ground."

"Decipher the note," the woman said.

"I will," Dale said. "Put your foot down. Please."

The woman slowly lowered her leg back onto the parapet.

There was a loud *bang* from behind, and Dale jumped. The door to the stairwell flew open, and three cops ran out onto the roof.

"Go," Dale said to the guard, motioning toward the cops.

The guard nodded and ran to the door, his arms up, urging them to stop.

The police wouldn't be able to help. Dale knew just how deeply these people on the roof had been hoodwinked. Brainwashing was a powerful thing. The only way to get these folks down was to play the kidnapper's game.

He had one shot at saving them.

ORCA. His mind went into frantic overdrive. *Orca*'s only use in the English language was for the whales. Orca whales. *Killer* whales. Death. But what was the damn connection?

There had to be a tie to the Dare Stones and the Lost Colony. Dale was no marine biologist, but he figured that even though killer whales had a large range, sightings off the modern-day North Carolina coast would be rare. And, besides, if the Roanoke colonists had spotted one, it seemed the sort of thing they'd leave in the historical record.

"Your time is running out," the woman said, still not turning to face him. "Make your decision." She extended her leg away from the building again.

The crowd below screamed.

The answer to the riddle would be subtle. Something to do with the word itself. Nearly all taxonomical names were derived from Latin, and though he didn't have the scientific name in front of him, he could hazard a guess that *orca* derived from the whale's genus name, which itself would have been derived from the name *Orcus*. This was a Roman god of the underworld, the one who dealt punishment for broken oaths. But the name *Orcus*—like that of the king of the underworld, *Hades*—could also be attributed as the name of the underworld itself.

The death theme could be the kidnapper's sick way of telling Dale what was planned for the rest of the hostages—reinforced by the four people prepared to jump from the roof.

"We are to give you but a minute," the woman said. "Your time is almost up."

The remaining three Marshallites stuck a leg out over the edge of the building.

More screams from the crowd below. Dale heard footsteps approach from behind. The cops had seen enough.

Orcus = death. Could it be that simple? Of course, the kidnapper wasn't alluding to whales, but was a Roman god really the answer? Certainly death could be a connection—the potential death of the hostages and the disappearance of the Roanoke colonists—but was that a strong enough connection? It just wasn't gelling in Dale's mind. It felt off.

He looked at the note. *ORCA.*

"Ten seconds," the woman said.

Seconds. He had seconds left.

The letters? Maybe it could be an acronym. *Original Roanoke Colonists ... Attacked?* Yes, that fit. Being attacked by Indians was one of the possible fates of the original Roanoke colonists.

Dale felt a tingle of hope. But in his last moments of

remaining time, he had to double-check. Rearranging the letters, perhaps. If he put *C* first it might—

There it was.

Of   course.   *CROA*.   The   unfinished second *CROATOAN* message that the Roanoke colonists left behind. The colonists may well have fled to Croatoan Island.

ORCA = death. CROA = survival.

"C-R-O-A. Croatoan!" Dale shouted. "The unfinished second message of the Roanoke colonists!"

There was an agonizing beat as the four people continued to stand with their legs extended. Finally, in unison, they all retracted their legs, turned around, and stepped down onto the roof.

Dale released his breath, which came out choppy and hoarse. He hadn't realized that he was holding it.

A cheer came up from the crowd below.

The cops rushed past Dale toward the Marshallites. Dale looked at the security guard and took another deep breath. The guard nodded at him respectfully.

———

When you barge into a corporate headquarters, accost a security guard, fire your weapon within city limits, and talk four individuals out of suicide, there's a lot of paperwork. If there was anything more loathsome in the world than paperwork, Dale had yet to encounter it.

When he was done with that detestable task, he found himself back outside the Norfolk and Western headquarters. He looked down Jefferson Street, to the corner and the tree where he had been standing earlier. He saw the stone with the writing on it. All during the fiasco with the people on the roof, a thought was sitting in the back of his mind—*there will be another riddle on the underside of that rock.*

A second stone. A second riddle. Back at the library, he'd learned that there had been forty-nine Dare Stones altogether. If the kidnapper decided to follow that pattern, this assignment could damn well kill him.

He walked down to the tree. When he picked up the rock, he found that, unlike the one in the Marshall Village, it appeared to have been buried recently. The kidnapper would have known that he couldn't count on a stone remaining buried for years under a tree in the middle of a big city.

He ran his finger along the letters making the *Look up* ↑ message. The handwriting—or would that be stone-chiseling?—was the same as that of the other messages so far. He turned it over and brushed the dirt from the bottom.

As he expected, there was another riddle.

go to the rounded, razed top of a land that's royal, plotted, and taken

The riddles were getting easier. He had seen this before. The creeps who left taunting riddles started by making them difficult for the police but, fearing they were going to completely confuse them and thus end the game, eventually panicked and made the clues easier.

Thus far everything connected to the story of the Lost Colony and the Dare Stones. The only royalty involved in those tales were Queen Elizabeth and Sir Walter Raleigh.

And, conveniently enough, there was a city named for the latter. Raleigh, Virginia.

A car skidded to a stop beside him. Dale grabbed the stone and stood up.

Wilson hopped out of his station wagon and hurried over to him. "You okay?"

"I'm fine. Thank you," Dale said, still looking at the stone.

Wilson glanced at the chaos surrounding them. The

crowd hadn't entirely dissipated, and the police and fire-fighters were still loitering.

"Can't take you anywhere, can we?" Wilson said.

CHAPTER TWENTY

DALE'S FEET pounded the pavement, and his legs burned as he took another one of Staunton's steep hills. He sucked in a deep breath and cleared the top. He was in the downtown area, a picturesque region of pretty brick buildings, lampposts, and Southern charm by the bucketful.

Staunton was one of the most offbeat places in his old stomping grounds. In 1902 it became an independent city, so despite still being the county seat, it was no longer a part of Augusta County. Unlike other Shenandoah Valley towns, Staunton came out of the Civil War relatively unscathed, and there were buildings in town dating back to the eighteenth century. Staunton had a dark side, too, as it was home to Western State Hospital, a one-time lunatic asylum that had been under the command of infamous eugenicist Dr. Joseph DeJarnette, a place of lobotomies, electroshock therapy, and forced sterilization. Staunton was also well known for being the birthplace of President Woodrow Wilson.

Dale's Wilson—he of the station wagon and sensible neckties—had still been asleep next door when Dale woke up. Later that morning, when the library would open, they would follow up on his lead about Raleigh, and, with any luck, they'd be on their way to that city by lunchtime.

Running usually cleared Dale's mind, but right now it was still spinning from the Roanoke ordeal. He hadn't seen mob mentality like that in years, and it scared him as much today as it had then.

After working at the *Worldwide Weekly Report* for a couple years, he received the assignment to cover the Collective Agricultural Experiment. He went to the camp as a legitimate member of the press. Certainly no one was under any false impressions that the *WWR* would soon be rivaling the *New York Times*, but by that point they had yet to begin investigating lake monsters and UFOs shot down by farmhands.

The biggest challenge was convincing the CAE that he and Spencer were truly interested in the organization's philosophy. It was a socialist group based upon a foundation of extreme Christian zealotry. Dale grew up as afraid of communism as he was of the bogeyman in a home without religion. His mother had turned her back on church when his father left shortly after Dale's eighth birthday, claiming to have done so based on a message from God.

That said, convincing the people at the CAE that he wanted to devote his life to socialistic Christianity was a challenge, but what he lacked in knowledge, he made up for with feigned enthusiasm. Dale's PI had always been able to compensate for his numerous inadequacies with some smooth words and a flashy smile.

The world of the Collective Agricultural Experiment that Glenn Downey had created was nothing like Dale anticipated. Thirty-six buildings of cinder block construction, most of them residential cottages holding a dozen people each. There were administration buildings and two communal structures—the dining hall and the most important structure on the grounds, the Pavilion.

It was a large, open area with a roof overhead and a cement slab floor—an oversized picnic pavilion. Four thirty-foot poles sat at the corners of the building's grounds. The poles held floodlights and the huge speakers from which Glenn's droning words could be heard throughout the camp.

Randomly, Glenn would use these speakers to assemble his followers at the Pavilion. In the middle of the afternoon. At three in the morning. He used these gatherings to rant about the various groups of people he felt were opposed to the CAE's mission. Civil rights organizations, concerned churches, the American government. But more than anything, the meetings were tests. He was testing his followers' resolve. He'd call them out, questioning them as to whether they would give their lives for the CAE. And they always agreed that they would.

The bulk of the camp was made up of the fields where Dale and the others worked each day harvesting the crops that sustained the community. Darnell Fowler and his Blue Guard patrolled the fields. Hovering along the edges. Walking down the rows. Always with batons and usually with an automatic rifle strapped across their chests. They wore the same uniform as the rest of the CAE staff—baggy, white, linen shirts and tan pants—with the addition of a deep blue armband.

Darnell had been under Glenn's complete control—the lieutenant from hell ... with a particular distaste for Dale's PI. Dale never figured out if Darnell was inherently sadistic or if it was something that Glenn Downey brought out of him. And he would never know for sure because when the rest of the Blue Guard died in the firefights outside the camp, Darnell disappeared. No one had seen him since.

But what Dale remembered most of all was the subservience from Glenn's followers, their unwavering belief in Glenn Downey and his message. Unconditional faith and love were dangerous. This would be confirmed repeatedly to Dale later in life as an agent. He once encountered a serial killer's wife who truly believed that her husband was "a decent soul" and stood by him until the day he fried. Beautiful, in a way. But dangerous.

Nowhere had he seen this phenomenon more than at the Collective Agricultural Experiment. There were chants. There were songs. A group of seemingly normal, intelligent adults somehow all came to call a man "Father" and "Dad." They would say and do anything that Glenn Downey commanded.

It rocked Dale to his core, more so than anything he'd ever seen.

The Marshall Village was a lot like the CAE. A group of people all following a leader with a seemingly ideological vision. The ones on the roof had been brainwashed. That much was clear. And, if the pattern from the CAE held true, Dale knew who was controlling them.

A jog always got Dale's analytic juices flowing.

He rounded a bend, and the drab Ashbury Motel appeared before him. Wilson was sitting on one of the lawn chairs in front of their rooms. A phone was on his lap, the handset between his shoulder and his ear. Dale ran up to him.

"He's here now," Wilson said and hung up.

"Father and the Man in Black, Wilson," Dale said between breaths. He put his hands on his knees. "That's all the girl at the hospital would say. At the CAE, Glenn Downey had his people call him 'Father.' There are two men behind this. The Man in Black brainwashed those people on the roof, but there's someone else running the whole thing. It's the damn professor, Wilson. I just know it is. We need to find Camden Marshall. Immediately."

"No need," Wilson said. "That was Sheriff Brown on the phone. Camden Marshall just turned himself in."

CHAPTER TWENTY-ONE

WILSON AND DALE barreled down the interstate.

Dale had spent a lot of time on I-81. Growing up in the Shenandoah Valley, 81 was a way of life. But it seemed like in these last two crazy days he'd been traveling up and down the highway more than ever. If he had to spend another minute in Wilson's big, green, faux-wood-covered Custom Cruiser, his mind was going to melt from mundanity. He missed Arancia in a bad way.

He was putting on a green dress shirt that he'd snatched from his room before they left. "When did this happen?"

"Half hour ago. During your jog," Wilson said. "He walked into the Sheriff's Office and confessed."

Dale pulled his arm through his left sleeve.

Wilson leaned away. "Hey, watch it, would ya?"

"You kiddin' me? We could toss a football in here."

Wilson frowned and looked Dale up and down. "What's with the grown-up clothes, anyway?"

"I like to make a good first impression with these creeps. What did Marshall confess to?"

"Everything. Said he abducted all those people. Every man, woman, and child."

"I'm guessing that this isn't going to wrap up with a nice little bow." If there was one thing that Dale learned since joining the BEI, it was that there were no simple answers.

"Not exactly," Wilson said. "He's admitted to abducting the people, but he won't tell us where they are."

Dale fastened the top button, flipped the collar up, and pulled the tie around his neck. It was light brown with thick, diagonal stripes. Nice and wide. His leather jacket looked smart with a shirt and tie under it. And *everything* looked good with 501s. Dress them up, dress them down. Fantastic.

"How much does he want?"

"That's the thing," Wilson said. "He's not asking for money. Not making any demands at all. He only wants to talk to the fed in charge. That would be you."

Dale slid a half-Windsor knot to his neck then exhaled as he leaned his head back. "Well, no one ever said it was gonna be easy."

————

Dale and Wilson arrived at the Augusta County Sheriff's Office and entered the viewing area of an interrogation room. It was dark and sparse, and their footsteps echoed. On the far wall was a large window, about eight feet wide—the backside of a two-way mirror. Visible through the glass was a man sitting at a table.

Sheriff Brown stood in front of them. His arms were crossed over his chest. He was chomping on gum and shaking his head as he looked through the window.

"Sheriff," Dale said as he and Wilson entered.

Brown extended a hand to Dale. "Hey, hero. Heard you found yourself some trouble down there in Roanoke."

"Trouble finds me wherever I go, big guy." Dale looked toward the window. "So, he's confessed?"

Brown led the agents across the room. "Damndest thing. Walks right into the office, nonchalant, not a care in the world. Says he'd like to make a confession. He's Camden Marshall of the Marshall Village, and he kidnapped the one hundred forty-seven missing people."

Dale looked through the glass.

Camden Marshall looked just like he had in the picture. The years had done little to change his appearance. His posture was perfect, and he sat with his hands placed one on top of the other on the table in front of him. He had a well-maintained beard and wore a flannel shirt and tan corduroy pants. He stared straight ahead, patiently, a small grin on his face.

"Actually, Sheriff, there are one hundred forty-one missing people," Wilson said. "One hundred forty-seven, less one in himself, less the girl in the hospital, less the four in Roanoke."

"How was he able to kidnap so many people?" Dale said.

"He's not talkin'," Brown said. "Won't tell us how he got the people or where they are. Only wants to talk to the man in charge."

"I guess that's me." Dale gazed at Marshall, who continued to face forward and grin, holding very still.

There was the flush of a toilet. A door on the opposite side of the room opened. Out walked Special Agent in Charge Walter Taft. He was zipping his fly.

Dale felt what little joy was in the room evaporate.

"Oh my god," he said, not trying at all to lower his tone or conceal his bewildered disappointment.

"Sorry about that," Taft said as he strolled across the room. "Had to drain the main vein." He smacked Dale hard on the back and pointed at the two-way mirror. "Looks like he landed right in your lap, you lucky son of a bitch."

"Not feeling too lucky at the moment, sir. What are you doing here?"

"The main suspect in my prime case turned himself in. You bet I'm here. Get used to it, pretty boy. I'll be around through the remainder." He reached into his pocket and grabbed some pistachios. "Glad you cleaned yourself up." He pointed at Dale's tie.

"You got your work cut out for you, Conley," Brown said.

"How so?" Dale said, slowly pulling his tractor beam of disbelief away from Taft.

"He's a real smug son of a bitch. Thinks he's smarter than everyone who tried questioning him so far. He's probably right, but that's beside the point."

"I can handle a cocky college professor."

"But that's not all," Brown said. "He's one of those types that won't budge. Not an inch. Isn't making any requests. Doesn't want a damn thing. And when you got nothing to lose, there's nothing you can be threatened with. Funny thing is, we usually see this with lowlifes. Real pieces of crap. But this guy—this guy's different. Educated, successful. No prior record. Just doesn't make sense."

"Then we'll have to keep playing his games," Dale said. "When there's no way to bargain with him, what other choice do we have?"

Brown shrugged. "You're gonna have to figure that out as you go."

CHAPTER TWENTY-TWO

DALE OPENED THE DOOR. The interrogation room walls were cement blocks with a smooth, polished surface. Greenish-brown in color. Dim, sickly light came from a set of humming fluorescent lights. Everything was dull, pea green.

He walked into the room with confidence. This was something he'd learned in training. Interrogation technique was one of the most important skills he gained at the Academy. New BEI agents went to the FBI Academy in Quantico, Virginia, posing as traditional incoming FBI agents. A BEI recruit left the twenty-week program after just sixteen weeks, at which point the FBI recruits were told that someone had washed out.

Unlike college, which was composed of as much nonsense as it was quality information, Dale found the Academy curriculum to be wholly useful. Of course, any guy would enjoy shooting guns and hand-to-hand combat, but the courses on subjects such as law and surveillance were also incredibly practical. Dale loved practicality.

Interrogation was a finer art than he'd imagined it would be. Most of his training had been finite, with a focus of time-tested techniques, but ultimately the most useful tip he'd gotten was one piece of general advice from an instructor. *Start gentle. You can always get sterner, but you can't go backwards.* Dale didn't know if he'd be able to apply that principle to Camden Marshall. It was taking all his mental discipline to restrain himself from jumping over the table and tearing the man's limbs off.

He straightened his tie and pulled out a chair.

Marshall continued to grin. He smiled bigger when Dale sat across from him.

He was striking in appearance. Pleasant features, tall, broad-chested. He was model-level good-looking, one of those older models they have tossing a baseball with his "son" in a picture-perfect yard, a golden retriever waiting faithfully in the background.

He locked in on Dale with a pair of green eyes. Distinguished-looking crow's-feet sat at the corners. There was a sinister quality to his gaze, but the little grin lingered on his lips. If he was trying to make Dale come unhinged, he was going to need to try a lot harder. Dale had seen it all, and he wasn't going to buckle to this nut-job.

"Good afternoon, Professor Marshall. I'm Agent Conley."

"Good afternoon, Agent Conley. I'm Camden Marshall." He imitated Dale's intonation.

Dale eyed him. "You have something I need."

"Oh?"

"One hundred forty-one missing people."

Marshall tilted his head. "Thought you'd start with some chit-chat."

"Not my style."

He nodded. "I admire the direct approach."

"Where are they?"

"The *really* direct approach. Very good."

Their eyes locked. A game of chicken. Dale didn't fold.

"They're somewhere safe enough," Marshall said finally.

"Where?"

"I've given you five people so far. The girl and the four on the roof. You keep solving my riddles, and I'll keep releasing them. A few at a time."

"These people have family who want to know they're safe. Tell us where they are. Let us get these people home."

Marshall raised his eyebrows. "Mmm. So you're a liar, Agent Conley? Everyone in my village either had no familial ties or broke all connections."

"You don't think these folks have *anyone* who cares about them?"

Marshall shrugged. "They were with me for years. No one came knocking."

"What's the plan, Camden? You going to keep running us around on wild goose chases indefinitely?"

"Aw, didn't like my first two riddles, did you? Well, you're a big buck of a boy. I think you can handle this. Wait till you see some of the other stones I've left for you. Just smile and play my little games if you want to see any of those people alive."

Dale leaned forward. "Why are you doing this? What do you want?"

"The local fools have already asked me that. There's nothing with which you can negotiate, no way to buy me off. I trust you've begun working on my latest quandary. Have you figured it out yet? *Go to the rounded, razed top of a land that's royal, plotted, and taken.*"

Dale paused. He had a strong feeling the riddle was leading to Raleigh, but he couldn't be sure yet. And he couldn't give Marshall the wrong answer. To do so would be to appear vulnerable. In a situation like this, that was a death wish. So he had to bite the bullet. If he was going to find the Marshallites, he didn't have time for pride. "No, I have not."

"That's a shame. You haven't much time. So let me get you started. Focus on the word *plotted*."

Dale uncrossed his arms. "What do you mean, I haven't much time?"

"Oh, did I forget to mention that little parameter?" Marshall said with a shit-eating grin. "It is so very tiring carving out all those messages."

"Spit it out, Marshall!" Dale had been maintaining a facade, but he could feel it cracking.

"Temper. You didn't think I'd make them all so easy, did you? This riddle needs to be solved by the end of the day."

"Midnight?"

"Oh, no, no, no. Close of the business day. Banker's hours, in fact. Three p.m." He leaned over and looked at Dale's watch. "Just under seven hours." He opened his mouth wide in feigned surprise. "Well, go. Go, agent! Time is of the essence. People's lives are hanging in the balance."

Dale eyed Marshall coldly before he stood up and walked to the door.

He put his hand on the doorknob and glanced back. Marshall waved at him, fluttering his fingers.

CHAPTER TWENTY-THREE

"*Seven hours*," Wilson said, rushing toward him.

"Don't worry. I got it." Dale loosened his tie. "He said the key word is *plotted*. Raleigh was a planned city, one of the earliest American examples. Eighteenth century. And the land was *taken*, as the clue says, when state officials bought a thousand acres from—"

"Dammit, Conley," Taft said. "We don't need a history lesson. What are you getting at?"

"It means I'm right, sir. They *are* in Raleigh."

"Son of a gun," Brown said, looking through the window. A prison guard was escorting Marshall from the room. "He's playing us like a five-dollar fiddle."

"At the moment, I'm at a loss for other options," Dale said. "And I need to borrow your car, Wilson."

The thought of driving Wilson's lumbering station wagon made Dale a little ill, but desperate times called for desperate measures. All in the line of duty. Oh, how he missed Arancia.

Wilson handed Dale his keys. "Don't wreck my car, Agent Conley." He narrowed his eyes.

"I'll try not to, Agent Wilson." He turned to Taft. "Sir, I need my own car delivered here by the time I get back."

"Exactly why?"

"Since Camden Marshall is going to keep sending me after these riddles, I'm gonna need faster wheels. And I'll need a chopper, too."

Taft's lips curled. "You little ... *Fine*." He stormed toward the exit.

"So I'll you see you back at the Ashbury Motel?" Dale called out behind him.

"The Ashbury?" Taft spat, his hand on the doorknob. "I'm staying at the Stonewall Jackson." He slammed the door.

Dale jingled Wilson's keys. "Here goes nothing."

"You know what, Conley?" Brown said. "Until you get that fancy car of yours, I think I can do you one better than Agent Wilson's station wagon."

———

The airplane shook all around Dale, and he clenched the seat. He'd never been airsick—he was, in fact, a great flier—but right now he felt like his lunch might resurface at any moment.

It was a small crop duster, and its best days were distant memories. Everything rattled and squeaked. When Dale looked out the window, he saw the wing was covered in patches of rust and shook violently each time it cut through a pocket of rough air.

To Dale's left was the pilot, a portly good ol' boy named Butch, who controlled the plane with short, jerky movements of the yoke. Dale was wearing cups, and Butch's voice came through the speakers sounding all scratchy.

"Darn glad Carl was able to find me," Butch said.

Sheriff Carl Brown was the kind of man who knew "a guy"

for every situation. He'd called up his second cousin and set up the trip within a matter of minutes.

"I was just about to fly this thing out to Waynesboro to pick up my nephew."

"Sorry to ruin your plans," Dale said.

"Just glad to help. Any friend of Carl's is a friend of mine."

Dale rapped a knuckle on the dash. "What the hell is this thing?"

"Beaver."

"I beg your pardon?"

"She's a U-6A Beaver. Old Army plane. This baby was in Nam."

"Looks like she barely made it out alive." The plane hit a pocket of turbulence and dropped a few feet. Dale was aware of his stomach once more. "How much longer we got?"

"Not long. Five minutes. Now hold on. Here's where it gets dicey."

Butch made a sudden, hard bank. Dale's face smacked into the window.

CHAPTER TWENTY-FOUR

IT WAS A DAMN WEIRD BUILDING.

The tower was cylindrical and well over two hundred feet in height, the tallest building in Raleigh.

Go to the rounded, razed top of a land that's royal, plotted, and taken.

The tower was perfectly round, but the top was flat. *Razed.* It was, of all things, a Holiday Inn.

The hotel staff had already let him check the roof. No Marshallites. The last time he stood at the bottom of a building trying to locate victims, he'd found a clue scratched into a stone. But he'd searched under every bush, looked around every tree and found nothing.

After walking the length of the parking lot, he crossed the road to a neighboring group of buildings to expand his search. He was getting desperate. Panic shivered through him. Maybe he was wrong. Maybe he wasn't supposed to go to Raleigh after all.

Something moved in the alley. A piece of paper fluttered from the sky, hitting the ground a few feet away from him. It was an envelope. Written on the front, in the now familiar scratchy handwriting, was:

Dale glanced up.

On the fire escape above him, a man wearing a black hooded jacket was climbing upwards.

The Man in Black.

They'd been following him.

Dale stuffed the envelope in the back pocket of his jeans and ran to the fire escape. He yanked on the ladder, and it clattered down, hitting the ground with a bang. He climbed and looked up. The Man in Black disappeared over the top of the building.

Dale's boots dug into the metal rungs. His hands scrambled to pull him up. He reached the top and hoisted himself over the edge just in time to see something he didn't expect.

On the opposite side of the roof, the man he was chasing jumped off the ledge.

The man flew across the gap between the building and the adjacent one. The other building was shorter, and it looked like the guy was going to make a giant red splat, but he rolled a time or two, absorbing the shock.

"Shit," Dale said. He jogged to where the man had jumped and saw him running away across the roof of the next building.

Dale looked down. The ground, four stories below, shrank and wavered. He knew what he had to do, but he hated that he had to do it.

He raced back to the opposite side of the building. This was gonna take a running start. He took a deep breath.

The things he did to keep the world safe from psychotic riddlers...

Dale sprinted.

The edge of the building drew closer. He saw the foot-tall parapet around the edge of the building. For a split second, he thought of how rotten it would be if his foot got caught and he fell face first to the cement fifty feet below.

Each stride of his legs brought the empty void between the buildings nearer. It now looked more like a canyon than a three-yard gap.

The ledge was within feet. He tensed his thighs.

And leapt.

His legs treaded empty air, and his arms pumped in circles around his body, as though he could pull himself across the empty space. He sensed the ground so far below, and its presence seemed to pull him downward like a magnet. His tie flapped behind him. The other building loomed before him, all too distant, frozen in time and space.

But slowly he drifted over the edge of the new building. For a lingering instant, he hovered over his new surroundings. A door, gravel, some vents. Everything felt foreign, like the moment your flight lands and you adjust to the new surroundings.

Then there was the pain.

In Dale's mind, he pictured himself landing like Dirty Harry, rolling a couple times and then casually hopping off the ground to continue his pursuit. But that's not how it happened. His legs crumpled beneath him, as much by accident as by will. Throbbing pain burst in his right ankle, and the gravel on the rooftop tore into his palms.

The chaos ended. He skidded to a stop.

He planted his hands into the ground and turned himself right side up. The Man in Black was at the other side of the roof, standing on the parapet with his back turned to Dale just as the Marshallites had stood in Roanoke. Dale pulled out his gun.

"*Freeze!*"

The man didn't respond. He slowly stuck his arms out to the side, forming a T-shaped pose. He remained like this.

"Turn around now!" Dale said. He tried to stand, but the pain in his ankle was too sharp. He slumped back onto his stomach.

The Man in Black leaned forward, slowly tipping over. He dropped off the building and out of sight.

Dale gasped.

He pulled himself up. The pain in his twisted ankle shot up through his leg, and he hopped on one foot to the opposite side. He braced himself for the sight of a mangled body and a splash pattern of blood.

But when he looked down, he saw the Man in Black climbing out of a giant pile of cardboard boxes. The bastard had this planned the whole time. He sprinted over to a nearby pickup truck, got in, and sped away.

Dale watched, panting, as the truck drove off. He sat down on the roof and wiped the sweat from his brow. He touched his ankle. It was swelling up, but he could tell it wasn't broken.

He took the envelope from his pocket and opened it. Inside was a piece of paper.

nice try, agent.
but you've misinterpreted the clues.
this is not the royal, plotted, taken land.
try again.
time's running out.

Dale loosened his tie, unbuttoned the top button of his shirt, and looked at his watch. 11:42. Earlier he'd been worried that he only had seven hours. Now he had just over three.

For the second time, he felt a wave of panic. A cold sweat flushed over his body. He froze, not knowing what to do.

Go to the rounded, razed top of a land that's royal, plotted, and taken.

Royal ... king, queen, prince. Knights, like Sir Walter Raleigh. *Plotted* ... planned, organized. Schemed? Or maybe the word was referencing *plots* as in holes. Burials. Could a *plotted land* be a graveyard?

Dale smacked his thigh in frustration, sending a surge of pain through his ankle. He was getting nowhere fast. He had to get back to Staunton. There was a chance of getting this thing solved with the people and resources back at the base of operations. But he was 200 miles from Staunton. What if he went that far just to find out that he'd backtracked? Given the scant time that remained, doing so could prove fatal for the Marshallites that were hidden at the end of this riddle.

Looking down from the roof, he spotted a filling station with a pay phone. He hobbled over to the fire escape and limped across the road to the phone. He deposited a dime, and a moment later the desk sergeant at the Augusta County Sheriff's Office connected him to Wilson.

"Conley," Wilson said. "What happened? Did you find them?"

"Dead end. I'm headed back to Staunton. Is my car there?"

"A time like this and you're worried about your dang car?"

Dale gritted his teeth. Just like The Animals, he couldn't stand being misunderstood. "I need a fast set of wheels. The clock's ticking."

"So what's our next move when you get back?"

Dale paused. "I don't know yet."

Honestly, he hadn't the foggiest idea.

"I'm glad I got you on the phone," Wilson said. "You need to find that pilot and get your butt back up here. She's talking."

"Who's talking?"

"The girl from the village."

CHAPTER TWENTY-FIVE

DALE WAS BACK in the girl's hospital room. With him were Susan and Brian. The nurse looked askance at him with a simmering but timid glare.

Dale knew he was running a risk by coming here. There were only two hours left. But he was up the proverbial creek with no paddle, and the girl was his only hope.

She was sitting up and looked quite alert. There was something about her appearance now that was completely different from the last time he had seen her. Her eyes weren't dead. She looked like a normal girl.

"You got her talking?" Dale said.

Brian lifted his chin. "Yes, we——"

"I was asking the doctor."

Brian's mouth moved. Small sputtering noises came out but no words.

"She's fully responsive," Susan said. "She's a little confused and very scared, but otherwise she's acting like a perfectly normal girl in her situation."

"What did you do?" Dale said.

Susan started to answer, but Brian spoke over her.

"She gave her the sedation and rest that you and the sheriff didn't think she needed."

It was clear that he'd been calculating his words. He said them like a scared freshman at a forensics tournament.

Dale took a step toward him. "How old are you?"

"My age isn't—"

"How *old* are you?"

"I'm twenty-eight."

Dale turned to Susan. "And you?"

"Thirty-one."

"He's your *younger* brother and your nurse, yet you let him do all the talking?"

Susan looked away.

"Is it right?" Dale said. "What he said about the sedative and rest?"

"Yes," she said. "If you'd just *listened* to us in the first place, it all would have worked out."

"I need to—" Dale started to make a demand but quickly changed it to a request. "May I talk to the girl?

"That would be fine. But remember, she's just a child. She's been through a lot. Take it easy. None of your usual clowning around."

Out of the corner of his eye, Dale saw Brian slip out the door. He kept himself from scoffing and turned to Susan.

"Tell me, has she mentioned royalty? Anything about a king, queen?"

Susan gave him a baffled look and shook her head.

Dale knelt beside the bed. The girl looked at him. Those eyes that had at first looked so demented were now clear and blue, a pretty blue, the kind they put on cars. There were deep bags beneath the eyes, though.

"Hi, sweetheart. My name's Dale. I wonder if I might ask you a few questions."

The girl nodded.

"What's your name?"

"Caitlin."

Dale put his hand on the bed rail.

"Caitlin. That's a pretty name."

The girl smiled weakly.

"Do you know how you got here, Caitlin?"

She shook her head.

"Can you tell me about where you were living not too long ago, the Marshall Village?"

She nodded. "Kind of."

"Kind of? What do you mean?"

She shrugged, twisted her blanket between her fingers. "I don't remember much."

Caitlin was eight years old. She had been in the village just a couple of days prior and had likely been there for a very long time.

Dale looked at Susan. She mouthed, *I don't know*.

"You don't remember?" Dale said. "Weren't you there for years?"

Caitlin nodded again.

"But you don't remember that much?"

She shook her head.

"Can you tell me what it was like?"

She opened her mouth and spoke slowly.

"They made us do things we didn't want to do." She looked down at the blanket she was holding. "With words. The words made us do it."

The way she said that... The way she clearly defined that *words* had controlled the Marshallites. Dale began to suspect something of the Marshall Village that he hadn't yet. The implanting of subconscious thought. Waking suggestion.

Hypnosis.

"Who used the words?" he said.

"Father told us what to do, and the Man in Black used special words."

Father would be Camden Marshall, and the Man in Black was his man on the outside, the man who'd just escaped in Raleigh.

"Was Father the king of the village?" Dale said.

Caitlin looked up from her blanket. She raised one of her little eyebrows.

"Did anyone ever talk about a king or a queen?" Dale continued.

"Yes. The Man in Black taught us about King Roosevelt."

There it was. Roosevelt.

Franklin Roosevelt.

Susan knelt beside him. "Who's King Roosevelt?"

"FDR. When he instated the New Deal programs to put an end to the Great Depression, some people thought it was a godsend. But some thought he was overstepping his authority, becoming a tyrant, a monarch." Dale took out the paper on which he'd written the latest riddle. He pointed to the last words—*a land that's royal, plotted, and taken*. "One of the big New Deal projects is minutes away from here. Shenandoah National Park."

"But Roosevelt didn't *take* the park."

"He most certainly did. By force, as a matter of fact," Dale said. "The CCC carved the park out of the wilderness. The Civilian Conservation Corps. One of Roosevelt's New Deal programs that put shovels in the hands of the unemployed. Only problem was, there were already people living on the land. Hundreds of people. Entire communities were forcibly removed from their homes."

Dale was satisfied. A small smile came to his lips. But then he looked at the riddle again.

go to the rounded, razed top of a land that's royal, plotted, and taken

He was going to Shenandoah National Park. But where? The park covered more than 300 square miles.

"*The rounded, razed top,*" Dale said, pointing at the note. "That's what's throwing me off. The park is in the mountains, so the *top* has to be one of the peaks. They're small mountains, so they're all pretty much *rounded.* But *razed?* How can a mountain be razed?"

"It's that one with the rocky peak," Susan said sensibly.

Dale paused. "You're right. Old Rag Mountain. It's one of the tallest in the park—or the *top.* And its summit is rocky, barren. *Razed!*"

He could have kissed her. But he didn't. Which was good because her reaction to the hand he put on her shoulder was chilly enough. He quickly removed it.

And now he had to get his ass to Old Rag. The clock on the wall read 1:28. He had an hour and a half.

He stood up and looked at the girl. "I need to leave now. Get to feeling better, Caitlin."

He put his hand to her cheek and smiled. As he quickly turned to leave, Caitlin grabbed his wrist. Tears welled in the corners of her eyes.

"I don't want to go back. I don't like it there."

Dale knelt down again. "I know, sweetie. You won't ever have to go back there."

"You're here to stop them, aren't you? That's why you're here, right?"

She cried.

"Yes. You don't need to worry about Father and the Man in Black ever again."

Dale hugged her, and she sobbed on his shoulder. He looked at Susan. She reached out, and Dale gingerly transferred the girl into her arms.

He watched the two of them. Susan lifted her eyes to his. They glistened. She smiled painfully. Dale nodded at her.

Then bolted for the door.

CHAPTER TWENTY-SIX

As the elevator doors opened, Dale pushed his way past the two nurses standing with him in the car, apologizing as he did so. He sprinted across the lobby toward the main entrance, where earlier he'd seen a line of pay phones.

Dale was kicking himself. He needed his car more than ever. As it was, he'd have to call the Sheriff's Office to arrange transportation.

He put a dime in the phone, picked up the receiver, and was about to push the first button when he heard it. A rumbling. Very faint but still audible. It was coming from outside and far away, but the noise was so deep and resonant that he could hear it through the walls.

He hung up and rushed out the front doors. The noise was coming from the south. He stepped over to the opposite side of the parking lot and stood on a sidewalk, facing the sound.

It was louder now. Getting closer.

A man and his son stood on the sidewalk as well, staring into the distance, frozen in confused paralysis.

Dale grinned.

The sound that was approaching from the other side of the horizon was unmistakable to the aficionado's ear, but to the father and son, it must have sounded like a piece of construction equipment run amok. Dale knew just what it was—the throaty exhaust of a De Tomaso Pantera.

It was Arancia.

He'd wondered why Wilson wasn't at the hospital when he arrived. Now he knew. Wilson had left to deliver Dale's machine. The thought of having a strange uniformed officer driving her for 150 miles—not knowing what he was doing to her—had been bad enough. But now that rotten Wilson was driving her. At least, Dale reasoned, Wilson's anal-retentive qualities ensured that he wasn't doing anything wild with her.

A glint of light appeared over the crest of a hill in the distance. It was her well-polished paint shining brightly in the daylight, adding a second sun to the sky. He could now just make out her form—a sleek, low-slung shape pulling itself down the road toward him while its engine bellowed. Dale didn't usually get to see Arancia in motion from an outsider's perspective, and it made him smile.

The Pantera was an Italian-made machine, a sports car, small yet beefy as a Big Mac. It floated low to the ground with long, sexy lines that were a tantalizing mixture of curvaceous and angular. The wedge-shaped hood extended well beyond the two-seat cab. Behind the wide rear tires, the form abruptly ended with a gorgeous rear end and four exhaust tips, two for each of the dual exhausts.

From those mufflers came about the most beautiful noise that could come to a man's ears. Low and grumbling. Angry and edgy. A symphony of metal and a pacifier for frayed nerves. The noise began a few feet north of the car's exhaust from the mid-mounted Ford 351 Cleveland V8, an absurd mass of steel belching out 330 horses.

She was orange in color. Not bright orange. Nothing

gaudy. A faint, yellow-orange. He'd named her Arancia after the Italian word for the fruit not the color. It was a sensuous name, the kind you whisper into the dark void of a sultry night. *Arancia, Arancia.* Funny how Italian makes any word, even a piece of fruit, sound sexy.

Dale crossed his arms and nodded his head in appreciation of his girl's beautiful form. Next to him, the boy now grinned ear-to-ear. His father kept a firm grip on his shoulder.

"Holy mother of God," the man said to Dale. "What do you figure that is?"

"It's a De Tomaso Pantera."

The man squinted and turned to Dale. "What are you, some kind of car expert?"

"You might say that."

Arancia slowed as she turned onto Cantrell Avenue. Her turn signal was on. Dale could see Wilson now behind the wheel. This made him cringe. The boy next to Dale giggled with excitement as the car drew nearer.

She waited for another car to pass in the opposite lane, and then Arancia pulled into the parking lot, stopping right next to Dale. The man shielded his son with his arm.

The driver-side door opened, and Wilson got out, struggling to pull himself from the low position. He straightened his suit jacket and stepped up to Dale.

"Agent Conley?" he said with a smile. "I understand you're in need of some fast wheels."

"I am."

Wilson handed him the keys. "She's all yours."

Dale smiled as he looked over the metal beast before him. He put his hand on the roof, feeling the mirror-smooth finish. "Indeed she is."

He slid into the black leather bucket seat, leaving the door open. He looked over the brilliant instrument panel, the series of switches and gauges that looked more akin to an airliner than a passenger vehicle. It had only been three days since he'd last seen her, and he'd had severe separation anxiety. He had a problem. He knew this. But he didn't care.

He put his right hand on the shift knob and looked back to Wilson. "Only got room for one today," he said, pointing to the passenger seat where there was a pile of equipment from his stakeout of Willard Ledford. Cameras, tripods, microphones. He shut the door then thrust the key into the ignition, depressed the clutch and turned the key. The V8 thundered to life, a giant awoken from a peaceful dream. He pushed a button and lowered the electric window. "I don't have much time. I'll catch you back at the station." Dale looked at the man and his son. They hadn't moved. The father was still staring with a kind of mild dread. The boy was beaming. Dale winked at the boy. "Gentlemen."

Reminding himself of the urgency of his mission, Dale stomped the gas pedal and pulled off the clutch. The big tires in the back squealed, and the rear end tore to the left. But Dale's expertise easily calmed Arancia's thrashing nerves, pulling her back into line. Dale slowed down briefly to check the traffic and then hammered the gas again, screeching off through Harrisonburg.

CHAPTER TWENTY-SEVEN

DALE HAD ALWAYS WANTED a performance car.

His initiation had been through American muscle. The idea of a big hunk of metal hurtling itself down the road through sheer force of a gigantic engine was thrilling and purely U.S. of A.

He watched the muscle cars progress through the years and for a time considered getting one. He particularly liked the Camaro, Challenger, and Torino. But he always found his mind wandering back to F1 races and the European sports cars that he so loved. Slinky bodies that clung to curves.

The answer to his automotive prayers arrived in 1971 in the form of the Pantera, a joint effort between De Tomaso and Ford. The Italian styling and engineering was paired with Ford's massive V8. This was as perfect a blend as Dale could have hoped for—the raw, insane power of American muscle planted squarely in a true sports car. And at ten thousand dollars, though certainly not cheap, this was a vehicle that was available to more than just the superrich.

At times like these, an Italian supercar sure came in handy.

Arancia roared up Highway 33 toward Shenandoah National Park. Heading out of Harrisonburg, it was a straight shot through the Valley, hitting the towns of McGaheysville and Elkton. Massanutten Mountain with its sloped southern peak passed on the left. Picturesque rolling meadows and patches of woods spread out on either side, and the blue mountains of the park sat directly ahead, looming in the distance. It was a beautiful drive and one that Dale had taken countless times during college. But today it flew past him in a blur.

Arancia's siren wailed, something Dale had installed when he first joined the BEI. He had a red emergency light that he could hang from the rearview mirror when needed—he didn't like the idea of using one of the magnetic types on the roof. The chances of paint scratches frightened him.

As he swung the light side to side with his right hand, the cars on the highway pulled over for him. They were slow to react, evidently unaccustomed to lights and a siren emitting from a sleek sports car.

Dale smashed the accelerator and kept his hand poised for downshift at a moment's notice. Arancia's pointy nose sliced a path, the whole car pulsing with energy as though it was tearing a rift in the very air surrounding it. Dale's ears echoed from the screaming of the V8, which sat right behind him in its mid-mounted position.

The Valley ended, and Dale was hurtled up into the mountains, following the tortuous road through the thick, green trees. Arancia's wide tires twittered as Dale pulled her around the sharp curves, his hands holding tight to the wheel. He throttle-steered her around one final curve, and her back end kicked around, sliding side to side until he stabilized her.

He entered the park.

———

Minutes later he slid to a stop in a gravel parking lot, kicking up a cloud of dust. He looked at his watch.

1:50. Just over an hour to go.

At the trailhead was a wooden sign with an informative panel. Across the top of this structure in big, yellow, carved letters was "Old Rag Mountain." There were rows of pamphlets at the bottom, and he grabbed one of them. He pulled it open and traced the trails with his finger. It was a decent enough hike—3,000 plus feet of elevation. He checked his watch again, stuffed the pamphlet in his back pocket, and sprinted into the woods.

———

The group of hippies shouted as Dale pushed through them. He apologized as he ran by. They had been laughing and carrying on, but now they were all yells and jeers.

"Hey, man," one of the men said.

"Love assassin!" screeched a woman who looked like Janis Joplin.

Dale continued running, not turning around.

He was sweating profusely. The trail was steep. It wasn't the sort of trail that would usually give him trouble, but he wouldn't normally take it at a run. He was going as fast as he could, but he was slowing rapidly.

———

Ten minutes later. Halfway up the mountain.

The front of his T-shirt had patches of sweat, and he could feel that the rear was completely soaked, clinging to his back. His running had downgraded to a jog. His calves had ignited. His thighs were steel blocks. The forest was shady and cool, which was helpful, but the rocks and roots crisscrossing the trail exacerbated his challenge. He checked his watch.

Fifty minutes to go.

He pushed on.

———

He had completed this hike a handful of times, but it felt like the mountain had grown a couple thousand feet since his last visit.

Finally, though, the sign appeared before him, the one with an arrow that read "Old Rag Summit."

He was within yards now.

CHAPTER TWENTY-EIGHT

THE MAN in Black was so excited he could hardly stand it. Now was the time he was going to reveal himself to Dale Conley.

He was at the edge of the woods near the outcropping of rocks at the peak of Old Rag Mountain. He fidgeted with the mask in his hands. He was delaying on putting it on. There were a lot of people milling about the rocks in front of him, so he didn't want to draw attention to himself until he had to.

He'd had quite a scare back in Raleigh, and he knew it was because of his own carelessness. Unlike the Norfolk and Western headquarters, where he'd taken careful precautions to disguise himself, he had chosen not to take any measures to hide his face. He'd been wearing his hooded sweatshirt, after all, and he didn't think there was any chance that Conley would take more than a fleeting glance at him.

He certainly didn't anticipate that Conley would chase him up a fire escape. But that's what he liked about the guy, that indomitable spirit.

Conley would be arriving at any moment, and when he did, the Man in Black would emerge from the forest, wearing his mask and his all-black clothing. It was all going to be very dramatic. This was the first time Conley was going to come face-to-face with the Man in Black, so it had to be impactful.

There was a noise in the distance, from the direction of the trail. Commotion, raised voices. Then he saw a figure running up the trail headed toward the rocks. It was Conley.

The Man in Black put his mask on.

"Showtime."

CHAPTER TWENTY-NINE

DALE REACHED THE SUMMIT.

He burst out of the woods into the open, treeless peak. A stone expanse dotted with people lay before him. The sudden rush of sunlight made him squint. He took out his sunglasses and checked his watch. 2:54. Six minutes left.

The top of Old Rag Mountain was an area of large, rounded stone, something like a lumpy pile of gray ice cream, which, along with its impressive views, lent to its popularity. The green tips of the mountains created a rolling expanse that could be seen all the way back to Harrisonburg. Since the hike up the mountain was tame—that is, if one wasn't sprinting—it wasn't surprising that there were a couple dozen people relaxing on the stones. Dale scanned the scene, looking for anyone wearing antique clothing. There was a family sharing Wonder Bread sandwiches. A young couple necking. Some college girls taking pictures.

Then someone caught his eye. A man dressed all in black standing in the woods behind the stones. All by himself. The black hood of his jacket was pulled up over his head, and he wore a black Halloween mask—a smiling jester face.

The Man in Black.

The two of them looked at each other. There was a warm breeze on the peak of the mountain that seemed to be channeled in the space between them. No one crossed their line of sight. The Man in Black touched his arm where a watch might be and made a dramatic swipe of his arm across his forehead, as though wiping away sweat. Then he pointed. Toward the rocks.

Dale turned. Barely visible over the crest of one of the stones were the head and shoulders of a man and a woman. He could just make out that the woman was wearing one of the Marshall Village bonnets. They appeared to be sitting.

Dale glanced back at the Man in Black, who made a "shoo" motion with his hands urging Dale toward the people.

When Dale climbed over the top of the large stone, he found the couple sitting on a checkered blanket and gazing out at the view. There was a picnic basket next to them. They were holding hands beneath a fold in the blanket.

Dale leaned over and stepped into their line of vision. Their blank stares never broke.

"Hello?"

"Hello, Agent," the man said.

"Are you two okay?"

"We are fine," the woman said. "We've been waiting for you. We were told to ask you a question."

Dale looked at the area of the blanket covering their entwined hands, a small mound under the cloth. He furrowed his brow. Something didn't look right, something about the shape. He motioned toward the blanket. "May I?"

"Yes," the woman said.

Dale slowly pulled back the blanket. Underneath, the couple's hands were not holding each other. Instead, each hand held a handgun, and the weapons were pointed at the opposite person.

Dale took a step back.

"We have been told that if you cannot answer our question we are to fire," the man said.

"And you'll do this?"

"There is no greater glory than to die for the Maker, our Father, and the Man in Black," the woman said.

"What's your question?" Dale said.

"What do you call a challenging seed?" the man said.

Another goddamn game of word association. The kidnapper's modus operandi was as predictable as Wilson's wardrobe. Dale took a deep breath.

A challenging seed ... *Germ, grain.* From *Macbeth:* "If you can look into the *seeds* of time, And say which *grain* will grow and which will not." A *grain* of truth? A *nugget* of information?

"Your time is almost up, Agent," the woman said. "You have less than a minute left."

Dale glanced at his watch. 2:59. He ran a hand through his hair. Acid rose from his gut.

Seed. That was the key. That was the word he needed to focus on, the one that was going to have a second meaning. *Kernel, spore, cell.*

The man and the woman turned to each other. Each of them raised their guns and pointed at the other's head. Their arms remained perfectly still as they held the weapons.

One of the college girls who had been taking pictures saw this and screamed, "My god, look!"

A wave of yelling and panic flashed over the people on the rocks as they began to see what was happening. Some of them went screaming for the trail. Others crowded around at a cautious distance.

Seed ... nut? No, something different. Something more abstract. *Concept, notion.* Maybe something along those lines. Like *core beliefs. Faith.* But what about *challenging? Testing, taxing.*

They cocked their weapons.

He put the two words together and blurted out the best answer he could form. Something that fit with both words. Something that fit with the theme of the Roanoke colonists, a group of people who'd crossed an ocean to a new land that was little more than legend. "A challenging seed is a test of faith."

"I'm sorry," the man said. "That answer is wrong."

They didn't give Dale even a split second to stop it.

Two shots. The sound was loud and heavy, and it echoed over the rocks. The woman fell first, just a fraction of a second before the man. Her head snapped hard to the right. The man fell forward, and his body slid down the rock. Blood sprayed over Dale, a warm mist dappled with heavy, hot droplets. He felt it on his cheeks.

The crowd screamed.

Dale dropped to his knees. The man's face was covered in blood. The woman had been struck in the side of the head. Brain matter leaked out.

And then it hit him. *Challenging grain.* A *challenge* is a dare. And *grain* can mean *stone*—as in a seed, like a peach stone.

Dare Stone.

He whipped back around and faced the crowd. People were screaming, crying.

"Is anyone a doctor?" Dale yelled.

A man in a yellow polo shirt and flared corduroys ran up. "I am." He kneeled down beside the people.

Dale reached out to pull the Marshall man's body closer. "I think that—"

The doctor shoved him away. Dale lost his balance and fell to his butt. "Don't touch. Just go. Give me space."

Dale pulled himself up from the rock, his eyes not leaving the slouched bodies. He panted. The blood was congealing on his face. He slowly backed away then climbed down the rocks. The crowd looked aghast at his blood-covered form as he approached. They split before him, creating a path.

And then he remembered. The Man in Black.

He scrambled to the top of a tall rock to his right and looked back to where he had seen him. The Man in Black was gone. Dale cursed but knew that if the pattern remained from the other incidents, the Man in Black would have left him another clue on a stone. From his perch high atop the rock, Dale scanned the area around him.

He was completely surrounded by stones. Stones of all shapes. Big stones, small stones. Thousands of stones. It would take days—hell, a lifetime—to go through all of them. It seemed like the Man in Black's main goal was to run Dale ragged, humiliating him all the while.

And he was doing a damn good job of it so far.

Dale put his hands behind his head.

Then something occurred to him. The Man in Black wouldn't want him to fail at this. Going through all of these rocks, while humiliating, would be impossible. No, the Man in Black would have left the next clue somewhere more obvious. But aside from the rock outcrop, there was just the forest and a trail. So the only logical place ...

Was exactly where the Man in Black had been standing.

Dale climbed down and jogged over to where the Man in Black had been standing at the edge of the woods. There were no stones. He pushed the grass aside with his foot, looking left and right.

Nothing.

He kicked the grass out of frustration. The last two stones had a time limit. Odds were this stone would have one too. He didn't want to piss his time away looking for the damn stone itself. And he couldn't be certain that the stone wasn't out there with the thousands of rocks behind him.

He kicked at the grass harder now, and his boot

connected with something hard, stubbing the big toe on his right foot and causing him to curse.

It was a stone, about a foot across with letters carved onto it. Dale got on his knees. The message was brief.

talk to marshall

They were ramping up the face-to-face. Good. Dale had no problem with looking scumbags in the eye. In fact, he excelled at it. At least there wasn't another damn riddle; though chances were he'd get a riddle from Marshall himself.

Like the first two stones, there would be writing on the bottom side. Dale dug his fingers into the dirt and pried. He rocked the stone a time or two, and it came out of the ground with a heave, crushing the grass behind it. As before, he brushed the dirt off the backside. Letters began to appear. The beginning of the new message—*you've done well so far*— didn't raise his eyebrows, but when he brushed the dirt away from the last two words, his heart stopped.

brad walker

It was his PI, his Prior Identity. They knew his *real* name.

He looked at the message in disbelief, thinking that somehow it might change. But it didn't.

you've done well so far, brad walker.

Cold sweat flashed over his body. He took a step backward, his eyes never looking away from the stone.

Brad. Brad Walker.

A BEI agent's PI was the most guarded secret of a very secretive organization. BEI agents didn't exist. They had no social security number and paid no taxes. This was what kept the small selection of geniuses ahead of the darker geniuses they aimed to stop. BEI agents were created to be shadows, whispers, the only thing that could stop the world's most sophisticated criminals.

Dale couldn't remember the last time he'd been called Brad. Mom had been diligent with her promise not to use his real name, despite her vehement objections. She was the only person he was in contact with who might use his PI. The Bureau had wiped his old personality from existence. He had no birth certificate, no death certificate, no school records, no debt. Brad Walker no longer existed. He was dead.

Brad Walker was so dead that when Dale looked at the name on the stone, he hardly recognized it. When your past has been obliterated as much as Dale's had, it was easy to forget your name. Especially when you wanted to.

What was tying his stomach in knots, though, wasn't seeing his PI again. It was knowing that the kidnapper was in a situation to know it. BEI security had been breached. If the kidnapper was this well informed, what could that mean for the rest of the investigation? He cringed to think that the Man in Black had been following him the whole time. He scanned the trees around him for the masked man.

Dale put a hand to his forehead. It was sweaty. He looked back to the stone.

you've done well so far, brad walker.

He ran his tongue over his dry lips and tried to say something, though he didn't know why.

"My ... name. They know who I was."

CHAPTER THIRTY

DALE WAS STILL dirty and covered in sweat and blood. Facing him, standing not a foot away on the other side of the bars of a jail cell, was Camden Marshall. He wore an orange prisoner's jumpsuit and a smug grin. There was a glint in his lifeless green eyes.

"Brad," Marshall said. "You look like you've seen a ghost."

"How the hell do you know my real name?" Dale's jaw was clenched so hard it hurt.

Marshall laughed. "You BEI fools think that you're so secure. There's a lot that we know about you."

Dale flinched at hearing "BEI" come from Marshall's lips. There were very few people in the world who knew about the Bureau of Esoteric Investigation. "Who are you?"

Marshall gave him a confused look. "We're the Marshall Village, of course."

"What do you want?"

"You asked me that already. Earlier today. In the questioning room."

Dale jabbed a finger at Marshall's face. "I'll find out how you know these things."

"Careful, Agent. Aren't you supposed to ease into this? Start gentle and get more aggressive?"

Dale gritted his teeth. "I'm willing to make an exception."

"Now, now. Remember, I have what you want. I have all those people."

"And you're releasing them a few at a time. But you never ask for anything."

"Then there's no time to waste. I'll let you know how to find the next group of Marshallites. But first you're going to have to do something for me."

Dale scoffed. "*Me* do something for *you*?"

"I have the people. And the last stone did tell you to talk to me. Don't be so obstinate. You're only making it worse on yourself."

"What the hell are you talking about?" Dale suddenly had a really bad feeling.

"My little project outside Staunton wasn't so different from the Collective Agricultural Experiment, of which I understand you were a member. I heard that Glenn Downey used to have some really interesting ways of punishing his dissidents. I even heard that when one of his favorites tried to leave, he gave them a very special punishment. Did you get a special punishment when you tried to leave, Brad?"

"What are you implying?" Dale said.

But he knew exactly what Marshall was getting at.

Marshall leaned closer, put his hands on the bars. "Oral sex. Fellatio. A blowjob. Did you give Glenn a blowjob, Brad?"

"*No.* No, I did not." Dale had not. But he knew that Spencer Goad, the photographer intern who had gone on the assignment with him, might very well have faced that fate.

"Too bad." Marshall took a step back. He lowered his eyes and smiled.

"Piss off, creep!" Dale's heart pounded. The fear came

rushing back to him, the fear he'd felt when he and Spencer were captured the first time they tried to escape the camp. His eyes focused on Marshall's neck, and he pictured his hands wrapping around it, fingers piercing through skin and muscle and tendon.

"Don't worry, Brad," Marshall said. "I'm not going to ask that of you. I want something else entirely."

"What's that?"

"I want you to bark."

"Bark?"

"Bark. Like the dog you are."

Dale knew what Marshall was trying to accomplish here. Humiliation. This was something that Glenn had also used back at the CAE. Small things. Constantly. Things that were crafted to suck every drop of dignity and character from a person. At the end of every conversation with the Father, Glenn required his children to "close it out" with a groveling, mortifying speech.

And now Marshall was trying to humiliate him. But he had another thing coming. "Again, I say you can *piss off!*"

Marshall tsked. "Brad, Brad, Brad. You really don't want to save those people, do you? Remember, you need to be extra nice to me, or I won't tell you when and where you can find them. Come now. Bark for me."

Dale did nothing. He could feel his nostrils flaring.

"Bark."

Dale was damn near hyperventilating. He thought of the people Marshall had kidnapped. Locked away in a barn. Or a cellar. Or cages.

"Bark!"

He knew what he had to do. But he couldn't give that part of him away. There had to be another way.

Marshall smacked his hand against the bars. "*I said bark, goddamn it!*"

Dale barked, quietly, his eyes firing smoldering contempt right into Marshall's.

"Louder!"

Dale grabbed the bars and leaned right into Marshall. And he barked. He barked loud. So loud it burned his throat.

"Louder!"

Dale barked louder. The room was so loud he felt the noise closing in around him.

"Louder! *Louder, louder, louder!*" Marshall jumped up and down.

Dale's neck expanded. His eyes watered. He barked. He felt his throat tearing apart.

Marshall clapped his hands. Dale couldn't hear it. Just the sound of his own barking. Marshall waved, and Dale stopped. The room echoed. Dale was lightheaded, and he steadied himself with the bars. He was short of breath.

"Very good," Marshall said with a bout of laughter. "You've earned your reward, your next riddle. Remember the ringing of that terrible bell? Go there. To the bell. At midnight."

Dale took in a breath. "*What did you just say?*"

Marshall grinned, big and wide. "Lovely. You solved my riddle already—'terrible bell,' my reference to the CAE."

"The only people who know about the bell were directly involved with the Collective Agricultural Experiment. How the hell are you connected to the CAE, Marshall?"

Marshall shrugged sheepishly. "Another riddle for you to unravel, I suppose.

Dale turned to leave and stopped. He looked back at Marshall. "I *will* find out what's going on here."

"One hundred thirty-nine people left, Brad. And I'm the only person who knows where they are. Remember that."

Dale glared at Marshall.

He had thought Marshall and Glenn Downey to be similar before. But now that Dale knew Marshall was somehow connected to the CAE—and with the psychological torment he'd just endured—it was as though Glenn was in the room with him, smiling back at him from the other side of those bars.

Dale turned and paced off. But he could still see Glenn Downey. In his mind. And he felt the same need to escape that he'd felt several years ago.

CHAPTER THIRTY-ONE

BRAD WALKER STOOD under the awning of the shed and looked out at the water. If he had the space to do so, he would have been pacing. As it was, with his need to remain hidden, he simply twisted his fingers around in his hands.

He'd heard a ship's horn.

They were to meet at sunset, but that had long since passed. It was already pitch black. He had no way of telling the time, but he knew he had to have been there for at least an hour. Something must have happened. Spencer hadn't arrived.

It had only been two weeks since their first escape attempt, when they were caught and beaten by Darnell and the Blue Guard. They had one shot at this. The boat arrived at 7 p.m., and the final inspection of the barracks was also at 7. Just when the boat would arrive, the guards would find that Brad and Spencer were gone. There was no turning back now. They'd both agreed to the risks.

Brad saw a light on the water in the distance. The ship was approaching. He looked back to the camp.

The road parallel to the generator shed by which he was

standing stretched about two hundred yards before reaching the main area of the camp. There was the Pavilion, lit by its tall spotlights on all four corners. Nearby was the kitchen where two guards stood watch, one on each side, AK-47s in hand. This was one of the places that Glenn kept under lock and key. Food rations had gotten smaller, even in the short time that Brad had been there.

He saw no sign of Spencer.

The small cargo ship arrived. The armed men on the dock waved it into position. Their backs were turned to Brad now. This was it. He couldn't wait any longer. Whatever happened to Spencer now couldn't be undone.

Brad got on his hands and knees and crawled through the tall grass toward the dock. When he got closer to the water and the grass thinned out, he lowered himself to his stomach. The ground scratched at the fresh wounds on his chest and sent fire through his body. He clawed at the earth with his fingers, pulling himself inch by inch. Mud packed under his nails. The surf lapped at his hands, and he pulled himself into the water. His clothes felt heavy, and in his weakened state he struggled to keep himself afloat.

The plan was to swim under the dock, approach the ship, and climb up the side. They would then stow away on the ship and use cover of darkness to get to its return destination —Charleston.

He made it to the dock and clung to one of the wooden beams, catching his breath. It was cold and slippery with moss. The voices of the CAE men and the ship's crew filtered down through the boards of the dock.

He pulled himself onto the rope net on the side of the boat. It was tough going, and after he tugged his tired body into the net, his final position left him twisted and bent in half—a sadistic hammock. His heart beat faster, and a feeling of guilt fell over him. Had he been too brash? Was it too early to attempt another escape? Spencer wouldn't be able to handle another punishment like they'd faced the last time.

Brad looked back to the camp. Still no sign of him.

There was shouting from above, and the whole ship shook around him. He held onto the wet rope. The ship's anchor retracted, and he began to drift away from the camp.

His stomach was empty, and it rumbled. He tried to think of how incredible a full meal was going to taste. He tried to think of anything that would distract him from the fact that Spencer was being left behind at the Collective Agricultural Experiment.

As the ship began to slowly pull away, there was a commotion. The men on the dock were shouting as they sprinted back toward the camp. They were focusing on something, but Brad couldn't tell what it was. Then he saw it.

It was Spencer.

The kid was running at full speed toward the ship. He was short and thin, but he still managed to push one of the men aside with his elbow. The man fell off the dock and into the water with a terrific splash. Brad was impressed.

Brad tried to stand. His foot slipped on the wet rope, and his leg fell through one of the gaps in the net, all the way. The rope hit him painfully in the crotch.

As Spencer ran toward the end of the dock, two men converged upon him. Spencer flailed his arms in the air, waving desperately at the boat.

The ship had cleared the dock by a few yards. If Brad could get himself free from the rope, he just might be able to get back. He clambered to pull his leg out.

As the ship drifted farther, Brad could make out less and less of what was happening on the dock. There was a guard on each of Spencer's arms, and still he thrashed about. One of the men released Spencer and brought his rifle into the air.

He cracked it down on the back of Spencer's neck, and the kid collapsed.

Rope tore into the flesh of Brad's inner thigh and wouldn't let go. He managed to get his right foot against the side of the ship, squeezing the net between his shoe and the hull. With a heave, he pulled his whole body up, freeing his imprisoned leg.

Back at the dock, the two guards were dragging Spencer toward the camp, each holding one of his wrists. He was conscious but just barely. Blood ran down the side of his face. He screamed out.

"Brad! *Brad!*"

Brad clambered to the top of the net. He froze. The ship was already a hundred yards away from the dock. If he jumped, it would take several minutes to swim back to shore. He'd never catch up to Spencer.

There was only one thing to do. When he returned to civilization, he would tell the rest of the world about what was going on at the Collective Agricultural Experiment. If he went back to the camp, he would never get this opportunity, and the rest of the people would continue to suffer.

So he had to let him go.

"*Brad!*"

He watched as the men dragged Spencer past the end of the dock. They walked through the last patch of lamplight and disappeared into the darkness.

CHAPTER THIRTY-TWO

ARANCIA GRUMBLED IN PROTEST. She was riding in the right-hand lane, the slow lane, a place that made her very pissy indeed.

Wilson was in the passenger seat, but Dale hadn't spoken to him for a good twenty minutes as they drove north on Interstate 81. His mind was elsewhere.

The investigation had taken an unexpected turn into painful remembrance. Now that he knew Glenn Downey was somehow connected to the CAE, Dale and Wilson were going back to the only place where he could look into this connection: *The Worldwide Weekly Report*.

When Dale's PI, Brad Walker, had been on assignment at the Collective Agricultural Experiment, his escape from the camp triggered a chain reaction. He told his story not only to his own paper but every major newspaper in the country. The story was a sensation, and government action came swiftly.

The feds closed in on the camp. After a month of failed negotiations, they found their reason to enter the camp by force. Intel indicated that fully automatic AK-47s had been imported into the camp, something illegal after the Gun

Control Act of 1968. The ATF and the FBI's hostage team moved in to take Glenn's followers by force and came face-to-face with the alleged AK-47s in the hands of Darnell Fowler's Blue Guard. The shooting began around midnight.

While Darnell held off the feds, Glenn called one final White Night, gathering his followers at the Pavilion for what he called "the ultimate resistance."

Mass suicide.

With federal forces closing in, Glenn convinced the people to consume fruit punch laced with cyanide. By this point, Glenn's teachings had reached a new level of insanity, due in no small part to his escalating drug addiction. But still they followed him, every word he said. Three hundred eighty-four people died from the poison.

The only ones Glenn didn't poison were his Appointed, the ones he favored. Glenn took the Appointed to the speedboats in a foolhardy plan to escape out the Chesapeake Bay and reach the sanctity of international waters miles off the coast in the Atlantic. The firefight continued on the water. In the process, several of the CAE's boats caught fire, including Glenn Downey's.

Nearly everyone on the boats died that night. And the whole world watched it happen. The media had been following the case since the feds first started negotiations. All month they'd lived in a makeshift town of vans and cables and cameras on the shoreline across from the camp. When the action began on the fateful evening, the cameras were rolling. Everyone in America saw the fires on the bay. They watched as the boats burned and the people died.

Glenn Downey had been at the front of the pack, using the boats behind him as protection, but even his boat could not escape. Soon it was ablaze too. He burned to death like so many of his followers before disappearing forever into the depths of the bay.

Spencer had been one of Glenn's closest Appointed. Of the survivors, he was the only one who had been on Glenn's boat.

The media had its way with the story. The government agents were labeled as murderers. They were accused of aiming for the boat's motors, trying to start the fires, purposefully killing the CAE members. The images of the burning boats were broadcast for weeks on end. A fresh wave of anti-government rhetoric spread through the country.

Though there had been three CAE survivors from the boats and five who evaded the poisoning, Brad Walker had been the only person to escape the camp *before* the ill-fated night. He told his story with a major book deal—*Break Free: The Collective Agricultural Experiment's Lone Escapee.*

Before joining the BEI, Dale visited the *WWR* from time to time, but he never worked there another day. Spencer, however, continued to work there to this day. That was going to make Dale's return visit all the more uncomfortable.

———

Dale and Wilson stood within the busy yet pleasant chaos of Rich's Diner, at the register, waiting in line for their to-go order. Dale could smell the apple pie. His mouth watered.

He also saw Julia, farther down on the opposite side of the counter, filling a coffee, chatting. She hadn't noticed him yet, and he wasn't sure if she would. Her hair was styled in the flipped, feathery look that women had been doing for the last few years. The Farrah Fawcett look.

Wilson, too, took in a big whiff of the diner air. "I need a coffee. Bad. So we're headed to Arlington, back to your old newspaper. What are you hoping to find?"

"Something. Anything. There's a connection between

Marshall and the CAE, and nobody has more info on the CAE than Vance at *The Worldwide Weekly Report*."

The customer in front of Dale and Wilson shuffled away, revealing the register. Julia stood behind it, looking right at Dale, smiling big and bright.

She *did* remember him.

"You look bushed, Mr. Private Eye."

Her perfume smelled nice. She was smiling, a playful smile, one that told Dale that she was ready to continue their little game of cat and mouse from his last visit.

"This assignment of mine has me and Wilson here running our butts off." He waved a hand between the two of them. "Julia, Wilson. Wilson, Julia."

Julia offered her hand to Wilson then returned her smile to Dale.

"Well, I'm envious of you," she said, still with a tone that let him know she was being playfully sarcastic. "I think it'd be a stone groove to figure out mysteries."

She handed them a pair of to-go coffees in a paper carrier and two slices of apple pie in clear plastic containers.

Wilson went for his wallet, but Dale waved it off, took out his own.

"I got this one, Wilson," he said as he handed a bill to Julia.

Wilson nodded his thanks.

Julia gave Dale his change, and he put the coins and a couple ones in the tip jar.

"Don't let this assignment stress you boys out too much," she said as Dale and Wilson started to leave. "You know what I always say, Dale? If there's something that's beating you, don't give it a helping hand."

Dale suddenly liked Julia a whole lot more. He had a policy of not taking himself too seriously. Dale liked that Julia recognized the value in this. He enjoyed a girl who could wax philosophical.

Plus, she remembered his name.

"Bye, Julia."

Dale and Wilson turned for the door, meandering through the crowd. Wilson held his piece of pie in front of his face, studied it through the clear plastic container.

"Best pie in the city, you say?"

"Best pie in the world. Enjoy the moment while you can. I have a feeling things are about to get really complicated at Vance's."

CHAPTER THIRTY-THREE

THE WORLDWIDE WEEKLY *Report* office sat in a run-down, industrial side of Arlington, Virginia, outside the nation's capital. When Dale worked there, he hadn't yet gotten Arancia. At the time he drove an old Chevy truck and didn't care where he parked it. But now, as he drove his De Tomaso Pantera through an area of crumbling buildings, wandering bums, and cracked sidewalks, he had considerable pause. Luckily the *WWR* had a parking lot, so he wouldn't have to park her on the street, but even that made him anxious.

It was a gray day. The sky and the buildings melted into one smoky blur. Still, when Dale opened Arancia's door and stepped out into the *WWR*'s familiar gravel parking lot, he felt some of the case's pressure lift from his shoulders.

The office was a converted factory, fifty feet tall, with a sign over the front entrance that read:

The Worldwide Weekly Report - Uncovering What the Others Won't Cover

Dale smiled. He was breaking about a thousand BEI regu-

lations by coming here. SAC Taft would be one grouchy bear
about this. Though he was given near carte blanche with his
investigations, he couldn't break the Bureau's basic regulations. Still, he did so with some regularity, and it made Taft's
blood pressure shoot through the roof each and every time.
But when times were desperate, when people's lives were at
stake, Dale did what he had to do.

As he and Wilson stepped through the doors and into the
office, the nostalgia hit him like a hurricane wind. It was just
as he remembered it. There was the main office below with
all the desks and the usual trappings of a busy newsroom—
clacking typewriters, phones ringing, people darting about.
Pictures of flying saucers, ghosts, and 1950s movie monsters
peppered the walls alongside some of the bizarre artifacts
that had been collected throughout the paper's investigations.
There was a mystery skull, a piece of metal from the Roswell
crash site, and Dale's personal favorite, the haunted
basketball.

Two huge objects dominated the office space. In the back
was "the Montana Monster," a stuffed grizzly bear with a
bizarre looking face, standing ten feet tall on its rear legs. A
rancher named Vernon Caldwell claimed to have shot and
killed the Monster after it ran off with three of his sheep. But
when he brought it to the *Worldwide Weekly Report*, the staff
soon discovered that the Monster's face had been heavily
doctored. The bones of the snout had been removed, and a
new metal structure had been put in its place, turning the
bear into something akin to a fuzzy crocodile. The fur, some
of which was synthetic, was stitched together in patches to
cover the new monstrosity.

Then there was the enormous hook that hung from the
ceiling. When he took over the old factory, Vance gutted the
building and sold off all the equipment. But he decided to
leave the hook. It dangled dead center in the room on forty

feet of chain with links the size of a man's hand. It came within a couple feet of the ground. The hook was a good three feet tall with a rusted orange-red patina. The sheer size and simple lines of its form made it look like a piece of modern art. With its pulley and housing, the whole apparatus easily dwarfed a six-foot man.

Vance had saved it not just for its visual appeal but also for its symbolic nature. In writing, the "hook" is the attention-grabbing moment that occurs early in a piece to grab the reader's attention and compel him or her to read the rest. When you have a newspaper concerned with ludicrous stories of alien abduction and mutant trout, a hook is of particular importance.

Someone across the room recognized Dale and began to walk toward him. It was Vance. He was two months younger and two inches taller than Dale. Even now, wearing a look of utter confusion, he crossed the newsroom with long, commanding strides.

"Br— I mean, Dale," Vance said as he approached. He tilted his head, narrowed his eyes, then smiled wide and pulled Dale in for a strong hug. "Didn't I fire you?"

"No, I quit."

It had been years since Dale had seen Vance, but in this briefest of exchanges, Dale felt like he'd seen him yesterday. That's how all good friendships should be.

Dale motioned toward Wilson. "My current partner, Special Agent Cody Wilson."

After Vance and Wilson greeted each other, Dale inspected Vance with a grin. "You're looking smart, as usual."

Vance was wearing a dress shirt and plaid, dark brown pants. He had a warm smile and New England good looks, sort of like a Kennedy, except Vance was no politician. He was the genuine article.

"Thanks." Vance flicked his shirt's butterfly collar. He

looked Dale over. "T-shirt and jeans. Nothing changes you, does it?"

"I wouldn't say that. But nothing comes between me and my 501s. I need your help with something, Vance."

Vance lowered his tone. "But ... you said you could never come back here. You in some sort of trouble?" He put his hand on Dale's shoulder and squeezed.

"The assignment I'm working has to connection with the CAE."

Vance paused. "And you want to look through the archives?"

"Right."

"I take it this is off the record?"

Dale smiled. "My friend, it's five miles off the record."

———

Vance's office was on the upper level of the building off the catwalk that looked down upon the old factory floor. Dale, Wilson, and Vance stood over a large table. Spread out before them was a collection of materials—bound copies of *The Worldwide Weekly Report*, newspaper clippings, magazines, photographs. Vance had rolled up his sleeves. They were looking at one of the bound collections.

"Here's where you began working on the story." Vance put a finger on the front page of one of the issues of the *Report*.

THE COLLECTIVE AGRICULTURAL EXPERIMENT:
TERROR ON THE CHESAPEAKE BAY
by Brad Walker

There was a picture of the camp beside the title. It was a photograph Spencer had taken. Images and memories of the CAE had been resident specters of Dale's mind in the years since he was there. But he had never gone back to the place, and he had avoided any photographs. His heart pounded now. The physical reaction to seeing the camp once more was greater than he thought it would be.

The buildings in the picture were all square and cinder block construction. Plain, monolithic. They had been in a rundown state even when the CAE was in operation. The camp had been a large storage facility at one point, but by the time Glenn moved his people in, it looked like some sort of abandoned Eastern Bloc plant.

Next to the picture of the camp was the photo of Brad Walker that adorned each of his articles. Dale hadn't particularly wanted his image to appear in the paper, but Vance, who always had more business sense, pimped out Dale's handsome mug to help sell copies.

Brad Walker stared at Dale now with a clean, casual smile and bright eyes. The picture was taken when he first started at the *WWR*. Dale was blessed with good genes, so he hadn't aged to speak of since the picture was taken. Nevertheless, the differences in the photo spoke volumes. Dale was embarrassed by Brad Walker.

He scanned over the article and saw nothing that related to Camden Marshall.

"My tell-all book was the only account of the CAE. And I didn't mention the bell. I'm certain of this because I never wanted to think about the damn thing again. But Marshall knew about it somehow, which means he must have been highly involved in the camp." He pointed to the some of the other sources at the back of the table. "Let's go back a bit further."

Vance pushed the stack of bound *WWR*s to the side. He stretched his arms out wide to pull the other stacks closer. The pile collapsed, creating an avalanche of books.

They dug into the materials. It was like the early days at

the *Report*, the days when it wasn't quite the rag that it would become. Sure, they wrote their fair share of articles about Kennedy assassination conspiracies and *el chupacabra*, but they put some serious research into their work. These were long nights of coffee and pizza—in a time before Dale's healthier diet, of course. Doing the work again, hunkering over the books with Vance as he had so many times, made him realize how much he'd missed having a friend.

About ten minutes into their searching, Vance shouted out. "Brad, look!" He covered his mouth. "I ... I'm sorry."

Dale shook his head. "Old habits die hard. What do ya got?" He took the article from him.

It was published a year before the Collective Agricultural Experiment began. Vance pointed toward a paragraph near the bottom.

Downey has had difficulty procuring sponsorship for his work. The mainstream churches have all rejected his requests. All of the grant proposals he has submitted have been denied. The main source of his initial funding, such as it is, has come from individual donors. The Neville Family of industrialists has agreed to a partial funding with the desire to learn more about small team labor dynamics. Two economics professors at Virginia Tech University have also donated money in hopes of further developing theories of non-traditional economies.

Wilson leaned over Dale's shoulder. "Camden Marshall is a Virginia Tech prof."

"Indeed he is," Dale said. "We're onto something here."

Vance handed him another article from the same time period. It was a yellowed newspaper article, and the content was focused on the two Virginia Tech professors' contributions to the CAE. A four-inch across sat to the right of the text.

Centered in the frame, larger than life, were Camden Marshall and Glenn Downey, shaking hands and smiling for the camera. Above their clasped hands they each held an end of an oversized check.

Dale read the first couple paragraphs of the article ... and suddenly stopped.

"You got that look on your face again, Colombo," Wilson said. "What did you find?"

Dale didn't look up from the article as he replied. "Camden Marshall was on sabbatical at the same time the CAE was operational—in South America, studying primitive tribes without monetary systems. He was in the wilderness isolated from mainstream society for years, shortly after he helped fund the CAE. He was gone during the entire time the camp was operational."

Vance stepped closer, crossed his arms. "Okay. So what's your point?"

Dale finally looked up at Vance and Wilson. "If the only people who know about the bell were *physically at* the CAE camp, then Marshall couldn't have known about it. And yet he used the bell as my latest riddle."

Wilson scrunched his eyes. "So how..."

"We've been had, Wilson. Marshall isn't the man in charge here. He's as brainwashed as all the other Marshallites. He's not the kidnapper. *He was kidnapped along with the rest of his village.* The guy on the outside, the Man in Black, has been running this thing the entire time. He's played us for fools."

Dale grinned, and a rush of excitement flooded over him. Sure, he'd just opened up a whole new mystery in this assignment, but for once, he felt like he was getting the upper hand.

He looked back to the photo of Glenn and Marshall. Glenn wore his tinted glasses and a baggy suit with a wide tie and wider lapels. His usual slimy sneer was slathered all over his gaunt face, and his eyes had their typical twinkle, somewhere between that of a department store Santa and a local union leader. Marshall wore a dark turtleneck and a blazer, looking every inch a college professor. His beard was longer and scruffier than it was now in the jail.

In the background, cut off by the edge of the photograph, was Darnell Fowler, standing like a sentry, arms behind his back. Fowler hadn't died on the boats like the others. He and his Blue Guard had stayed behind to fight off the feds in the woods surrounding the camp, and he was never seen again after that. Glenn couldn't have picked a more suited lackey. Not only did Darnell obey every command he was given, but he also shared Glenn's demented outlook.

"This is it," Dale said. He pumped his fist then turned to Wilson. "We gotta roll."

Vance lowered his head. "Before you leave ... the kid's still with us."

"Yeah. I know." Dale paused. "Didn't see him out on the floor."

Vance motioned to the catwalk outside his door. "He works part-time. I have him in one of the upstairs offices now, and, um ... he's here right now. You know, he might remember something about Camden Marshall and the CAE."

Dale nodded. "Is he doing well?"

"He's doing well at his job. I couldn't speak for how he's doing in the outside world." Vance glanced at the window. "Want to talk to him?"

"Not really." He put the newspaper article on the table. "But I should."

CHAPTER THIRTY-FOUR

DALE'S GUTS had just been pulled through the wringer with images of the Collective Agricultural Experiment camp and Glenn Downey. But those two things were going to be mere appetizers to the main course of seeing Spencer Goad.

He exhaled. And knocked.

There was the squeak of wheels from an office chair followed by footsteps, starting faint at the back of the room and getting louder. A dark figure appeared behind the frosted glass and grew larger.

An odd feeling fell over him, and a thought flashed across his mind.

Spencer is right on the other side of that door.

The handle jiggled. The door inched open.

A man familiar but quite different appeared. Spencer was on the short side and nerdy thin when Dale had known him. He'd bulked up considerably. He looked broader in the chest and fuller in the face, which had been covered in zits but was now acne-free. As before, he had a mop of sandy blond hair, parted on the left. Dale had forgotten how blue the kid's eyes were. Piercing, ocean blue, like two shiny marbles.

Neither of them moved nor said anything. Dale couldn't react. There was nothing on Spencer's face either. His lips were a thin line.

Dale tried to say something but nothing came out. He flirted with something profound, something that was fitting of the occasion, but all he could say was, "Hi, Spencer."

It came out piteously, like the dying putter of a lawn mower as it runs out of gas.

"Long time no see ... Dale? That's your name now, right?"

"That's right. Dale Conley."

Dale was encouraged. 'Long time no see' was something that the Spencer he knew years ago would not have said. It was far too casual, too easygoing. Plus, it looked like he'd been exercising. This was all encouraging. Dale always thought Spencer was a bright, good-looking kid. He just needed some confidence.

When he and Vance gave him a hard time, called him the "whipping boy," it was all good-natured. They wanted to help the kid. He was smart, and he had a good heart. Dale knew that both of these things could easily get him eaten alive in the real world.

"Well, come on in, Dale." Spencer opened the door wider and walked into his office. He leaned against his desk, folding his arms across his chest and crossing his legs. "What are you doing here?"

Again, Dale hesitated. "I'm working a mass abduction case I think might have a connection back to the CAE. I know this is incredibly awkward, but I need to ask you something."

"Shoot."

"When you were helping me with the background research on the CAE, do you remember anything about the connection with Camden Marshall?"

Spencer cocked his head to the side.

"He's a professor who partially financed the camp," Dale continued, "and he's the man who abducted my missing people. Does his name ring a bell?"

Spencer shook his head. "I'm not remembering that name. Sorry."

"It was a long shot, I know. But worth asking," Dale said. He chewed his lip.

Silence again.

They looked at each other.

There was an elephant in the room that neither of them wanted to talk about. An overgrown, restless elephant.

With normal guys, a nod could express all that was needed. But with a guy like Spencer, a nod wasn't going to cut it. Dale was going to have to face this thing head-on. He had to do something he avoided like the plague.

He needed to emote.

"Spencer," he began. He looked down to the floor and back up. "I never got a chance to say anything about the night I left the CAE. I tried to get you out of there with me. I couldn't wait any longer. I had to leave."

Spencer's expression didn't change. Dale didn't know whether that was a good thing or a bad thing.

"I know," Spencer said.

They looked at each other. Before another awkward silence could present itself, Dale said, "I'd better get rolling. We should get together some time. Grab a bite to eat."

"I'd like that," Spencer said.

But Dale knew it would never happen.

There are some experiences people share that keep them from ever having a normal relationship again.

"You take care of yourself, Spence."

"You do the same." A slight pause. "Dale."

Dale turned. When he reached the door, he looked back. Spencer was still leaning against the desk.

Dale looked at him for a moment then gave him a nod after all.

Spencer nodded back.

CHAPTER THIRTY-FIVE

"THIS WON'T TAKE LONG. I promise," Dale said.

Dale and Wilson slowly drove down Main Street in Front Royal, Virginia. Arancia's Cleveland engine grumbled, and its deep resonance bounced off the brick walls of the two-story businesses on either side of the road.

Brad Walker spent the second half of his childhood in Front Royal before moving to Harrisonburg for college. Later, at the same time that Dale Conley joined the BEI, Brad Walker died in a hiking accident. Dale wanted Brad to die attempting to break the land speed record on the alkali flats, but SAC Taft shot that idea down. As a youth, Brad had kept to himself, so since his death, Front Royal had yet to notice when his ghost would return to visit his mother.

Front Royal was a town of about nine thousand people, and its downtown area was quintessential Americana. It was, in fact, a perfect little place. It reminded Dale of all the small towns back in Hoosier-land.

Dale was born in the great state of Indiana. He was there through the age of ten, when his mother moved them to Virginia to live near family. She had been in and out of work for a couple years after Dale's father left, and Virginia held the promise of a solid job at her uncle's scrap metal yard.

Wilson stared out the window. "Cute town." He turned to Dale. "If Marshall was kidnapped along with the rest of his village, our connection to the CAE has gone dead."

Dale shook his head. "I'm gonna try to think more positively on this, Wilson. There were only a handful of survivors from the camp, which means we now only have a handful of suspects. Now as to tracking down those suspects ... your guess is as good as mine."

―――――

When she answered the door, Dale's mother was wearing one of her sweatshirts. Each one had some sort of picture on the front—an animal or some lettering or an image of a snowy scene. Today's shirt was hunter green with a silhouette of a dog sewn upon it. The dog was made of red plaid cloth with white frill around the outer edge.

She looked up at Dale and shook her head. Audrey Walker stood about five feet four inches. She had a mass of gray, curly hair and a little frame with a bit of extra padding. A stranger would take one look at her and assume she was a card-carrying member of the Sweet Grandma's Club. But there was pure piss and vinegar surging through her veins.

She didn't smile, just stepped aside and allowed him and Wilson to enter. In recent years her house was beginning to look like one befitting an old lady. The furniture in her living room was floral print. There was a dish of hard candy on one of the end tables. Her shelves were crowded with an ever-growing assortment of dust-collectors—deer figurines, decorative plates, a shell with googly eyes.

Dale sank down into the couch. The cushion was squishy,

and there was a musty smell. Wilson took the opposite end of the couch, and Mom sat in the chair across from them.

Mom remained stolid. "You freed up some time."

"Just a little. Wilson and I only have a few minutes. Sorry I had to miss our breakfast."

She waved it off. "I'm used to it."

"How have you been lo these eleven days since we last met?" He eased back into the chair, prepared himself.

"You know that salesman I was telling you about? He came back today trying to sell me a stinkin' set of knives. Know what I did? I tried to sell him some of my forks. Told him since he wasn't buying I'd stop by tomorrow at *his* house and try again."

Her negativity was like a drop of ink in a cup of water. It started off small and concentrated but soon dispersed to everything around it, tainting it all. When she got to rambling like this, Dale zoned out. It was better for his mental state, and it didn't make any difference to his mother. She was talking at him, not to him. Even if he was listening, she'd be upset if he opened his mouth.

Instead, he thought about the case.

Dale was the connection between the Glenn Downey and Camden Marshall. Brad Walker had been the only CAE survivor who had left without serious mental issues. He was the only one who escaped. And now he was the agent investigating the disappearance at the new utopian community. It was all way too coincidental.

Which begged the question he'd been left with after he flipped over the stone on Old Rag Mountain—how did they know his PI? The BEI had been meticulous about destroying his past. There were only a handful of connections to his former life remaining.

Then his stomach dropped. One of those connections was sitting right in front of him. His mother.

She was still going. "... so the doctor told me I need to stay off my feet. I told *him* that—"

"Mom, did anyone come here asking about me when I was at the CAE?"

She put her hands on her knees. "My story not good enough for you? Got your mind on that secret mission of yours?"

"You have to tell me, Mom. Did anyone come asking about me while I was there?"

She huffed and crossed her arms. "No. No one came here asking about you. What an ego."

Damn. He was positive that he was on the right track. He scratched his chin. "You're certain?"

"I haven't lost my memory just yet. The only people who've come here looking for you were all those damn reporters when you made it big with those books of yours. And the two men who did your background check for your secret agency."

An alarm went off in Dale's head. "*Two* men?"

"That's right. Some grouchy fella..." That would be Taft. "...and another guy, asked a lot of the same questions as the first one."

It hit him like a smack to the face. The second man who visited his mother was tied to his current assignment. To the Marshall Village. And now that he knew the assignment and his time with the CAE were connected, it all added up. The Marshall Village was established right when Dale joined the BEI. That was how they knew his PI. That was how they had stayed one step ahead of him the entire investigation. They'd been meticulously planning this thing for years. Following him, monitoring him.

Then a strange notion crossed Dale's mind. A wild notion. One that the conspiracy nuts he chased after would have sunk their teeth into. He couldn't believe what he was thinking, whom he was suspecting. There was a man he hadn't seen in years who could very well have been the one to visit his mother. A man who disappeared when the CAE was destroyed and was never heard from again. Glenn Downey's right-hand man.

Darnell Fowler.

Dale glanced at Wilson and then quickly looked back to Mom.

"Do you remember what the second guy looked like?"

She thought for a moment. "No."

"Mom, it's important. What did he look like?" He needed to hear that he was wrong, to hear that the man she saw wasn't the same sneering, evil man he had once known.

"It was years ago. I'm a senile old lady, remember?"

"Was he short? What color was his hair?"

"I don't know."

Dale had to get back to Staunton. And fast. The whole thing was coming together, and he knew who was at the center of it all. Dale Conley.

Or, rather, Brad Walker.

He stood up and walked over to his mother. "Mom, I gotta go. Love you." He kissed her on the cheek and left.

"Yeah, nice seeing you too," Mom yelled out behind him.

CHAPTER THIRTY-SIX

BACK AT STAUNTON, Dale had been told that SAC Taft was momentarily out of the sheriff's office. So Dale returned to the motel to pour over the materials he'd gotten from Vance. It was getting later and later in the day, which meant it was getting closer and closer to the time Dale would need to return to the CAE camp. His nerves were beginning to shred. But instead of distracting himself from the CAE, he was doing the complete opposite—studying everything he could about the camp. He had to examine the information as thoroughly as he could ... no matter how badly it hurt.

He'd allowed himself half an hour for a jog and some pushups. Otherwise he'd been immersed in his studies of Darnell Fowler and his connection to the CAE,.

He was shirtless, wearing only his 501s, and he had the air cranked to bring his body temperature back down after his hot shower. An old magazine was in his hand as he walked circles around the room, reading. There was a knock at the door.

Wilson.

Something must be up. Maybe his iron wasn't working properly.

When Dale looked through the peephole, though, it wasn't Agent Wilson on the other side.

It was Susan Anderson.

For a moment he couldn't believe his eyes. This was the last person he would have expected to come knocking on his motel door in the middle of the night. His heart thumped.

Sure, maybe she was there to give him an update about Caitlin, but if that were the case, she could have just called him.

His T-shirt was on the chair to his right. He reached for it but then thought better of it. He put his hand on the doorknob, paused, fluffed his chest hair out a bit, and opened the door.

She was wearing a sweatshirt and jeans. She'd gone for the *au naturel* look, eschewing makeup. Her face showed no trepidation or uncertainty.

"Well, now ... What's up, doc?"

"May I come in?"

"Sure."

His heart thumped a littler harder yet.

He stepped aside, and she walked right in. Her assertiveness was intoxicating.

"How do you do it?" Susan said.

And with that, Dale knew Susan's visit wasn't of the playful variety. Her tone wasn't arousing. It wasn't even intriguing. It was concerned, a little scared.

And her question made no sense.

"I'm sorry?" Dale said.

"How do you stay so cold? How do you make all those jokes? So flippant. Caitlin earlier..."

Dale could understand why she thought he was cold, but what she didn't realize was that he wasn't being flippant. He was putting up a shield. Humor kept the dark reality of his work at bay. If he couldn't protect himself from the awful things he saw—things like murders and rapes, things like a brainwashed eight-year-old girl—then he wasn't going to be strong enough to do his job.

"Sometimes jokes are the only way to get through it," he said.

"But did you see the look on her face? Didn't you see how scared she was?" Susan's eyes began to look wet. "When you left, it took her a full ten minutes to stop crying. She told me how they used to control her, how scared she is now."

She covered her mouth with her hand. The hand began to shake. She breathed deeply two times, releasing the breaths slowly, trying to control herself. Then she cried openly.

Dale was lodged firmly between a rock and a hard place. He'd never known how to deal with tears. The best he could do was reach out to touch her shoulder.

She stepped nearer to him, just a little, wanting but not asking to be hugged. He put his other hand on her and slowly pulled her closer. She allowed her head to fall onto his chest. Her arms were folded up between the two of them, and she cried harder. Dale hugged her.

The tears quieted, and she looked up. Her eyes were pink, and the wetness magnified the hazel centers, making them look clear and deep. They fixed on him, blinked. Then she leaned up. Her mouth met Dale's.

There were tears on her lips, and the taste of saline mixed with that of a thin layer of lipstick. Again, Dale didn't know what to do.

So he let her lead at first. She began with small kisses, gentle movements, her lips slowly gliding over his. Then she became more passionate, and Dale kissed her stronger, putting his hand on her lower back.

Just as he sensed her tongue, her lips began to tremble.

She cried again. Dale paused and began to pull away, but she put her hands into his hair, at the back of his head, and drew him closer.

Dale knew this had to end.

He placed his hands on her shoulders and pushed her away.

"You don't want to do this," he said.

"Yes, I do." She wiped a tear away and lunged at him.

Dale stepped backwards. "Susan, listen to me. You'll regret this. And I'm not going to let it happen."

Susan rubbed her face. She was breathing hard. "I feel like a fool."

"Don't." He motioned to the chairs at the table by the window. "Sit. Please."

She nodded and slowly sat down. "Thanks, Dale."

He pulled out a chair and sat across from her. "You bet."

———

A plate of Mrs. Baker's cookies sat in the middle of the table. They'd polished off a handful of them, and three more remained. Oatmeal raisin. Mrs. Baker had a good handle on the crispy-to-chewy ratio. The cookies were golden brown on top, a little darker on the edges, and moist in the middle.

They'd been chatting for a good ten minutes. Dale now knew that Susan had joined the medical field from a desire to help people. As a child, she wanted to be a nurse, but when she got a little older and women started becoming doctors, her career goals changed. She channeled her own maternal instincts into her studies and pursued pediatrics.

"And why did you become a federal agent?" Susan said.

Dale took another bite of his cookie. "Because they gave me a shiny badge and a gun."

"See, there you go again."

"What?"

"Those little gags of yours. You're hiding. You don't want to go head-on with those pesky little human things called emotions."

"Oh, geez. Are you a pediatrician or a shrink?"

She cocked her head to the side and crossed her arms. She wasn't going to let him weasel his way out of the question.

"Okay, fine," Dale said. "I always wanted to do something for my country, but I dragged my feet for some time. You've probably noticed that I'm tad quirky, so I wasn't sure where I could fit in. One day, I'd finally had enough of my procrastination. I was just about to walk into a federal law enforcement recruitment fair, when I heard a guy call out to me from the parking lot." He lowered his voice, doing his best to imitate Walter Taft's gravely tone. "*Hey, pal. I heard you're a historically-encyclopedic, sect-escaping genius.*"

Susan raised an eyebrow. "Um ... what?"

Dale struggled with his response, with how much he could say. "Before I became an agent, I was ... Well, my agency was keeping tabs on me, thought I'd make be a good fit. My name was famous at the time because ... um ... Look, it's not important. The important thing is that I got my chance to serve."

"You don't strike me as the federal agent type."

Dale scoffed and wiped some cookie crumbs from the T-shirt he'd put on. "What makes you say that?"

Susan smiled.

"You, on the other hand," Dale continued, "look every inch a doctor."

She really did. Poised. Professional. And with an aura of intelligence.

"I imagine it's tough being a doctor in your situation."

She squinted, confused. "How do you mean?"

"Having your little brother as your nurse."

Susan stuck out her tongue and made a gagging noise. "There's a huge chip on Brian's shoulder. He always thought he'd be the doctor and I'd be the nurse."

"Why do you take that treatment from him? He's your younger sibling and your subordinate. Show him you got some backbone."

She shook her head. "Backbone wasn't encouraged among the females in my family."

"So what? You're a big girl now. A professional. A doctor."

"We're not all as supremely confident in ourselves as you, Dale Conley. What do you suggest?"

"I think you oughta pop him right between the eyes." He was only half joking. "You're a good doc. And your work speaks for itself. You don't need Brian to validate that. You seem so tense, like he's a constant stressor for you. Why don't you let your hair down?"

She shrugged, took her hair tie between her fingers, and pulled it down the length of her ponytail. Her hair fell down in big waves.

She looked to her shoulders. "Not bad. Not bad at all."

CHAPTER THIRTY-SEVEN

THE MAN in Black pulled his car into the gas station parking lot and killed the engine. He couldn't stay long. It would look suspicious.

He looked out across the parking lot at the Ashbury Motel. Brad was staying in room seven, and his partner was in room eight. The Man in Black could see Brad's figure behind the drapes pacing, reading, working really, really. How like Brad. How diligent. How honorable. How nauseating.

Brad's car sat right outside his door, the sleek, ostentatious monstrosity. Brad's partner's car—an odious station wagon of some sort—was a couple spaces away, and between the two was another car, one the Man in Black hadn't seen yet on his trips to the motel. It was a Volkswagen Beetle, brown in color. He recognized all the other vehicles, and the motel had no new check-ins as far as he knew.

Curious.

A silhouette appeared against the drapes in room seven. The Man in Black sank down in his seat. There was little chance that Brad would be looking out his window, let alone that he would notice the Man in Black's car, but he wasn't taking any chances. The silhouette in the window turned, revealing a second silhouette. There were two people in the room. Brad had wrangled his partner into his late-night, paranoid research. That probably hadn't gone over well. His partner seemed like the type of man who ironed his socks.

The door to the room opened, and the Man in Black sank further into his seat, peering over the bottom edge of the driver-side window frame. Out of the room came not Brad's partner but a woman. A beautiful young woman in a sweatshirt and formfitting jeans.

Interesting.

An idea came to the Man in Black.

Brad stepped into the doorway. The woman approached the mystery Beetle and opened the door. They exchanged some parting words, and then the woman got in the car and started the engine.

The Man in Black's pulse quickened. The best part about meticulous planning was that when something new presented itself, it almost always served as an asset not a liability. This new development was certainly an asset.

The woman backed the car out. Brad waved at her and shut his door.

"Interesting," the Man in Black said aloud. "Very interesting indeed."

CHAPTER THIRTY-EIGHT

"My holy hell, Conley," SAC Taft spat. "What on God's green earth were you thinking going back to your old newsroom?"

The two of them stood in a janitor's closet. It was the only private place Taft could find in the Augusta County Sheriff's Office, and Taft was a firm believer in *Praise in public, admonish in private*. Dale regularly found himself alone with Taft in his office or pulled aside into an empty conference room.

Taft's face was red and his neck purple. Dale called this Stage 6. There were seven stages altogether. Considering he was nowhere near solving the case yet, Dale was proud he'd gotten Taft this far. He fought back a small grin. Still, he had to be careful. Taft was pissed enough to yank him off the case. He'd done it before.

"Do you have any idea how many BEI regulations you broke by going back there? You're gonna get someone hurt with these tactics of yours. You're impulsive, you're reckless. You're like a ... like a..."

"A loose cannon, sir?"

"Exactly. I got the Attorney General breathing down my neck about this case, and my investigating agent is out taking a trip down his PI's memory lane. Your carelessness is a blight on the whole Bureau. You're off the case, Conley! In fact, I oughta take your badge and gun for this."

"Don't you want to know what I found out, sir?" Officially he was off the case, yes. But if he played his cards right, he could bring Taft back around.

Taft ran a hand over his shiny, mostly bald dome. He looked to the back wall, then to Dale. His lips curled in disgust, and he quickly looked away again. He crossed his arms. Turned his back, faced the mops and brooms. Paced a few steps. Looked at Dale. Narrowed his eyes. "Okay, Conley. Tell me what you found."

Again Dale suppressed a smile. "Two things. First, Camden Marshall isn't the mastermind. In fact, he's another one of the victims. We need to transfer him out the jail and to a medical facility. He needs help. Lots of it."

Taft let out a growly sigh. "And the second thing?"

"My mother told me that there were multiple men who stopped by for the background check when I first joined the Bureau."

"What the hell are you talking about? I was the only one who did your background check."

"Exactly. Meaning someone's been following me around since I started with the BEI. Just like how someone's had this whole abduction at the Marshall Village planned out for years."

"You're thinking the two are connected?"

"There's a connection between the Marshall Village's founder and the Collective Agricultural Experiment, and they know my PI. Yes, that's exactly what I'm thinking."

Taft shook his head. "Dammit, Conley. If there was one

guy in the Bureau who this whole mess would be tied back to, I could've guessed it was you."

"Since I'm off the case, I'll just go and write up a quick report and get it to Wilson. Time's ticking away." He stuck his hands in his pockets.

Taft took a deep breath. "I don't like your tactics, Agent Conley." There was a long pause. "But you get results. What the hell is your next move?"

"Does that mean I'm back on the case?"

"Yes, goddammit!"

Dale smiled. Taft always ended up seeing things his way. "Is the helicopter I requested here? I'm gonna need it. There's a hunch I need to follow up on."

Taft scowled. "It's here. What kind of hunch?"

"I think I know who visited my mother and claimed he was completing my BEI background check. Darnell Fowler."

"Wasn't that the creep guard from the CAE? The guy who disappeared?"

Dale nodded. "I'm putting out an APB on Fowler."

"Christ, Conley." Taft ran his hand over his face. "I don't know who's gonna put me in the grave first, you or Peggy." He headed for the door.

"Where you going, sir?"

"I need a smoke."

Before he could open the door, though, there was a knock at it. Taft threw it open.

"What?"

It was Deputy Miller. He looked past Taft to Dale.

"Agent Conley, Harrisonburg police just received a call from the hospital. There's a gunman with hostages on the pediatrics floor. He's got the little girl."

CHAPTER THIRTY-NINE

Arancia belched out growls, and Dale had to restrain her from running right into the sheriff's rear bumper. He was following the sheriff as close as he could, and though the sheriff's Ford was hauling some serious ass down the road, the Pantera was still ready to overtake it at any second.

Dale had the windows down. The roaring wind and the blaring siren from Brown's car poured in, a loud concoction of mayhem.

Darnell Fowler. The creature from the camp. The man who took pleasure in whipping people. He was in Caitlin's room right now.

Dale's grip tightened around the shift knob.

The sheriff and Miller were leading in the Ford, Arancia was in the middle, and Wilson was struggling to keep up in the Custom Cruiser. A caravan of justice cutting through the Shenandoah Valley. Any other time, this would have been intoxicating to Dale. A fringe benefit of his job. But now all he could think about was the little girl who had already been through so much. And Darnell Fowler.

Dale pushed harder on the gas pedal.

The hospital came into view, and they slowed momentarily to pass a squad car with its lights on serving as a roadblock. The sheriff's car skidded to a stop outside the front doors, and Arancia slid in right beside it. Wilson pulled up behind them, and the four men got out.

There was a group of other police cars surrounding the hospital. The new, two-story Emergency Room sat on the corner of Mason and Cantrell with the main tower behind it, a square-ish, brick monolith. A crowd of gawkers had gathered on the sidewalks, and police officers held them at a distance.

The rest of the cops were positioned behind their squad cars. One of them had a megaphone, and everyone was looking up at the third floor of the tower. There were two silhouettes against the closed drapes of one of the rooms—a larger silhouette of adult size and a smaller silhouette of a child. A gun was evident in the hand of the adult.

A Harrisonburg officer strode over from one of the cars. "We have men posted at the front and rear. There are five officers and a security guard outside the room. He's saying he'll blow the girl's head off if we enter."

Dale nodded. "Come on, Sheriff," he said to Brown and headed for the front entrance.

"Somehow I knew your crazy ass would want to get right in there."

Inside, Brown led Miller, Dale, and Wilson toward the elevators, but Dale pulled him in the direction of the stairwell. "No time."

They stormed up the stairs. The agents and Miller took three steps at a time. The sheriff was panting heavily when they reached the third-floor landing.

Dale burst through the doorway. Halfway down the hall, a handful of cops, a few nurses, and a security guard were standing outside the door to Caitlin's room. The cops were shouting into the room.

Dale flashed his badge as he approached the group.

"He has himself barricaded in there," the guard said. He jiggled the doorknob. "Sprayed something in the lock. Can't get the key in."

Coming out of the keyhole was thick, translucent glue. It looked like honey. Dale touched it. It was sticky to the touch but had already set up considerably.

Sheriff Brown came from behind, panting. He put his hands on his knees.

"How long have they been in there?" Wilson said to the guard.

"A good fifteen minutes now. He hasn't said anything for five."

"Let me try," Dale said to the cop standing closest to the door. "He's looking for me." Dale faced the door and spoke loudly. "This is Special Agent Dale Conley. You can have me. Just let the girl go."

There was a thud from inside the room, like someone falling to the ground. Dale and Wilson looked at each other.

"Dear God," the guard said.

Dale grabbed the door handle and twisted. It didn't budge.

The sheriff's radio sounded. "The child just collapsed, Sheriff!" an officer said. "I repeat, the child collapsed."

Dale pounded on the door. "What the hell's going on in there?"

No reply. Complete silence.

Dale leaned back and lined up his boot for a massive kick. The door was sturdy metal, and the impact hurt his foot. The door didn't budge.

He looked up and down the hall for resources. In situations

like this, his mind went into instant search mode. No problem was insurmountable. You just had to find the right option. And the right option had just presented itself. In the corner at the end of the hall by the elevators was a bronze bust on a pedestal.

Everything works out if you give it time.

He approached the bust, a stern-faced man with a mustache and a bald head. The inscription read:

ALBERT CLANTON, MD
1893 - 1968
RMH'S FIRST HEAD OF PEDIATRICS
CAREGIVER, RESEARCHER, INNOVATOR

"Sorry, Doc," Dale said. He lifted the bust from its pedestal. It was even heavier than it looked, and his arms dropped a little with the weight. Perfect.

Brown stared at Dale wide-eyed as he shuffled back to the door. "You're not thinkin' of doing what I'm thinkin' you're going to do…"

"Depends on what you're thinkin', Sheriff."

Dale stood in front of the door, and the other men quickly cleared out. He turned the bust so that its base was facing the door. It was wide and flat—an ideal surface. Plus, it would help to minimize the damage. Dale sure didn't want to desecrate a man's memorial.

Dale pulled Dr. Clanton back and gave a solid swing. There was a terrific clang of metal-on-metal impact and a ringing noise that made the other men yell and cover their ears. The vibration in the sculpture quivered all the way up Dale's arms to his shoulders.

The door swung open and smacked into the wall. Clanton flew out of Dale's hands and bounced across the floor, clanging loudly.

The scene was staggering. Caitlin was duct-taped to her

bed. Her mouth too was duct-taped. She was screaming, crying, struggling. The nurses and uniformed officers ran up to her and tore at the tape.

On the windowsill was a cassette player. A CPR dummy lay on the ground by the window. It was a torso only, cut off at the waist, and about the size of a child. Next to it was a plastic skeleton, standing vertically on a metal stand, holding a toy gun in its hand and draped with a black jacket.

The Man in Black's jacket. Darnell's.

This was the jacket that Dale had seen at each of his three encounters with Darnell. He approached it and took one of the sleeves in his hand. It was lightweight, a bit heavier than a sweatshirt, and made of rough canvas material. There was a musty odor.

He turned the jacket's hood inside out. There would be hair samples in here. Leaving it behind was careless on Darnell's part. Too careless. Why had he taken it off in the first place?

Miller was helping the others with Caitlin's tape, and Dale pulled him aside. "You said that a doctor called this in?" Dale said.

"That's right."

"Was it the girl's doctor? Dr. Susan Anderson?"

"Yes, sir."

The hair on Dale's arms stood straight up. Something was wrong. Something was very, very wrong.

"She said she hadn't been away from the girl for more than a minute or two when she came back and found her all taped down," Miller said.

Dale looked at the people trying to free Caitlin. The tangle of duct tape holding her down was massive. It would have taken more than a minute or two to lay it all down on a scrappy girl who was surely fighting back.

He turned to Brown. "And the hospital's been on lockdown?"

"Yup. Security contained it for us immediately. No one in or out. Except emergencies."

"Emergencies going in *and* out?"

"Of course. I can't shut the whole place down. It's a hospital."

Dale weighed the jacket in his hands. Darnell had somehow gotten in, tied up the girl, and disappeared. How had he escaped unnoticed?

The cops and nurses freed Caitlin from the bed and removed the tape from her mouth. She sobbed on the shoulder of one of the nurses, who put her arms around the girl.

Dale noticed the nurse's lab coat. White, long-sleeved. Her name was stitched on the front of it.

He looked back at Darnell's jacket in his hand. "Oh god..."

CHAPTER FORTY

DALE SPRINTED up to the hospital's front desk where a young receptionist with wispy hair sat reading a magazine and chomping on gum. When she looked up and saw Dale bounding toward her, she slowly wheeled her chair backwards.

"Have there been any patient transfers since the lockdown?" Dale said the instant he crashed into the desk.

"I'm sorry, I can't give out that inf—"

Dale pulled out his badge. "Police business. Who's left the building?"

The receptionist's mouth opened in stunned disbelief. "Just one ambulance. A doctor and a patient."

"A female patient?"

The receptionist nodded. "And a male doctor."

"Did the patient look okay?"

The receptionist gave him a confused look. "I'm not sure. She was on a stretcher. Unconscious."

Dale sucked in a breath. "Where were they going?"

"Some hospital in Staunton. I hadn't heard of it..." She looked at a clipboard. "Western State Hospital."

———

Dale flew down I-81. Arancia's siren blared. The emergency light hanging from the mirror flashed. He kept one hand gripped tightly on the steering wheel and the other on the horn, blasting it in long bursts. Cars parted to either side before him.

Susan was somewhere out there with Darnell Fowler. He thought of the things that Darnell had done. Brainwashing, hypnotism. What he could do to Susan was literally limitless. His fingers felt like they were about to tear the leather-wrap from the wheel.

Western State Hospital. The old lunatic asylum. Where there had been electroshock, lobotomies, sterilization. It was more of Darnell's demented mind games.

A couple more cars cleared the way for him, and then he saw it ahead of him on the crest of a hill—an ambulance with its lights on. Dale could picture Darnell behind the wheel, his small, ugly face laughing.

Dale dropped the stick into fourth gear, and the engine bellowed. His head whipped back into the headrest. The rear tires tried to slide out from under him, but the limited slip differential did its job, keeping them where they should be.

The ambulance was giving everything it had, but it couldn't match the Pantera, a 159-mph vehicle. Dale came right up behind it.

The ambulance didn't brake. Its movements were jerky and erratic, swerving like it had a drunk behind the wheel. Its tall form teetered on soft suspension, ready to topple over at any moment.

Cars pulled over left and right. The ambulance came within inches of them as it continued to swerve. It clipped a pickup truck that was trying to move to the side, spinning the truck around halfway. If Dale couldn't bring the ambulance to a stop, Darnell was going to run someone over.

The main exit into town was drawing near—Jefferson Highway, the road that led to the mental hospital. But as they came upon it, there were no brake lights from the ambulance. Was he leading him into the countryside?

The ambulance jerked to the right so fast that Dale barely dodged it, coming within a few inches of smashing into the back. He whipped his head around to see the ambulance topple over. It hit the sheer rock face along the right side of the off-ramp, where the exit for Jefferson Highway had been dynamited from the hill. But instead of falling to the ground, it barreled down the off-ramp like this with its top angled against the rock, two wheels on the ground and two in the air. The metal screeched along the rock and sent out a shower of sparks. The ambulance slammed back onto four wheels, swerved, then continued on toward the highway.

Dale laid on the brakes and fought the fishtailing of Arancia's rear end. The tires squealed, and the whole car shuddered. He flew right past the exit.

He flicked his eyes to the rearview mirror. No cars immediately behind him. He had the room. So he pulled back the handbrake and yanked the steering wheel to the right, using the car's forward momentum and out-of-control energy to his advantage.

Arancia spun around, centrifugal force smashing Dale into the door. He held on tight and guided the car's slide to the outside shoulder of the road. The interstate was divided—a copse of trees separating the north- and southbound sets of lanes. So he had one option to get back to the exit.

He downshifted, smashed the gas pedal, and laid on the horn as he drove down the shoulder against the traffic. There was enough room for the Pantera, just enough. The cars in the right-hand lane, the one closest to him, panicked at the sight of an orange car flying right at them. They moved into the other lane. Horns blared. Cars came to a halt, narrowly avoiding each other.

Dale surged past the pileup. Avoiding the cluster of cars, a Chevelle shot into the shoulder, coming right at him, and Dale yanked Arancia's steering wheel to the left. Her tires dipped into the gravel at the side of the road.

He pulled past the Chevelle and onto the off-ramp, again using Arancia's momentum to pull him ninety degrees around, oversteering then realigning her back down the off-ramp. The ramp was an open shot for him—no vehicles. He rev-matched into third and thundered toward the highway.

At the light, the cars heeded his siren and cleared a path for him. He turned to the right, toward the mental hospital. Ahead were the lights of the ambulance. It was about half a mile down the road, pushing through the traffic that was pulling over for it. This was to Dale's advantage. Given that both his vehicle and the one he was pursuing had sirens and lights, cutting through traffic was the least of his worries.

Arancia rocketed toward the ambulance. The open path in front of him allowed him to pull in like he was on a high-power winch. He was back behind the ambulance again, three feet from its bumper.

They flew right past Western State Hospital. Dale had figured that wasn't the real destination. Darnell was trying to get Susan to wherever he was keeping the Marshallites.

The ambulance continued past the Stonewall Jackson Inn. They were headed into downtown. Right into the little businesses and restaurants.

Where all the foot traffic would be.

Dale took out his Model 36. He had to shoot out the tires. Susan was in the back, yes, but there was an immediate danger to everyone else on the road. He stuck the gun out the window, steadied his arm on the mirror. He aimed down the gun's small, fixed sights. The ambulance's tires weaved. Dale tapped the brake, gave himself a little more space.

The ambulance dropped in front of him, going down one of Staunton's steep hills. Arancia followed, and Dale was pushed back into his seat, his stomach sinking like the first hill of a rollercoaster. The ambulance went up the other side of the hill and sailed over the crest. Blue sky appeared beneath it, and the wheels sank, dropping below the frame. The whole vehicle tilted to the right in its flight, and it came back to the ground hard, spitting out a burst of sparks.

Arancia's sleek profile was much more suited to air travel. Dale dropped his gun onto the passenger seat then held on tight with both hands. The crest of the hill appeared before him. Then there was nothing but sky. His gun drifted up, its shiny, nickel-plated form suspended in the air. A tiny satellite. Arancia's engine, now unencumbered by tire-to-road friction, screamed. Then the gun dropped, and so did Arancia's nose, bringing the horizon back into view. Arancia touched down hard but, mercifully, completely on her tires. No metal.

The ambulance took a couple of hard right turns, putting it on Beverley Street. The heart of downtown Staunton. Dale grabbed the gun. There were flocks of people milling about downtown. He had to bring this vehicle down. Right now.

He took the corner onto Beverley tight, clipping a crate of fruit outside the corner grocer. The crate erupted with—fittingly—oranges that thumped over Arancia's hood and top. They popped beneath her tires.

Dale pulled in close to the ambulance. It started to swerve in big arcs, left and right, snaking its way down the street and glancing off the edges of the sidewalks. People standing outside the stores and restaurants screamed, ran inside.

There was a sandwich-style barricade sign by an open manhole cover on the left side of the road, and the ambulance pulled to the right to miss it. This gave Dale a chance. He shot once from the Model 36, double-action, missing.

The ambulance swerved again, and then, with a cloud of torched rubber smoke and a shrieking sound, it turned sideways and headed into an alley.

Dale guided Arancia right behind it, sticking to it like a magnet.

It was a wide alley, and the ambulance had enough room to continue its swerving tactics. A pile of cardboard boxes sat outside one of the buildings. The two vehicles crashed through. Corrugated paper flew in all directions.

Brake lights. The wheels on the ambulance locked up, smoke billowing from the rear tires. There was a brick wall at the end of the alley. A dead end.

Dale slammed on his own brake pedal. The Pantera's four-wheel disc brakes brought it to a sudden stop. His chest slammed into his seatbelt.

The ambulance had a harder time with it, rocking and jolting to a halt several feet away.

Dale slapped the stick into neutral, yanked the parking brake, and jumped out. He crouched behind the door and took out his gun. Sometimes he had to use Arancia as a shield. He hated it. He ought to be taking a bullet for the Pantera, not the other way around.

He flicked off the siren. The emergency light remained flashing.

"Step out of the vehicle!"

The ambulance was motionless. Dale watched, looking for movement. Nothing.

He stood up, paced toward the ambulance. His gun swung back and forth between the driver and passenger side.

Darnell could sneak out either way. Chances were, he was armed.

The sound of Dale's footsteps was just audible over the two idling engines.

Another step forward.

He repositioned his grip on the gun.

The ambulance's reverse lights came on. Tires squealed, and it lunged backwards. Coming right at him.

And Arancia.

Dale fired three shots into the passenger-side tire. It exploded into long, flapping shreds. The rear corner of the ambulance crashed to the ground. It swerved to the right in a tight arc.

Dale barrel-rolled to the side as the ambulance flew by him. It smashed into the brick wall. The impact shook the buildings. The rear corner of the ambulance crumpled—right where Susan would be. A hubcap zipped toward Dale, rolling in circles until it clanked on the ground.

He stood. The ambulance now rested at an awkward angle against the wall. The two wheels on the driver side were off the ground. They spun to a stop.

He raised his gun at the driver side door and sprinted to the rear of the ambulance. The right door was smashed. The left was intact. He tried the door handle. Locked.

"Susan?"

No reply. Both of the windows in the back doors were shuttered. He tried to peer in but could see nothing.

He banged on the door. "Susan!"

Again there was no response.

He moved to the side of the vehicle and cautiously crept toward the front. The driver's door, angled as it was, hid Darnell from view. Dale could see only his shoulder.

He smacked a fist against the ambulance. "Federal agent. Get out of the vehicle."

There was the *click* of a seatbelt detaching. The door began to open. It creaked on its hinges, and Darnell had to push against gravity to get it open. When the door fully opened, Dale saw something he didn't expect.

It wasn't Darnell Fowler in the seat.

The gun dipped in Dale's hand. The man was in his mid-thirties and wearing Marshallite clothes. He stared at Dale with an empty smile. That familiar glassed-over look was in his eyes.

Dale took a step back to make room for him, keeping the gun aimed right at him. "Get out and put your hands over your head."

The man did as he was told, struggling to pull himself out of the upturned cab and then clasping his hands behind his head. His smile grew wider.

"Open the back of the vehicle."

"Not who you were hoping to find, am I?" the man said in a singsong voice. "You were expecting Darnell Fowler, the Man in Black."

"I said *open it.*"

The man walked to the rear of the ambulance. Dale took a few steps back and kept the Model 36 fixed on him as he opened the back doors. The man swung the door open wide.

There was nothing there. Just shelves, supplies, and two empty gurneys.

Dale's mouth opened.

"You were hoping to see Susan Anderson," the driver said. "I am certainly sorry to disappoint you once again."

Dale rushed forward and grabbed the man by the shirt. "Where is she?"

"She is with the Man in Black. He has asked me to pass a message to you. You need to return to the Sheriff's Office. Otherwise you might miss his call."

"What call?"

"That is all I'm permitted to tell you."

Dale looked from the man to Arancia and back to the man again. He patted the man down. He was clean.

Dale groaned and put his gun back in its holster.

"Get in the damn car."

CHAPTER FORTY-ONE

THE MAN in Black was driving south down Highway 11, the historic staple of the Shenandoah Valley, headed back to Staunton. Such a gorgeous day. Bright blue sky, big clouds. He had the window down, and the breeze felt nice. If anything, it was just a bit too warm. His back was starting to sweat a little.

Brad Walker would be in no position to enjoy the lovely weather. Right about now, he was busting into the hospital room. Hopefully he would even take the bait and chase after the ambulance. The Man in Black was particularly proud of that little scenario he'd concocted with the ambulance, and it would be a shame if it went to waste.

In the seat next to him was Susan Anderson, the woman he'd seen coming out of Walker's hotel room the last night. She was unconscious.

His man in the ambulance had met him at the predetermined location five minutes prior, the parking lot of an abandoned store not a mile away from the hospital where they transferred the woman between the vehicles. It had been a risky operation, but it went off without a hitch.

He had unbuttoned her blouse down to her stomach. Her breasts were big and soft-looking. They shook with the motion of the drive. He'd promised himself that he would do no more, that he wouldn't do the things that Father had done. It was an exercise in ascetic self-control.

But seeing them shake like that, he decided he would give himself one small treat. He reached out and grabbed one of her breasts. It was velvety and warm and made him moan out loud.

The car hit a bump, and her head rolled to the side. Her lips were open, as were her eyes, ever so slightly, slits revealing a little white.

He still couldn't believe the luck that he'd had when he saw her leaving Brad's motel room. What had already been a foolproof plan was now bordering on genius. When life presented opportunities, he always took advantage of them.

If Brad Walker had one weakness, it was the ladies. The Man in Black was disappointed in himself for having not already thought to exploit this weakness. He was systematically attacking everything that made Brad what he was. The riddles in his ridiculous books. His sense of honor. Now, he got a chance to destroy his weakest link—women. And soon enough, he was going to strike a lot closer to home.

If Brad was worried about Susan, wait until he saw what the Man in Black had in store for him next. The problem was going to be getting there. It was another flight of fancy on his part, and it was gonna be a headache. It would take hours just to get there and back. In that time, he'd have to incapacitate Susan again, and that was yet another chore. All the work, though, would be worth it in the end.

But first, he had a phone call to make.

CHAPTER FORTY-TWO

DALE WALKED across the lobby of the Sheriff's Office to where Brown, Wilson, and Taft were circled around a desk. Behind him, a sheriff's deputy escorted the ambulance driver, now in handcuffs, across the room.

"How's Caitlin?" Dale said.

"She's as panicked as a corncob in a hen house, but she'll pull through," Brown said. "Did you catch the son of a bitch?"

"I caught the wrong son of a bitch, as it turns out. Get that man some medical help, Sheriff. He's going to need it."

"What in the world do we do now?" Wilson said.

"I'm waiting for a phone call."

"A *phone call?*" Taft said. "Conley——"

The office phone rang. Dale held up a finger.

The desk sergeant who took the call scrunched his face and looked out into the office. He put his hand over the receiver. "Sheriff, is there someone named Brad Walker around?"

Dale sighed and walked over to the desk sergeant. "It's for me." He took the receiver. "Who's this?"

A menacing voice came from the other line, but it wasn't

that of Darnell Fowler. It was cool and even, with a hint of Texas twang. "So snippy. Is that any way to talk to an old friend?"

It was Glenn Downey.

"Glenn?"

A freight train of confusion crashed through Dale's brain, shredding synapses as it went.

He reached for the table in front of him, caught himself, tried to make sense of the fact that the man was alive. The man who had nearly destroyed his life was talking to him once again—a man who was supposed to be nothing but a charred corpse at the bottom of the Chesapeake Bay.

"That's right," Glenn said. "The notorious. Back from the dead. By now I'm sure you've figured out from my little clues that things are connected back to the Collective Agricultural Experiment and that Camden Marshall was merely one of my pawns, so I thought I'd call and congratulate you on making it this far."

"This can't be real."

"It's very real. But do you really want to spend your time arguing with me on whether or not my existence fits with your perception of the past? Glenn Downey is back. And the question is, how are you going to deal with that as you move forward with your investigation?"

"What do you want, Glenn? Why are you doing this?"

"'Glenn.' The last time I saw you, you were calling me 'Father.' Call me 'Father.' Now."

This was the sort of thing that Glenn used in the camp to maintain control over his subjects. The use of titles. The strong, commanding language. As the lead investigator of the case, if Dale allowed Glenn to think he could control him now, it could prove disastrous.

"No," Dale said.

"If you want to see any of these people alive again, you

will address me as 'Father.' But I know what you're thinking right now—*he's bluffing.* Allow me to prove how serious I am. Look out the window."

Dale grabbed the base of the phone and walked to the window.

Across the street, a man in Marshallite clothing stood on the sidewalk by a pay phone. He made eye contact with Dale, put a revolver to his head, and fired. The *crack* of the shot roared through the office.

Dale sucked in a breath. Wilson, Taft, and the sheriff ran out of the building.

"I assume I now have your attention?" Glenn said.

"Yes."

"Yes...?"

Dale thought of the barking incident with Marshall. The humiliation. When people did these things to another human being, its purpose was two-fold. One reason was to break the other person's spirit. The other was the thrill, the same thrill gained by rapists and rotten bully kids, a putrid sort of satisfaction.

But, like in the interrogation room, Dale knew that he had to do it.

"Yes, Father."

"Good," Glenn said. There was a pause, and he exhaled. Dale could hear saliva smack between his lips. "There are one hundred thirty-two souls left. I suppose I've left you dangling on the line long enough. I'll let you know what I want in exchange for the rest of the people."

"Which is?"

"You."

"Me?"

"Yes. You're the only one who escaped, the only one who I didn't touch forever."

Glenn's erroneous megalomania hadn't changed. "You're

wrong," Dale said. "Five people fled that night. Five people were strong enough to not take your poison."

"Yes, but those people will never be the same. Not after that last night. No amount of head-shrinking will ever take that night from their memory. I'll be with them forever. With all of them but you."

Glenn was wrong again. Spencer too had survived and regained his identity. Thank goodness.

"So what do you want from me?" Dale said.

"I want you to come out to the ol' homestead. Tonight. Unarmed and alone. Truly alone this time, not like those little stunts you pulled in Roanoke and Manteo. You bring anyone else, and I start killing these people. You got that?"

"Yes."

"I'll have snipers posted all over the camp. As you've seen from recent events, these folks really are quite loyal to me. They'll have no qualms shooting one of your associates."

"Alone. Got it. What have you done with Susan?"

"Ladies always were your Achilles heel. Don't worry. We'll keep her safe and warm. I'll see you tonight, then. Close it out."

Dale shuddered.

Glenn was telling him to use the standard closing for any conversation between the Father and one of his children at the CAE. It was another one of his methods. Everything was some form of control over his followers.

"I said *close it out*," Glenn barked when Dale didn't immediately respond.

Dale spoke slowly. Despite having tried to forget them for years, the words came back to him perfectly. "Dearest Father, I am a sinner, and I beg forgiveness. For all that you give, I am thankful."

Dale felt unclean.

Glenn chuckled. "Very good. Until tonight."

There was a rattle of the phone on the other end, and the line went dead. Dale slowly lowered the receiver from his ear and handed it back to the sergeant.

Dale's pulse was supersonic. He had known for some time now that there was a connection between the CAE and the Marshall case, but now he knew there was much more than a connection. The two were one and the same. Glenn Downey was back in his life.

Knowing he would face Glenn again was terrifying enough, but the memory that was forced to the forefront of his mind was even worse. The memory of leaving Spencer behind. He'd watched from the ship as they dragged him back into the camp. He left him with Glenn. Even after Glenn warned him what would happen to Spencer if they ever tried escaping again.

After the meeting in Dale's cottage.

CHAPTER FORTY-THREE

BRAD WALKER STOOD in his cottage. It had been less than seventy-two hours since he and Spencer tried to escape through the woods. The lashes across his chest still blazed and made his skin feel tight and rigid. His muscles were weak from the blows, and it was hard to stand. But he was not backing down from this confrontation.

Glenn Downey was in front of him. It was a muggy day, and his shirtsleeves were rolled up, buttons undone halfway down his scraggly chest. He had expelled all the other people from the cottage, leaving just him and Brad.

Brad's hands were rigid and twitchy, ready to curl into fists at any moment. He was prepared for anything. Glenn's temperament had been hurricane-violent lately, and many of his children had suffered the cost. The man's eyes were bloodshot, and there were sweat rings on his shirt. His chest was glistening wet. None of his children believed he was any less than the Son of God, even in this current state, but Brad recognized the signs of a junkie.

"I'm glad to get a chance to talk to you alone. Man to

man," Glenn said. "I've come to propose a gentlemen's agreement."

"About what?"

"I fully understand that the rest of the people here only converted because they see something in me. Something that they *wanted* to see. But you and your little buddy came as spies. It takes a lot of extra work to convert the resistant mind, but it can be done."

"Not this mind."

"Not yet, maybe. You're like the stallion that just can't be ridden." Glenn smiled. "But your little colt—he can be broken. It's already happening. You've noticed."

Brad had indeed seen the changes in Spencer in the three days since the night they tried to escape through the woods. The night they were caught. Tied to the beds. Beaten. Since then, Spencer was different. It showed in the way he spoke, the way he conducted himself at the meetings. If Brad didn't get him out of here soon, Glenn would own his mind like everyone else's. Brad would be the only one in the camp that Glenn didn't control.

But he couldn't let Glenn know that he'd seen the change. "You'll never own Spencer either."

Glenn sneered. "Somehow I think he'll come around. And you know that too. Which leads me to believe that your attempt to flee the other day won't be your last. That's why I came to talk to you. I hope you realize by now that escaping the CAE is impossible. If you do try again, the little punishment you two received the other day will seem like a tap to the nose. That Darnell—you've only seen a bit of what he has to offer. Between you and me, he's a bit of a backwater hick. But that doesn't mean he's stupid. Darnell's real genius is his work. Try again and I'll set Darnell's full wrath upon you. It'll be especially bad for Spencer. Thin and frail as he is, I don't know if he'll make it."

As much as Brad tried to avoid letting Glenn affect him, he couldn't force Spencer's howls of pain from his mind. The thought of Spencer receiving even harsher treatment made Brad begin to doubt his plan for a second escape.

"And I'll be there this time," Glenn said, "to see if the lesson might actually sink in. In that sense, I hope you do try again. I think I'd really enjoy seeing you under the whip." He turned on his heel, went to the door, and held it open before exiting. "That head of yours isn't as strong as you think. It will be mine soon enough."

He left.

CHAPTER FORTY-FOUR

DALE HAD VOWED that he'd never go back to the CAE camp.

He drove down the mottled gravel road in an old Jeep CJ-5 he'd borrowed from the Augusta County Sheriff's Office. The access road to the camp had been rough enough during operation, and it had been years since anyone had owned the land. Now it was riddled with potholes and debris. Arancia wasn't going to cut it out here.

The road was two miles long, snaking through the forest to the main camp. Glenn had chosen the camp's location because of its seclusion, and a big part of that was the natural buffer zone between the camp and the highway.

The forest was pitch black. His headlights lit the tree trunks as they slowly rolled by. They had the bright, unnatural look that objects get when artificial light steals their cover of darkness.

He had to stop twice to move fallen branches that blocked the road. Along with dodging the gaping potholes, it took him several minutes to reach the gate, a seven-foot steel affair with cinder block towers. Years ago, there would have been two guards standing on either side. Only authorized vehicles were allowed beyond that point. Now the entire structure was corroded and on the verge of collapse.

There was a rusty chain and padlock on the fence. He hopped out of the Jeep and tugged on the padlock. Not budging. He grabbed a large flashlight from the back of the truck and walked around the side of the gate.

He began to hike the last half mile to the camp. Wet gravel sloshed beneath his boots. He pointed the light toward the tops of the trees. They closed in on either side, forming a black tunnel around him.

A thought kept intruding into his mind—Glenn Downey could very well want to kill him. Everything to this point now made sense. Glenn had systematically attacked everything about Dale. He had tried to humiliate him, to ruin him. The next logical step was to kill him. Dale tried not to think about it, but his chest was ready to explode. He felt a strange, conclusive melancholy. He thought about his mother.

After ten minutes, every inch of him began to tense up as the muscle memory in his legs told him that he was drawing close. Right on cue, the road in front of him opened up. His flashlight showed the first structures of the camp in the distance. They were just as he remembered—square in shape and gray in color with all the purpose and charm of a Soviet missile silo. The doors and gutters and window frames were all rusted, and there were dirty veins of sediment staining the walls.

The camp was three square miles with over forty buildings, so whatever Glenn had planned for him, he had plenty of spaces from which to jump out and scare the shit out of him. Before Dale had a chance to enter the veritable fun house and ponder all of these possibilities, a figure slowly strode out from one of the first buildings.

The Man in Black. He wore the usual attire. Black pants and a black jacket, different than the one he left behind at the hospital. The hood was pulled up over his head, and he wore the same black mask with the jeering jester face.

Dale stopped. They were twenty feet apart.

"Thank you for coming," the Man in Black said. The voice was Glenn's airy Texas drawl.

"I'm here. Let the hostages go."

"Don't rush things. I need to savor this." He put his hands behind his back. "Here he stands. Brad Walker. After all these years. The one who escaped. I want to remember this moment forever."

Dale turned his face. "Here. This is my best side. For posterity."

"Oh, that tongue of yours. Such sharp wit. I suppose you think you've figured out why you're here."

"I have a pretty good idea." The melancholy feeling rushed over him again. It was somewhat relieving, even. Somehow dying didn't seem as bad as it was cracked up to be. As long as he could help the missing people.

"You think you're here to take the poison you escaped the first time. And you'd do it, too, wouldn't you? To save the lives of these people."

"That's right."

"So noble. So, so noble."

"Where's Susan Anderson?"

"And coming to a woman's rescue too. What are you, an Eagle Scout?"

Dale took a step forward. "Let's get on with it."

"No, Brad. You're going to serve a bigger purpose. But first, I'm afraid I haven't been entirely truthful with you."

Dale narrowed his eyes.

The Man in Black put his fingers on the bottom of his mask and lifted upward. After the surprises Dale had been witness to during this investigation, the fact that it wasn't Glenn Downey beneath the mask didn't shock him. It was who was there in his place that was surprising. A young face. A face that was lean, somewhat pleasant-looking. Sandy blond hair. Blue eyes.

"Spencer..." Dale said.

There was a sharp pain to the back of his head, and he collapsed. His face smashed against the gravel of the road. Just before he lost consciousness, he saw the boots of a Marshallite man who had emerged from the woods behind him.

CHAPTER FORTY-FIVE

DALE'S EYELIDS SLOWLY PARTED. He was somewhere dark. There was a throbbing sensation at the back of his head and pain in both of his wrists. He felt oddly cool.

He peered up. It was dark except for a shaft of rust-colored light focused on him like a spotlight. Wherever he was, it was cavernous. He could feel the weight of open space around him, crushing him. He squinted at the light. It was far above him, fifty feet or so.

He was bare-chested. His arms were outstretched. On each of his wrists was a strap connected to a chain that hung from above and disappeared into the darkness. His body-weight had been resting on the straps while he was unconscious, putting pressure on his wrists. He planted his feet and stood up, sweet relief coursing through his arms.

Like the moment of reminiscence that follows an early morning alarm clock, his memory flooded back to him. The Marshall Village case. Taking the gravel road to the CAE camp. The blow to the back of the head.

Spencer.

His heart raced, and there was a surge of dread. His bare

flesh suddenly felt even colder, and he fought to keep himself from shaking. Or screaming.

He was back at the CAE camp.

He tried to think of his training. There were rational ways to avoid panic and resist jeopardizing the Bureau and its mission. But the thought kept intruding.

He was back at the CAE camp.

He was at the old camp, tied up in one of the warehouses, completely vulnerable.

Deep breaths. Slow and controlled. He visualized the situation as an outsider. Disassociation. He was a camera floating above, looking down upon a half-naked man chained to a ceiling, his arms spread in a Christ-like posture.

Deep breaths. This wasn't him. The situation was not his. Deep breaths.

There was a noise in the distance. A metallic *bang*. A large door opening. The sound was deep and hollow, echoing through the vast blackness around him. Then a slow tapping of footsteps.

His heart thumped harder again, and all the deep breathing and meditation techniques flew right out the window. He was tied up in an empty warehouse. And there was someone walking toward him.

The footsteps stopped momentarily. There was a *click* in the distance, and the patch of light around him slowly got a bit brighter. The circumference of the light expanded, revealing several shapes a few feet away from him.

They were wheeled chalkboards, the type used at business meetings. Six feet across, pivoting in the center. They were arranged in a circle around him and were covered in photographs. Black-and-whites. Taped one on top of each other, haphazardly. The images were of corpses. Dale knew what he was looking at. They were the dead people of the

CAE. Glenn Downey's followers. The ones who took the poison.

Bodies on the ground. Lying in the dirt. In the puddles. Curled lips. Bared teeth. Vomit. Rolled eyes.

The footsteps grew louder. They continued at a slow, even pace.

Tap, tap, tap.

They were coming from straight ahead of him. He peered forward and squinted, trying to look through the gap between two of the macabre collages.

A figure materialized from the darkness and stepped into the circle of chalkboards. It was Spencer.

Somehow seeing him calmed Dale's nerves. Sure, he was half-naked and in bonds, but this person was someone he knew, someone he could easily outwit.

Spencer gestured at the photos. "Do you like my pictures?"

"You always did have talent with a camera. What's the point of all this, Spencer? Did you really do all this because of me, or was that just part of your Glenn act?"

"Yes and no. I do have a bigger goal, but first I needed to see if you could take it." Spencer put his hands behind his back and began to pace before Dale within the confines of the small patch of light.

"Take what?"

"My little series of tests. Pretty amazing, huh? The whipping boy outsmarting the puzzle master? But I think you know the real reason behind everything."

Dale just nodded. Of course he knew the reason.

"I saw you, Brad. I saw you on the boat. On the side, clinging to the ropes."

"I tried to get off and—"

"You did *nothing.*" His voice echoed off the walls somewhere in the distance. "You watched them capture me. You watched them drag me back to the camp."

"I would never have caught up with you in time."

"Maybe, maybe not. I suppose we'll never know. Remember that promise that Glenn made to you after the first time we tried to escape?"

The conversation had played in Dale's mind a million times since then.

"Let's just say he made good on his promise," Spencer said. He unbuttoned his shirt, slowly, and pulled it open.

Dale gasped.

Spencer's chest was an uninterrupted surface of scar tissue, bumpy and mottled. Long lines crisscrossed the mass. They were lash marks. Purple-pink with jagged edges. Dale had his own scars for a time, after the first punishment he and Spencer endured. His had now faded almost entirely. But these were worse than Dale's had ever been. Much worse.

"My god..." Dale whispered.

Spencer ran his hand over his chest, circling the entire area. "Most of this is from the fire. I was on Father's boat. You know that, right?"

"I do." Of the Appointed survivors, Spencer had been the only one who had been on Glenn's boat.

"I was covered in fuel. Burned me raw. But it still wasn't enough to get rid of these." He traced his finger along the most severe of the lash marks, the one that ran diagonally from his shoulder to his hip. "Darnell sure enjoyed himself that night. He was a vicious son of a bitch. Father watched. Then later he gave me one of his personal punishments."

Spencer was a wall of mangled skin. There were dark furrows in the scars, deep enough you could stick your finger in. His nipples were gone. But still the lash marks persisted, a large crosshatch pattern covering all of him.

Dale stared. Words tried to escape his lips. "Spencer ... I tried ... I couldn't..."

"You wouldn't believe how satisfying it was to watch Father burning to death, sinking beneath the water." Spencer paused. "He was talented, wasn't he? Controlling all those people. I've done so much better than he did, though, Brad. He couldn't do it as well as I could. I've added another element."

"Hypnotism."

"That's right."

"But you couldn't possibly have hypnotized a hundred forty-seven people. When a hypnotist works with a group, there are as many people who *can't* be hypnotized as can."

"Exactly. The mind has to be willing to believe. It has to be weak. Who's more willing to follow than people who joined a utopian community?"

Suddenly Spencer didn't seem so witless. In fact, he seemed like a demented genius. Of all the populations who could be controlled by hypnotism, a group of people already devoted unconditionally to an idea would be most gullible. The folks at the Marshall Village had unequivocally accepted Camden Marshall's concepts, leaving the door to their minds wide open. And Spencer barged right in.

"Marshall himself was the hardest," Spencer said. "It took a while before I got through to him. But once I did, I was able to slowly convert his utopian community into a cult like Father's. And eventually we all left, just as the Roanoke colonists did."

Taking advantage of people's most fundamental beliefs was about the most despicable thing Dale could think of.

"You're sick, Spencer."

Spencer walked closer. He stopped six inches away and looked at Dale with an oily smile that was all too reminiscent of Glenn Downey's.

"The thing about hypnotism is you can have someone entirely under your control," Spencer said. "They're at your mercy. Just like you were minutes ago when you were unconscious."

"Except I'm quite certain you didn't have me clucking like a chicken."

Spencer ran his hand along Dale's cheek, tracing his jaw line to his chin. Dale winced.

"Oh, you never know," Spencer said. He took a step back and began buttoning his shirt. "You could have been anyone or anything while you were asleep. Like a dream." He paused. "I really had you going, didn't I? You really thought I was Glenn Downey?"

"Yeah. You got me. Congratulations."

"A man you *knew* to be dead. A man everyone knows is dead. It was on TV, for Christ's sake." He threw his arms in the air. "All I did was imitate his voice, and suddenly you believed he miraculously rose from the dead. See how easily the human brain can be hoodwinked? Even one as brilliant as yours."

Dale didn't respond.

"The best part," Spencer said, "was that I had you believing for the longest time that I was Darnell Fowler. I have two degrees of separation now. Who would ever suspect me? They'll be out chasing Darnell. Of course, they'll never find him."

"What makes you so sure?"

"Thought you might ask that." Spencer stepped back into the darkness and returned with a cardboard box about eight inches wide. He opened it up and pulled out something the size of a volleyball. Something grayish brown and dry. A head.

Spencer held up Darnell's familiar visage by its scruffy, red hair. The eyes were closed, and the mouth was open and contorted. The skin had turned to wrinkled leather, and it clung to the skull beneath.

Spencer shook the head in his hand. "*Hey, Brad, old buddy. How's life been treating ya?* I caught up with Darnell out in the woods that night before making it to the boats. He didn't even get the satisfaction of going down with the rest of the Blue Guard."

He made a slicing motion across his neck then dropped the head back into the box. It rolled, Darnell's face coming to rest against the side. It looked like one of those shrunken heads in *National Geographic*.

This certainly explained why Dale's APB on Darnell Fowler yielded no returns.

"Christ, Spencer," Dale said. "What happened to you?"

"Let's just say I was kinder to Darnell than he deserved. Listen, I have something I need to ask of you." He snapped his fingers.

Two men in Marshall Village clothes who had been hidden in the shadows stepped forward. Their sudden presence made Dale jump. And to think, they'd been there the whole time.

The men pulled on the opposite ends of Dale's chains, which had been lying on the floor in the darkness. The chains fell from the ceiling, and Dale collapsed to the cement. He was weaker than he thought. The sound of the chains hitting the floor echoed through the building. The men walked over and began to free his wrists from the straps.

"What do you want?" Dale said as he lay like a discarded rag. He was in no position to act like a tough guy, but he did what he could.

"Money," Spencer said.

Even with the two men hovering over him and Spencer standing only feet away, even while being broken, beaten, and tied, Dale couldn't stop himself from laughing out loud. It always came back to money. "Of course. The truth comes out. It's been about money. Just another common thug."

"Oh, really? I haven't told you my plans for the money. Those people at the Marshall Village aren't just any ol' sycophants. They are the descendants of Virginia Dare."

"Um ... come again?" Dale had heard some whacky things in his time at the BEI, but every now and then he still heard something that took him by surprise.

"Haven't I given you enough clues?" He huffed and put his hands on his hips. "Each one of the Marshallites is a direct descendant of the first English-born person in the New World. As am I."

"Virginia Dare died as a child."

Spencer waved his finger. "That's what they want you to believe. That was the myth started in the sixteenth century and perpetuated with the first Dare Stone in 1937."

Dale stood up. His legs wobbled beneath him. "So what? If she did live and have descendants, so what?"

This angered Spencer. He got in Dale's face. "'So what?' Don't you see? It's the government. *Your* government, Agent 'Conley.' The Freemasons. They planted the first Dare Stone. For centuries they've been suppressing the natural descendants of Roanoke, fighting against Walter Raleigh and any other non-Mason of power. The colony didn't disappear. It was wiped out. But Virginia Dare survived. And so have her descendants." He whipped his back to Dale and paced a few feet away.

Dale hated Glenn Downey even more now. Glenn hadn't just wrecked Spencer's body; he completely destroyed his mind. And then Spencer had gone back to work at the *Worldwide Weekly Report,* marinating his brain in wild conspiracy tales. It was the worst possible place for a mind like that to go.

Even after seeing all that scar tissue, Dale felt worse now.

A bright and talented young mind had been completely anni-hilated. And without a mind, there wasn't a soul.

He'd been such a good kid.

"I'm sorry, Spence," Dale said. "So sorry." The words got stuck in his throat and escaped tiny and hoarse. Spencer didn't hear them.

Spencer turned back to him. "The Dare descendants will not be restrained forever."

"What about the people who died? You think you're protecting these people? You've killed three of them."

"Noble sacrifices. Every cause worth fighting for is one worth dying for."

"Let me help them, Spencer. Please." It was a pointless thing to say. His BEI experiences had taught him that trying to reason with a crazy person was like arguing with a traffic light.

Dale thought again about leaving Spencer at the camp and felt a pang of guilt. But then he remembered the two dead people atop Old Rag Mountain and the man who blew his brains out outside the Sheriff's Office. He remembered the terrified look on Caitlin's face as she bawled, duct-taped to a bed.

And the pity dissipated.

"Spoken like a true sheep," Spencer said. "But I need you nonetheless. Your shepherd government will provide me with two million dollars. Then I'll liberate these people by taking them to South America. We'll start a new community, free of the torment we've endured for the last four hundred years."

Spencer motioned toward the two men. One of them grabbed Dale from behind. The other began to tie Dale's hands behind his back.

"Be happy I need you," Spencer said. "Otherwise I would have left you alone to die. Like you did to me. By the way, how's that mother of yours? How's Audrey?"

White-hot rage coursed through Dale at the sound of his mother's name coming from Spencer's lips.

"What did you just say?"

"It's always important to check in on one's mother, Brad. Even when one has a secret identity. You really should check in on her more often up there in Front Royal."

"What have you done, Spencer?"

Dale, his hands now tied behind his back, lunged toward Spencer, but the large men grabbed him from behind. He thrashed and kicked, trying to get free. Spencer laughed casually.

One of the men pulled out some duct tape and slapped a strip over Dale's eyes. They dragged him backwards. A hand with a cloth clasped over Dale's mouth, and a pungent, cool smell filled his nostrils.

"I'll give you another call at the Sheriff's Office and tell you where to meet me," Spencer said just before Dale passed out. "Get me my money, Brad, or I promise you'll wish you had."

CHAPTER FORTY-SIX

DALE WOKE up on a metal floor. He felt movement. Though he couldn't see, by the ribbed steel beneath him and the road noise all around, he knew he was in the back of a van. The vehicle slowed, stopped, and after a moment sped off again, sending Dale sliding to the back. He slammed into the rear doors.

His wrists and ankles were tied. He managed to get himself to his knees and rubbed the duct tape covering his eyes against the side of the van. He worked it up and down but did little more than tear out his eyebrow hairs.

For maybe twenty minutes, the van was on a highway. Smooth, fast, uninterrupted travel. When this ended, Dale felt short stop-and-go motions of city driving and heard the occasional sound of the turn signal. This continued for several more minutes until the van took a left turn and came to a stop. He heard the doors of the cab open, followed by the crunching of footsteps on either side of the van. A moment later, the rear doors opened.

Four strong hands lifted him out of the back of the van. They dropped him, and he fell a good two feet to the ground, landing heavily against gravel and sending a dull pain throughout his battered body.

He heard the door shut then the sound of the van's tires spinning in the gravel before it took off with a roar. Dale was alone.

But not completely alone. He could hear traffic in the distance, and the gravel he'd landed on indicated that he was in some sort of parking lot or driveway. His analytical mind often left him labeled as cold-hearted, but in situations like this it easily countered what would have been a panic-inducing situation for most folks. Dale knew that they'd dropped him off somewhere where he'd be found. Spencer wanted his two million dollars. He wouldn't ditch Dale in the middle of the woods to die. More than likely, he'd dropped him off at the Ashbury Motel.

And with that, Dale's prophecy was proven true. Wilson's voice came from the distance. "Conley!" Dale heard footsteps approach at a run, stopping right beside him . "Hold still for just a second, bud."

"I'm not going anywhere," Dale said.

Wilson had called him "bud." Stressful situations truly do bring out some strange reactions. Wilson worked his fingers under the duct tape on the side of Dale's head. "This is going to hurt." His mater-of-fact-ness in action again.

Wilson yanked the tape from Dale's face with one swift motion. Dale's eyelids stretched off his eyes and slapped back down, eyelashes pulling out.

"What happened, Conley?"

Dale scrunched his eyes together, working some life back into the lids. "Untie me. We have to get to Front Royal."

CHAPTER FORTY-SEVEN

ARANCIA SCREECHED to a halt outside Dale's mother's home. The house's front door was ajar, and a sliver of light fell onto the front porch. The drapes in the front window were disheveled. Dale's heart dropped.

He killed the engine, and he and Wilson ran up to the house. Dale threw the front door open. A sickening feeling of unfamiliarity hit him as he looked in upon his childhood home.

A credenza that stood in the family room near the front door now lay facedown on the ground. The chairs and couch were out of position. One of them was overturned. Mom's knickknacks had been stripped from their shelves. They lay on the floor in a pile of painted sand dollars and shattered porcelain dog legs.

"Mom! *Mom!*"

There was no response, just the ticking of the grandfather clock, whose glass door was now shattered. Dale pushed through the chaos to the back of the house, dodging overturned furniture as he went.

"Mom!!"

He could hear water running. It was coming from the kitchen. He rounded the corner.

Every cabinet and drawer in the kitchen was open. Shattered dishes and silverware were scattered all over the counter and floor. The table, though, was unmolested. It was perfectly clear, save for a vase with a single black rose and, propped neatly against this vase, an envelope with a single word written on the front:

brad

He ran over to the letter, broken plates crunching beneath his boots. He picked it up and paused for just a moment. His hands shook. He tore the envelope. Inside was a folded piece of paper.

> *You've been good about solving the clues so far, but for you to really put your heart into the case, there has be a personal element. I trust this will suffice? Get me my money and leave the Dare descendants in peace and I'll consider returning your mother. Tomorrow evening. Croatoan Island. The old paper factory.*

Dale handed the note to Wilson, his hand shaking.

Wilson quickly read it. "Croatoan Island?"

Dale nodded. "When I was in the warehouse Spencer said something, almost in passing. He said the Marshallites left just like the colonists did. Many people think that when the Roanoke colonists left behind the word *Croatoan* they were referring to Croatoan Island, meaning that the colonists went to the island south of Roanoke. The island isn't called Croatoan anymore. It's Hatteras. In North Carolina. That's where we have to go tomorrow. Back to the Lost Colony. That's where this will all end."

CHAPTER FORTY-EIGHT

THE FOLLOWING EVENING.

Spencer looked at the dozens of people in the warehouse before him. He'd assembled them because he knew they'd soon have visitors. By now Brad Walker would have put all the pieces together and would be arriving with his federal goons.

The warehouse was the largest building in the factory, so it made sense to keep them there. But it was far from a perfect environment. It was cold, the cement floor was dirty, and the big fluorescent bulbs hanging from the ceiling put out harsh light that gave him a sad, sickly feeling. Still, these people would follow him into a sewer if he commanded.

They sat in rows of metal folding chairs, staring at him, not saying a word. Just exactly as he'd instructed them. Spencer had once marveled at Father's ability to brainwash people, but adding hypnosis had taken it to a new level. They would sit there as long as he wanted. They'd sit without food. Hell, they'd even shit themselves. Until he told them to move, they weren't going to budge.

When he sent Camden Marshall away to make his confession, Spencer told the Marshallites that their Father had died. There was great sorrow that day in the Marshall Village. But, of course, their beloved Man in Black assumed the mantle of Father. Spencer wished he would have had more time as Father, but in that short amount of time he'd achieved an exhilarating level of control. And it was all thanks to the little spark of brilliance he'd implemented years earlier.

He'd been fascinated by hypnotism since a visit to the county fair as a child. There, a hypnotist asked his audience to interlace their fingers. When he told them that their hands were now glued together, about half of the people could not pull their fingers apart. Those people were, according to the hypnotist, the ones who were capable of being hypnotized. He took volunteers from this group and had them do the most phenomenal things on the stage. He convinced one man that he was a country music star. This man proceeded to sing his off-key heart out despite the roaring laughter of the crowd. The hypnotist convinced a woman that her body was freezing. She shook violently.

What an awesome power to have! One important lesson Spencer learned from that hypnotist at the fair, though, was that as great as the power of hypnotism might be, it couldn't be used on just anyone. It wasn't until after his time at the CAE that he realized how he could utilize this power with an entire group of people.

He looked out on the faces of the former followers of Camden Marshall. When he first infiltrated Marshall's hippie village and put his plan into motion, he almost felt guilty. Marshall's followers thought of him not as a new messiah—as the people in the CAE had with Father—but as a symbol of hope, a beacon in a lightless world. And yet they were now about to serve their purpose not for Camden Marshall but for him, Spencer Goad.

Soon Brad Walker would arrive to personally witness what Spencer had planned for these people.

CHAPTER FORTY-NINE

IT WAS dark and quiet but for the sound of the surf to the east.

Hatteras Island was a slender strip of land, fifty miles long but with a varying width of only around 1,000 feet or less. It sat off North Carolina's main coast with the Pamlico Sound on one side and the endless Atlantic Ocean on the other. The abandoned factory sat isolated north of the town of Rodanthe. Back in the 1930s, it had produced paper goods. An eight-foot brick perimeter wall surrounded it.

Dale, Taft, and thirty SWAT members walked along the crumbling wall. Dale wore a bulletproof vest under his jacket. In his right hand was the metal briefcase, and he had a tape recorder strapped to his back. It was large and cumbersome, but he knew he might need it tonight. The ground was moist from rainfall earlier in the day, and the men's boots crunched on the cement. They approached the front gate—an iron monstrosity with the words *Bellevue Paper* forged in the center—and looked through the gates into the factory beyond.

There were a half-dozen buildings visible but no people. Weeds grew from cracks in the ground, and everywhere were piles of broken, empty crates. None of the lights throughout the factory were on—total darkness except for a thin line of light creeping out from the edges of a warehouse door in the back. Dale looked at Taft and pointed at this building. Taft grunted.

Wilson stepped up to Dale. He nodded at the briefcase. "You're really going to pay him?"

Dale opened it. Inside were neatly lined stacks of hundred-dollar bills. "A BEI mainstay. Forged bills. With serial numbers we can track. I get a lot of crazies wanting money."

Wilson rapped Dale on the vest. "If he starts shooting, have him aim for your chest."

"Thanks, Wilson."

Taft put his hands on Dale's shoulders. "Okay, Conley. Listen up. Go in swiftly—"

"But cautiously," Dale said. "Observing my surroundings for any contingencies. Keep my poker face on and my head up. Got it." It was the same speech Taft gave him every time he threw him into a life-threatening situation.

Dale took a deep breath and approached the gate. The other men slipped into the darkness behind the perimeter wall.

He tugged on the gate. It held firm in place. He pulled harder, and there was a whining, metallic noise from the corner. Just as he was about to give it another tug, there was a slicing sound and a loud *thwack*.

A bullet struck the ground inches from his foot.

Dale dove back toward the wall, falling on the ground and scraping his knee.

Loud cracks of rifle fire burst through the quiet nighttime air. Taft yelled something, his eyes bulging. Men covered their heads as they ran toward the wall.

The other men crowded in beside Dale, knocking into

him, everyone trying to find where the shots were coming from. The bullets hit the ground relentlessly, like workers hammering shingles into a roof. One of the bullets struck about six inches from Dale's hand, spraying small rocks that peppered his jeans and burned like bee stings. He took out his Model 36.

"Over there!" one of the SWAT members yelled. He pointed toward the corner of the factory grounds.

There was a sniper standing atop the perimeter wall. He had a scoped rifle and was wearing Marshallite clothing. Dale turned to the opposite corner. Another sniper. They had Dale's team in a crossfire.

The SWAT members returned fire. This slowed down the onslaught, but the snipers were able to easily draw cover behind the wall.

Dale aimed his Model 36 but hesitated before pulling the trigger. He remembered what Spencer told him back in the woods. The Marshallites had not only been brainwashed, but they'd also been hypnotized. He lowered his gun and turned to Taft. "We can't fire on those men, sir. They may be hypnotized."

Taft's eyebrows formed a jagged V across his forehead, and for a moment he resembled the Looney Tunes version of the Devil. He ran his hand over his face and looked back into the factory. He hesitated. "Goddamn you, Conley." A bullet struck the wall next to them, and debris fell on his hair. "You'd better be right about this."

Taft smacked one of the SWAT members on the arm. "No rounds! Use the gas."

The SWAT member whipped around. "*Huh?*"

"Just do it!"

"Put your guns away," the man yelled to the rest of the SWAT team. "We're using the CS."

They stowed their guns and brought out tear gas canisters. The lull in their return fire brought a reinvigorated attack from the snipers, which squeezed the men against the wall tighter. One of the SWAT team was struck in the calf and screamed out.

One by one the team began to toss the gas canisters, which clanked on the ground and the brick of the perimeter wall. Gas streamed out with hissing puffs. White clouds formed at each end of the wall, starting small and quickly growing in size. The bullet barrage stopped, and Dale could hear the snipers coughing.

The SWAT team handed out gas masks.

"Blow the damn gate," Taft yelled as he put his mask on.

Dale put a gas mask to his face.

Two SWAT team members darted out to the gate and quickly affixed small discs about three inches across to each side of it. The men ran back to the wall, and one of them took out a bag with a radio detonator.

"*Back!*" the man said.

Everyone took several steps away from the gate.

He pushed the button, and the gate exploded with a terrific crash. Dale felt his stomach pulled toward the gate for a moment, and he stumbled forward to keep his footing. Shards of metal and brick flew out in all directions, and large chunks of it clattered across the street beyond.

When Dale uncovered his face, there was a smoky, dusty, destroyed area where the gate once stood.

He called out to the other men. "Come on!"

They ran into the factory. The man running next to Dale dropped to the ground. *Whooshing* noises came from all directions. They'd run right into a fresh gun assault. Spencer's men had been waiting for them.

After what had been a ten-second reprieve, Dale found himself again in the confusion of high adrenaline and flying lead. Everyone around him scattered to the various buildings, seeking cover. Dale threw his gas mask aside and headed for a small building to his right that was elevated off the ground. It wasn't the greatest cover, but in the split second that he had to decide, it was his best option.

Taft and a couple SWAT members had scrambled to a building just in front of Dale. One of the men yelled out to Taft. "Sir, we *have* to use live ammo."

"Use it, goddammit!"

Though Dale hated the idea of using live bullets against mind-controlled people, in a situation like this, with flying death screaming all around, there was little choice. He held his Model 36 in front of him and dropped to the ground to check the space beneath the building. It was clear. He got on his hands and knees, crawled under the building, and went toward the front.

A couple of Marshallites with pump-action shotguns stood in the doorway of a building several yards away in front of the large warehouse. They weren't shooting but standing like sentries. The buildings funneled in that direction, which meant that as the SWAT team progressed to the warehouse, they'd walk right into a death trap.

The ground beneath Dale was muddy, and it seeped into his clothing. He did his best to stabilize himself and took aim at one of the men with shotguns, zeroing in on his left shin.

As his finger tensed around the trigger, there was a sharp sensation in his right shoulder. His gun fired just as he dropped it. The bullet struck the building above him, and chunks of wood drizzled down upon him.

Someone grabbed him and dragged him into the open. Standing over him was one of the Marshallites. Three inches from Dale's face was a rifle barrel.

CHAPTER FIFTY

THE PEOPLE SCREAMED AGAIN at another burst of automatic gunfire, this one even closer. Spencer raised his hands.

"Children. Children, please. Do not be alarmed," he spoke into the microphone before him. "This is the moment I've been warning you about. Have I not told you that the fascist American government would close in upon us? The time is here. They have come."

He looked out upon the faces. They sat in those chairs, just as he had told them, huddled with each other, looking to the south side of the building where the gunshots were coming from. Despite a full-out gun battle happening just on the other side of the stamped metal wall, they stayed exactly where he told them. This was the sort of power that Father had only dreamed of.

When the whole world came crashing down upon the CAE, a number of Father's supporters fled. The reality of the moment coupled with Father's insanity made them snap to. Father hadn't owned those minds. But now that Spencer was the Father, he had done things better. These people were under his complete control, and unlike Glenn Downey, all of Spencer's followers would go with him to the death.

The ones he had sent out into the real world to be puzzle pieces for his mind games with Brad Walker were weakest of them all. They would gladly kill themselves if Spencer asked. Three of them had done just that. It was going to take a bit more coercing with the majority of them, though. Asking someone to kill oneself could easily snap them out of their trance, as had been the case with Father. So he was going to need to take a shrewder, more calculating approach with the rest of them.

The children were crying, and the families held each other. Their wild eyes looked up at him, pleading for leadership in this most dire of situations. He would provide it. He would offer them a solution. He would do what Glenn could not.

They looked foolish sitting there in their old-fashioned clothes. They were dirty. They hadn't bathed in the six days since he'd taken them from the village. What kind of a mind would be so weak that it would turn over its entire self to one idea? To one *man*? This wasn't the kind of mind the world needed. He was doing the world a favor by erasing them.

"Do not be afraid. Parents, calm your children. Be quiet. This is not how we, as enlightened minds, free of all social constructs of this perverse world, this is not how we shall perish. We are not capitalists. We're not socialists. We're above all that. But for that we have been punished. Remember that there are people in this world who are suffering this very moment. They're suffering in ways you'll never know because you've had Father to provide for you. Haven't I led you in the right direction? Has Father ever steered you wrong?" He raised his hand.

They shook their heads. *No.*

"Then you must trust me now."

They watched him intently. Their eyes never wavered. He could do whatever he wanted. He felt his own power coming out of him like a light, something that would radiate out from the warehouse and touch the very skies. He knew that Brad Walker was out there in the gunfight. And he wanted to show him his light.

The time had come to fully exercise his power.

"Reach under your chairs and bring forth the meal I've provided," he said. "Don't be afraid to eat it. This isn't suicide. It's the ultimate resistance."

CHAPTER FIFTY-ONE

DALE YANKED the barrel out of his face just as the man fired. The roar of the shot crushed him. Instant deafness. Cold mud splattered his face. The gravelly smell of gunpowder burned his nostrils.

His hand was still on the warm barrel. He yanked on it, using it as leverage to topple the smaller man, who fell directly onto Dale. The sharp corner of the tape recorder smashed into Dale's back. A jolt of piercing pain.

He grabbed the man's wrist and yanked hard, twisting to the side, jockeying to a new position. The Marshallite was beneath him now, facedown in the mud. Dale pulled back a big, square fist and whacked it across the back of the man's head. But it didn't work. The son of a bitch was still conscious.

The Marshallite slipped out of his grasp and to his feet. Dale was about to to the same when he saw it—something shiny on the ground a few feet away. His gun. He reached for it, but the Marshallite's boot came crashing down on his wrist. Jolts of pain shot through Dale's arm.

The Marshallite dropped a knee to Dale's chest. The man

went for Dale's neck, and Dale blocked him. Their hands were interlocked. As their muscles quivered in deadlocked competition, their bodies began to squirm closer to the metal briefcase, which he'd dropped at some point earlier. It was inches from him.

A bullet struck the building beside them. For just a moment the other man released his grip. That was all the time Dale needed. He scrambled for the briefcase.

The Marshallite leapt at Dale, but he already had his hands around the handle of the briefcase. He swung it upwards in a a big arch—like a golf club—catching the man in the jaw. There was a sickly *crack* that can only mean a broken bone.

The man collapsed.

Dale took two deep breaths. He put his fingers to the man's neck. There was a pulse. Dale exhaled. A blow like that could have killed the guy.

Dale retrieved the Marshallite's rifle. He pulled back the bolt, cleared the round, and released the magazine. He tossed the cartridge and magazine into the darkness and grabbed his Model 36.

He went to the corner of the building, his gun held at chest level, and looked to the back of the factory. There was the warehouse, a line of light tracing the outline of its large, sliding door. That was where Spencer would have the people.

And that's where he had to go. It was time to face Spencer.

The men with the shotguns were gone, but bullets hissed through the air all around him. Getting to the warehouse was going to be a challenge.

Just as he was about to skirt his way along the perimeter of the factory, he noticed something at the front of the warehouse, illuminated by the light coming out of the door—half a dozen metal drums lined up along the wall. Their lids were gone. He had seen barrels like this before in a similar situation—when he went with government officials to the aftermath of the Collective Agricultural Experiment tragedy.

He'd seen the barrels Glenn Downey used to mix his poison.

Spencer wasn't taking the Marshallites to South America. He was going to follow in Glenn's footsteps.

Dale sprinted toward the warehouse.

CHAPTER FIFTY-TWO

SPENCER LOOKED DOWN at the bowl sitting on the podium in front of him. It wasn't quite like the bowls that the dozens of other people facing him held. His had the pudding and the vodka, but it lacked the cyanide.

One of the hippie-ass things that the Marshall Village sold at the Dayton Farmer's Market, aside from produce, was handmade jewelry. The man in charge of the jewelry-making had been a licensed jeweler in the outside world. When Spencer managed to take over the entire village, he used this man to his advantage. For months he had received small shipments of potassium cyanide, which was legal for the use of cleaning jewelry. Soon he had enough to make his special food.

The trick was to get the poison palatable. As much as any of these people were believers, Spencer knew that if the taste of cyanide touched the tongue, if a person really got the taste of death, then they would snap to. Just as some of Father's followers had. The poison had to be a tolerable experience, even a pleasant one. Thus Spencer mixed his cyanide into large amounts of pudding, sugar, and vodka to help numb the senses.

He held his bowl aloft.

"This is not something to be feared. This is not an evil. This is liberation. Very soon the government will be here. They will come for your children. The gunfight out there will soon spill into this space. And when it does, is that how you want to die? Do you want to die at the hands of an imperialistic regime? They'll take their machine guns to you. They will rape your children and gun them down too. They've done this before. We've seen it. They did this in Vietnam. They did it in South America, Africa. They're afraid. Don't you see? They fear a group of people less than one hundred and fifty strong. A group that wants nothing more than to live their lives in peace. But that's how afraid they are of anyone who knows, anyone who has caught on to their game. Don't die like that. Die like I will. Join me in this ultimate resistance."

Spencer actually did believe everything he had just said. With all his heart. And, in a sense, he truly did feel that he was liberating these people. But he wasn't trying to help them. Minds that weak were beyond help. He was trying to help himself, a true victim of Western imperialism, and they were just one more tool to achieve that end.

He dipped his finger in the pudding and stuck it in his mouth. He showed the crowd the clean finger. "There is no taste. There is no pain. It's just one more meal."

Spencer had tried a tiny amount of the real concoction earlier that day. In truth, there was a taste. Slight, but it was there. A bitterness.

"Raise your bowls with me." He held his bowl at chest height. Everyone facing him did the same. He loved that, when the whole group did exactly as he said, in unison, like troops marching. It thrilled him every time.

"Now. Now is the time—"

There was a loud screech of metal from the back of the room. The door pulled open.

Brad Walker darted into the warehouse.

What perfect timing. What unbelievable, beautiful timing.

CHAPTER FIFTY-THREE

DALE BURST through the doors and quickly assessed the situation. A group of people was seated facing a podium on a wooden dais. They were holding small bowls of what looked like chocolate pudding. Spencer stood before them, gazing out at the crowd.

At the sight of Dale, a good half of the people stood up, rage twisting their faces. They approached him. He didn't raise his gun, not yet. If he incited something here, he was facing certain death.

The missing Marshallites. He'd finally found them. Despite the fact that they looked ready to lynch him, Dale felt a wave of relief not quite like anything he'd experienced before in the BEI.

While the Marshallites were wearing their anachronistic clothing, Spencer was in a long robe, something like a Catholic priest would wear. The sleeves were wide and billowed out below his arms. He shouted at his followers.

"Children. Sit!" Spencer's voice rang out through speakers on either end of the dais. "Do not get up and face this man.

We are not like them. We will not face confrontation like them. We are a peaceful people. *Sit.*"

Those who had been standing went back to their seats. Every face in the room was turned around and looking at Dale, and each of those faces wore either an expression of wrath or fear. Most of the men looked like they could pop out of their seats at any moment. They began to jeer at him.

Government dog.

Come here, military man. See if I bend to your tyranny.

Kill him.

"Silence," Spencer commanded from his podium. "Be peaceful, children." The crowd quieted. "Did I not tell you? They are here. He is the first. This is indeed one of the government men. He is one of those who have come to end our journey. But, please, trust in me as you have before. I will handle this. Gabriel, please take his weapon."

An angry-looking man in the back row with a wide face and an even wider chest stood up and walked over to Dale. He'd never been in a situation before where he needed to turn over his Model 36, and when he handed it to the man, he felt naked and alone.

"Thank you, Gabriel." Spencer said.

The man walked away.

Spencer looked directly at Dale. "You can just drop that briefcase of bogus money right where you are."

The kid even knew about the fake cash. Dale put the briefcase on the ground.

"Now, my child, join me at the altar," Spencer said.

There was a rumble of protest from the Marshallites.

"Children, remember, trust my judgment."

Dale hesitated. Given the circumstances, he didn't have much choice. But he knew what was about to happen in this building, why all the people were holding clay bowls full of a dark brown liquid. Whatever purpose Spencer had in bringing Dale to the front, it had something to do with killing all these people.

"Child, I remind you," Spencer said, still looking right at Dale, "every soul in this room wants to tear you limb from limb. I implore you, join me at the altar." His look was bland and seemingly peaceful—just the sort of look one expects from a robed figure standing behind a podium that faced a group of followers. In Spencer's eyes, though, Dale could see more, a sinister, dark look with just a bit of cocky indignation aimed directly at Dale.

He had little choice but to listen. He walked down the center aisle toward the altar. The Marshallites' heads turned and followed him as he walked by. He took slow, purposeful steps. The smallest action could incite these people. They quivered with hate as he walked by. He saw their lips move. He was a man wearing a steak suit strolling through the tiger den.

Dale stepped onto the dais. The plywood squeaked beneath his weight. Spencer stood twenty feet away. The spotlight that was focused on him made his white robe shine and gave his whole visage the clean, unnatural look of an actor on a stage. Spencer waved his hand toward the podium, beckoning Dale forward.

Dale walked slowly across the dais, and when he got to the podium, Spencer put his arm around him, resting his hand on his lower back.

Spencer looked out onto the audience. "This man is one of them. It is true. But he is also another son of creation. Thus I am willing to give this man a chance, a chance to explain their intentions. For, as I have done with you, I will treat him with mercy."

The Marshallites applauded. There were some cheers.

Spencer turned off his microphone.

"What are you doing, Spencer?" Dale said.

"You came just in time, Brad. We were just about to have a little refreshment. Look."

Dale turned.

Everyone in the audience was holding their bowls of the brown goop. Even after the shock of his entrance, even with the continuous sound of gunfire outside, even with the thought of their own impending death, many of them smiled.

"All of these people are ready to make the ultimate sacrifice to their Father," Spencer said. "They're ready to ascend."

"You said you were taking these people to South America. That you were going to start a new society for the Dare descendants."

"I have to be honest with you, Brad. That was bullshit. These people are no one special. Just ignorant fools stupid enough to follow some hippie's dream of a resource-based economy. There aren't any members of the Dare bloodline in the Marshall Village. Except for me."

"I beg your pardon?"

"Think about my name. Spencer Goad. *Goad.* What does the word *goad* mean, puzzle man? A *goad* is a *dare*. The Dare family has been living in hiding for centuries, right under the Masons' noses."

Dale's face flushed. He'd had enough of Spencer's warped perceptions. "Spencer, dammit. You're not a Dare. It's a homonym! A coincidence! No one was looking for you until you kidnapped over a hundred people. The government's not trying to get you."

Spencer motioned to the door and the continuous *cracks* of gunshots beyond. "No? I find that hard to believe at the moment. But I tell you what, Brad. You wire *real* money to me, and I'll be on my way to South America and you can save all these people."

"My government doesn't—"

"Negotiate with terrorists. Yes, I figured that's what you'd say. Such a pity."

Spencer turned the microphone back on and looked out upon the people. "My children, this government rat has just told me their plan. They intend to torch this place to the ground. To burn every man, woman, and child like they did on the Chesapeake Bay. Dying like that, we will not make our final ascent. Raise your bowls with me now."

Everyone in the audience raised their bowls. Spencer raised his own bowl.

Dale pulled the microphone over. "Stop! You can't listen to this man."

There were angry jeers from the crowd. Some of them stood up, began to approach the podium.

Spencer raised a hand at the audience and leaned toward the microphone. "Children, sit. Before our ultimate resistance, I will allow him to speak. You should be able to hear from the very government's mouth what they have planned for you. Then you will see why our decision here tonight is truly divine."

Those who were standing returned to their seats, though there was still a current of hostility crackling through the crowd.

Spencer took a step back and locked eyes with Dale. There was a slight smirk at the corner of his lips. "Do what you may," he said under his breath.

Dale licked his lips and looked out before him. The crowd moved and shifted, waves in a solid mass. Whispers and shouts. Moving lips and clenched teeth. Curled fists. There were plenty of children, four in the front row alone.

"You cannot listen to this man," Dale said. "He's not who he claims to be. He's not a descendant of Virginia Dare, and he doesn't believe you are either."

There was a fresh wave of anger in the crowd, even

stronger than before. There was screaming. Women wailed. One of the men in the front row threw his chair toward the podium.

Spencer laughed. "It looks like that went over well. Face it, Brad. These people will do whatever I tell them."

"Not if I can get through to them."

Spencer glanced out at the screaming crowd again. "And how are you gonna do that?"

"Like this." Dale pulled the tape recorder from his back and smacked it down on the podium next to the microphone. Before Spencer even had time to react, he'd pushed play.

I have to be honest with you, Brad. That was bullshit. These people are no one special. Just ignorant fools stupid enough to follow some hippie's dream of a resource-based economy. There aren't any members of the Dare bloodline in the Marshall Village. Except for me.

The people in the crowd looked at one another and their surroundings. They spoke and shot scared, concerned glances up at the podium. In the front row, a woman quickly snatched the bowl from a child's hands and put it on the ground.

He'd gotten through to them. A wave of relief rushed over Dale.

Then something grabbed him from behind.

CHAPTER FIFTY-FOUR

SPENCER WRAPPED his arm around Brad's neck. He yanked hard and pulled him back, his heels dragging on the ground, toward the small door in the rear. Back at the *Worldwide Weekly Report* office, Brad had looked surprised when he saw how much Spencer bulked up. Now the bastard was getting an up-close demonstration of just how much stronger he'd gotten.

Spencer kicked the door open and pulled Brad outside. They were at the rear of the factory grounds now, isolated from the rest of the buildings. Moonlight shone off the water of the Pamlico Sound beyond.

There were sounds of gunshots in the distance, but they began to dissipate. The fight was dying down.

Brad finally got his feet beneath him and, despite the strong hold Spencer had on him, threw Spencer over his hip and onto the ground.

Spencer grunted.

Brad dropped to his knee and pulled his fist back. There was fire in his eyes, and Spencer loved it. He almost welcomed the punch, the pain. But he had to pose his next challenge.

"Don't you want to know where they are?" Spencer said. "Your women."

Brad hesitated, lowered his fist. "What have you done with them?"

Spencer laughed and flicked his eyes toward the river, showing Brad the little gift he'd left for him earlier.

In the distance, there was another fishing boat on the water. Just visible were the forms of two people. Brad's mother and his latest tramp. They'd put up quite a struggle when he'd tied them in. Especially the old bitch.

Brad's mouth opened, and palpable fear poured out of his bewildered eyes.

"Now you have a little decision to make," Spencer said and pointed to the dock, about ten feet away. "See those? One of them is for you. The other one is for me."

He'd left them earlier in the day—a shiny new speedboat and an aging fishing boat with a rickety engine.

"Mine's going to take me up the Pamlico Sound," Spencer continued, "toward *The Lost Colony* play. You know it, don't you, Brad?"

"Of course. In Manteo. First staged in 1937, the same year the first Dare Stone was discovered, and still running to this."

"Exactly. And it's where the blasphemous story of Virginia Dare's death is perpetuated. I've already loaded the stage with a hundred pounds of explosives. We're just out of range." He reached into his pocket and retrieved a small, black detonator with a translucent green plastic button in the center. "A mile north of here, this button will light up. All I have to do then is push it. Your choice is this. Use your boat to chase after the bad guy and save dozens, maybe even hundreds of lives, abandoning your two ladies. Or you can save the women and leave the people at Manteo to die."

"Save the women from what?" Brad said.

"From this." Spencer took out another detonator, this one with a lit, red button. He pushed the button. The detonator beeped, and the red light began to flash. "You now have three minutes."

CHAPTER FIFTY-FIVE

THE RAGE GREW out of Dale like a cancerous bulge. He gritted his teeth, and his arm instinctively swung at Spencer. As his fist came down to meet Spencer's face, he pictured it exploding in a mist of teeth and skin and eye.

Spencer dodged the blow, and Dale punched into the muddy ground. He immediately threw another punch, this one connecting and tossing Spencer's face to the side. It was amazing he didn't knock him out.

Spencer laughed and wiped blood from his lip. "Not bad, Brad. But you still haven't incapacitated the bad guy." He looked at his watch. "And look at that. You've already wasted twenty seconds. See ya."

Spencer quickly rolled to the side and sprang to his feet. He darted for the boats and tore off his robe as he ran, beneath which he wore a T-shirt and jeans. Dale sprinted after him. He reached for his Model 36 and found his holster empty before remembering that it had been seized back in the warehouse.

Spencer hopped into the speedboat and untied the rope from the cleat. Dale leapt in behind him and tore at Spencer's arms, pulling him away from the controls. Spencer threw a fist into Dale's ribs, and he staggered back momentarily before grabbing Spencer's arms and throwing him backwards. Spencer hit the rear end of the boat and tumbled onto the dock with a loud slap.

Dale rushed to the controls at the front of the boat.

"Forgetting something?"

Dale turned. Spencer was dangling a set of keys. Dale lunged to the end of the boat and tried to snatch them, but Spencer pulled them away.

Spencer looked at his watch. "Damn, Bradley. You're wasting an awful lot of time. Try as much as you want, but you won't be getting these keys from me. But as you'll see, the keys are there waiting for you in the other boat. The one I so graciously provided."

It was yet another game. The logical choice was to take the fishing boat. As to the choice of saving Susan and his mother or stopping Spencer from getting to Manteo, he knew how he was going to fix that problem as well.

Dale stepped onto the dock and leaned in closer to Spencer. "I've solved all your little riddles so far. I can solve this one."

Spencer stepped back and extended the arm holding the keys behind him. "Time's wasting."

Dale crossed the dock to the other boat, got in, and quickly threw off the rope. He started the engine, pushed the throttle to full blast and headed toward the women in the little boat in the middle of the water a quarter-mile away.

The temperature had dropped since earlier in the day, and the air whipping past his face made his eyes water. Dale had little experience on the water, and the boat bounced about viciously.

Drawing closer, he could see the women's faces. They were screaming. Each of them had their hands tied behind them at the waist. As he crossed the water toward them, he looked back.

Spencer took off from the dock going in the opposite direction. The sleek speedboat zipped across the water. Headed north. To *The Lost Colony* play in Manteo.

He began to hear the women's voices over the roar of his outboard. They were yelling at him for help, to hurry. Spencer had not bothered to gag them. He'd wanted Dale to hear their fear.

Dale tried to slow the boat down in time, but again his lack of nautical skills proved a problem, as he clipped the corner of their boat and went past them by several feet. Running against the boat's forward momentum, he dashed to the back and used the motor as a springboard, leaping off of it and running through the air. He splashed awkwardly in the water and swam to their boat.

He pulled his sopping body aboard, and the women yelled out to him.

"It's right there! Look, look!"

The women had each been tied to one of the boat's two seats. There was a box affixed to the boat under the seat in the back, Susan's seat. It was black steel, a foot wide, and had long, vertical grooves.

"Hurry, Waddy. Hurry," his mother said.

"I'm trying, Mom."

He dropped to his stomach and examined the box. A sense of dread filled him. Bombs were not his specialty.

There was a clock face on top of the box. It read thirty-three seconds.

CHAPTER FIFTY-SIX

SPENCER ENJOYED the fit and finish of a quality product, and this boat was a fine piece of engineering. He bought it seven months ago in preparation for this very night from a man upstate who had more money than sense and had only bought the boat because he saw it in a James Bond movie. To his credit, the man gave Spencer lessons on driving the thing before he left, and now Spencer had full command over it.

Spencer held the highly polished wooden steering wheel in his left hand and felt the power of the engine course through the throttle. Very soon, all his dreams would be secured. The briny air flowing past him and filling his nostrils tasted sweeter than it had any right to. By this time tomorrow, he would be on his way to freedom from the oppressive American government under which he'd lived his twenty-seven years. His only regret was that he would not be able to see how thoroughly he had destroyed Brad Walker's life.

At the rate he was flying across the sound, Walker would soon disappear from his sight, so he turned around and looked one last time upon the man who had taken so very much from him. Brad had abandoned his boat and was now in the women's boat.

Spencer smiled. "Any moment now."

He looked at his watch. He had synchronized a countdown. Twenty-five seconds left.

He would certainly hear the explosion and likely see the ball of flame. But he didn't have time to stop. Any moment now the feds would be wrapping up with the forces he left back at the factory, and they would soon figure out what had happened to him and Walker.

Spencer had been surprised when Brad headed toward the women's boat instead of chasing after him. He had been certain that Brad would take the option of saving more lives over saving two lives that personally matter to him. That would have been the more admirable decision. For once, Spencer had overestimated Brad instead of underestimating.

There was one more stop to make before he made his grand escape to South America. He thought back to earlier when he rigged the Lost Colony theatre with explosives. The damn thing had begun in 1937 and been performed continuously since then, perpetuating the lie that Virginia Dare had perished. It was a Freemason operation. Before he left the U.S. forever, he was going to correct one of its greatest historical errors.

There were ten pounds of explosives on each end of the stage, thirty pounds in storage shelters behind the stage, and fifty pounds spread throughout the seating area. When he pressed the button, the whole place would be destroyed. It was pushing 8:30 p.m. They would be into the second act by now, the audience drowsy with bellies full of food and lies. Spencer would make examples of all of them, especially those involved in tonight's performance. Whereas ruining and killing Brad Walker had been personal, this act was his gift to the world.

He never cared about the money anyway.

He looked at the detonator. The green button had not lit up yet. But it would soon. He was getting very close.

Spencer's motor began to sputter. He whipped around. He could see nothing wrong with it, but he was definitely losing speed. Rapidly. Then it began to make an awful coughing noise. And died.

At first he didn't know what to do. He just stared at the motor. Sometimes things just didn't work right. Hiccups. If he gave it time it might start back up. But several seconds passed, and nothing happened.

He stomped his foot on the bottom of the boat. This couldn't be happening. It wasn't fair. He'd planned things out so well. Everything was accounted for. He jumped up and down, smashing his feet into the floor. Hell, for all he cared he could crash right through into the water. He screamed and tried not to cry.

He lowered the throttle, wiped his eyes, and stepped to the back. He looked over the motor and found the problem. A small rubber hose on the engine had been cleanly severed, and it was spitting amber-colored liquid out into the sound. He put his finger in the stream and brought it to his nose. Gasoline.

He was stranded.

Spencer peered out at the other boats, just visible in the distance. He could see movement. That would be Brad trying to diffuse the bomb.

He looked back at the severed gas line on his motor.

It had been Brad. Goddammit, he just knew it had been Brad Walker.

CHAPTER FIFTY-SEVEN

DALE HOVERED over the bomb with his pocketknife in hand. He looked through the colors of the wires and wondered, like he had recently with the Willard Ledford situation, which one he should cut.

His clothes were soaked from his swim, but there was still a lingering smell of gasoline coming from his jeans. Moments earlier, as he jumped from the speedboat onto the dock, he deftly reached out with his pocketknife and cut Spencer's gas line.

Spencer had tried to present him with an unsolvable conundrum. Save the people he cares about, or save a group of innocent people he'd never met? Spencer had wanted so badly for him to be torn by this decision; he wanted him to anguish over it. But in Dale's experience, there was almost never an unsolvable problem. You just had to give it enough time.

And it never hurts to have a pocketknife.

Spencer's motor would be dying any time now, but Dale didn't have a moment to turn back and look. The bomb before him was reading ten seconds left.

The women screamed louder now, struggling in their bonds. Their words were unintelligible. Every part of him was focused on the bomb.

Seven seconds.

He didn't have time to figure out the color, and in his haste he could easily pick the wrong one. Not that he knew what the right one was.

So there was only one thing he could do. He put his hands on either side of the bomb and tried to lift. It didn't move. The housing must have been solid steel. That explained the grooves in the sides. Like the grooves in a grenade, these were designed to create huge pieces of shrapnel upon detonation.

Four seconds.

Dale planted his feet on the base of the boat, which shook unsteadily beneath him, and put his hands on the sides of the bomb. He thought about the squats he did at the gym, the strength that had built up in his quadriceps through all those years of lifting weights. He thought of his mother, his memories with her, and of his new friend Susan, the girl who'd finally let her hair down.

And he lifted with all he had.

His legs burned like fire, and there was pain in his lower spine. *Lift with your legs, not with your back*. He threw his shoulders back and dug in his heels. Blood rushed to his face. The bomb began to slip beyond his fingertips, sliding down and trying to escape his grasp. His right arm was weaker than usual, still smarting from the blow back at the factory.

He turned to face the water.

Two seconds.

He leaned toward the edge of the boat to toss the bomb over, but before he got a chance, it slipped from his hands.

As it dropped through the air, it rotated a quarter turn, and for a moment the clock looked him right in the face. The hand was one tick away from zero.

The bomb fell on the edge of the boat, and by the way it held this position, it seemed like it wanted to remain there. But then it shifted.

It slid off the side of the boat, and with a small splash it entered the sound.

The boat lifted, and there was a tremendous crack as it tore in half at the middle. It rose ten feet off the sound. A funnel of white water shot out in front of him, and Dale felt himself being pulled to one side of the crest. He and Susan were tossed to the back of the boat, and for just a moment he saw his mother in the other half clamoring to maintain her balance without the use of her hands. Then she disappeared behind a geyser of froth.

Dale felt an impact, and his body was upturned. Everything was black. And filled with a ringing silence. There was nothing before him, nothing behind him. He was engulfed in water. He was in the sound.

He held his arms out to the side and remained perfectly still. Nature would do its thing and pull him toward the surface. If he could just keep his composure, he would find the surface.

He drifted upwards, and with that he thrust his hands above him and pulled with what little was left in him. He broke the surface and sucked in a big helping of air.

Something touched his face. A board. The remnants of the boat were around him. Susan and Mom? Where were they?

The flotsam was piled thick around him, clanking against itself in the now choppy water. He grabbed onto a board and cupped his hand over his eyes. Something round was to his right, something that could be a person. It was Susan's brown hair plastered to her head. She was heaved over, her bound arms draped over a large piece of wood.

Dale let go of his board and swam over to her. She didn't move.

"Susan! Susan!"

As he got closer to her, he heard a noise. A low, constant noise. Moaning. Her back was moving up and down. Breathing. She was alive.

He touched her shoulder, and her head moved. "Susan?"

"I'm ... fine."

He could barely hear her. "Not sure that I agree with that prognosis, Doctor."

He'd found one of them. Now he had to find his mother. He looked about for anything that would resemble the sweatshirt she was wearing—blue with a dolphin painted on it. There was nothing. Only debris.

But then he saw something, something coming to the surface. It was blue, darker than her sweatshirt had been, as dark as it would be if it were sopping wet. Something white next to it. Her hair.

His mother broke the surface of the water and floated face up.

Dale didn't scream, he didn't panic. His training set in, and he pulled his body through the water with big breast-strokes, crashing through the debris like a drill through a piece of wood.

His mother's skin was pale, and the water lapped against her cheeks. In a flash, one of those moments where a million thoughts are processed at once, Dale visualized his entire future. A future that was without the only person in the world that he loved. The only person who knew who he was.

She was floating next to a large chunk of the boat's hull, eight feet across. He put an arm under her small frame and pushed her onto the piece of the boat before climbing on and straddling her. He initiated CPR. Her sopping sweatshirt sloshed beneath his hands.

Then he felt something. She was breathing. Just barely, but she was breathing. He could feel her heartbeat. She was out of it, that was for sure, but she wasn't dead. So he did the first thing that came to mind.

He slapped her.

She awoke with a jolt, and her eyes darted from right to left before centering on Dale. Her face registered confusion for just a moment. Then she scowled.

"That's a hell of a thing to do to your mother."

Dale smiled. "I love you too."

"Well, untie me."

Dale shook his head. Nothing could break Audrey Walker's spirit.

His pocketknife was still in his pocket, and he breathed a sigh of relief. It would've been heartbreaking to lose it. He sawed through his mother's binds. She frowned at the ropes, as mad at them as she was at the person who tied them to her.

"Mom, don't move."

"I'm not goin' anywhere," she said, rubbing her wrists.

Dale quickly swam back to Susan. She was still on the board where he left her. Her eyes were opened in pained slits.

"Susan?"

"Yes?" Her voice was little more than a whisper.

"Can you move?"

"No."

"I need your help. For just a second. I need you to climb onto my back so I can take you over to that big chunk of the boat. Can you do that for me?"

Susan groaned.

"Come on," he said. He left her hands tied together. Since she wouldn't have the strength to hang onto him, he could use her connected arms as a loop around his neck. After he turned his back to her, he put her left hand on his shoulder. "Now put your arms around my neck."

He lowered his face to the water. He could feel her slowly trying to raise her arms over his head. But she slipped.

And sank.

Her half-open eyes disappeared beneath the surface, not even registering the peril of her situation.

Dale spun around and dropped beneath the water. It was dark, terribly dark, but he could just make out Susan's form as she sank further into the nothingness. He swam toward her furiously as she fell. Just as she was disappearing completely into the inky depths, he grabbed the ropes around her wrists, and, as he did, their combined, sinking weight began to pull him down too.

He reached into his pocket and pulled out his knife. He hacked furiously at the ropes.

And then Susan looked right at him. Her eyes were wide open now. There was just a little bit of light from above, and as her face disappeared, Dale saw something in her expression. A calm buried somewhere beneath her panic. As though she was ready to die.

Dale wasn't going to let that happen, though. The moonlight disappeared around them. Total darkness. He gave the ropes around Susan's wrists two more strong hacks with the knife and felt them fall from her hands.

Dale wrapped his arm around Susan's midsection and kicked hard. Her face slumped down to her chest, creating more drag as he tried to get her up.

The moon peeked through the water above and taunted him. Every time he thought he was getting closer to the surface, he found that he had farther yet to go. The air in his lungs grew stale, and his chest got tight. But just when he thought they wouldn't make it, they burst through the top, catching Dale by surprise.

Susan was right side up and still breathing. He awkwardly paddled himself beneath her and got her onto his back. Her arms dangled over his shoulders like ice-laden branches hanging heavily off a tree. He had her face propped up against the back of his neck, and he did his damnedest to keep the water from lapping into her mouth. Her breath blew against his neck slowly, warm against the cold that surrounded him.

When he got back to his mother and the chunk of remaining boat, he pulled around and hooked his hands under Susan's arms. He guided her into the small hull. She slouched down against the remains of one of the boat's seats and opened her eyes. His mother immediately took to her, wiping the hair from her face and propping her up.

"Mom, this is Susan," Dale said. "I believe you've met. I need you to take care of her for me."

"And where do you think you're going?"

Dale scanned the water for Spencer's boat, just a small dot in the distance.

"To see an old friend."

She grabbed his arm. "Go get him, Brad."

Her lips raised into something resembling a smile, and her eyes, for once, registered encouragement. She'd called him Brad. But he would let it pass.

The boat that he had taken out there, the boat that Spencer had given him, was several hundred feet away. Thanks to his poor nautical skills, it had kept going for quite a ways after he clipped the corner of the women's boat. As he swam out to it, he looked to the east and found Spencer again.

He pulled himself into the boat, which felt foreign and strangely solid after the mess of the other boat. He took a deep breath. The rickety engine was still idling. He slammed the throttle down, barreling toward Spencer.

CHAPTER FIFTY-EIGHT

SPENCER WAS STRANDED in the middle of the water, and he was out of range to set off the explosion at *The Lost Colony* play. He looked at the detonator. Its green plastic light was dark, mocking him. How could this be? He thought for sure he was within range. He had tested it earlier, and he had only needed to get a mile north of the factory.

And yet here he was. With an unlit green light on the transmitter. Sitting helpless in the middle of the water. His plan had crumbled before his eyes. He hadn't gotten the money, and the lie of Virginia Dare's death would continue to be perpetuated. He had failed.

But for all that, he was so happy he could've yelled out to the heavens above. Brad Walker was dead.

The sound of the explosion had carried over the water, and he saw the bright flare for an instant before it disappeared, like a puff of flame from a fire breather's mouth.

He had killed the man and, before he died, wrenched his heart from his body. Spencer could taste Brad's agony, his sick dread at the moment he realized that he wouldn't be able to save his mother and his latest lady friend. Brad had known that he was once more responsible for destroying people's lives, right at the moment when he lost his own.

Spencer looked at the speedboat's motor again. It lay there dead, laughing. Brad Walker had given him a good parting shot, but Spencer would find another way to complete his plans. That was how he had gotten this far. Adaptability. It would be a long swim, but Spencer would be able to make it back to the shore. That was the least of his worries. Now he just had to come up with an alternate plan to duck the feds and get out of the country.

He took one more look to the distance where Brad had been blown out of this world. A smile formed on his lips as he thought again of the brilliance with which his plan of destroying Brad had come to fruition. As he looked at the boat, he saw something move. Spencer cursed himself for not bringing binoculars. He had been so prepared during this entire operation that he could forgive his oversight, but it certainly would be helpful to see now.

Whatever he had seen was in motion. It was large. And it was leaving the fishing boat's wreckage. Getting bigger. It was coming toward him. The boat. It was the rickety fishing boat that Spencer had given to Brad. It was headed his direction.

And as it got closer, he could just make out Brad Walker behind the wheel.

Spencer screamed out in pure, guttural rage, a sound something like that which he'd hoped would be Brad Walker's death throes. He screamed so loud that when he finished, his throat was raw. His heart thumped against his ribs, and for a moment he didn't know what he was going to do.

But then he went to the front of the boat and reached under the driver seat. He may not have been prepared enough to bring a pair of binoculars, but he'd had the foresight to remember firepower.

It was one of the old Soviet AK-47s from the Collective

Agricultural Experiment. He swung it around to the back of the boat and fired. This weapon wasn't a quality item in the same way that the speedboat was. It wasn't sleek, it wasn't textural. It didn't make you feel a certain way about yourself. But the AK-47 had it where it counted. The banana-shaped magazine. The reliability of decades of use.

The gun spat bullets out toward the approaching boat in the clackety manner of the Eastern European mainstay. He shot from the hip and wheeled it left and right, over and over, wide arcs that would lay out a fan of deadly metal. One of those bullets would strike Brad Walker.

Then he would finally be done with this mess.

CHAPTER FIFTY-NINE

DALE HELD on to the side of the boat. He had the throttle pushed all the way down, and he was keeping it in line with Spencer's speedboat, a small white shape that was getting larger and larger.

There was a noise in the distance, a snapping sound. Something plopped in the water next to him. The sound continued, louder now. It was a cracking noise, a steady flow, like a rippling electric current.

Gunfire. Automatic gunfire. Spencer was packing heat, and he was shooting at him.

Dale was closer to the speedboat now. He was close enough to see Spencer standing up in the hull. Bullets screeched by, and Dale lowered himself into the boat and blindly guided it forward.

A bullet smashed through the windshield. He flinched to avoid the shards of glass that sprayed down upon him.

He glanced up. Spencer's boat was rapidly drawing closer. There was a twisted, wide-mouthed jeer on Spencer's face, lit up by the fiery muzzle flash shooting from the barrel of his AK-47.

Dale's boat was right on course for a direct collision with Spencer's. Just as he intended. This was a kamikaze mission. There was a good chance that neither he nor Spencer would make it out of this alive. That was an acceptable risk. Somehow this lunatic had to be stopped.

Bullets hissed above him and to the sides. He was barreling right into an angry swarm of bees. One of them struck the side of the boat, and a large chunk of wood tumbled toward him, smacking into the seat beside him. Dale tightened his grip on the steering wheel.

Any moment now.

Please, oh please, let this turn out okay.

There was a sound and a jolt, so quick that he hardly registered it. Then Dale was weightless, gliding through the air with his back arched. His hold on the steering wheel weakened, and his fingers drifted away from it. Both he and the boat rose through the air, and there was a grinding noise beneath him.

The dash and shattered windshield floated away as he moved toward the back of the boat. His legs kicked aimlessly. His arms flailed. And his perspective of the boat changed. He was twisting around in the air. Or maybe the boat was. The boat turned to his right, and as he moved to the aft, the boat corkscrewed above him. The outboard hovered just over his hair, which was standing out in all directions, and for a moment he thought he'd be eaten by the propeller.

Smash. Something hit him in the side hard. A board, a piece of metal. He was under water once again. Surrounded by debris once again. Using what energy that hadn't been wrenched from him, he spun himself around so that when he floated up his lips would find air.

He drifted upwards. A chunk of wood brushed his face. And then there was air. He breathed. Chunks of destroyed boat surrounded him once more. He reached out weakly and grabbed at them with his arms and legs. His ears were still underwater, and the noises around him had a dull, muted quality. Water lapped on his cheeks. The undulations of the water shook him gently, peacefully.

There was peace. He could sleep here. If this was all there was left, he could handle that.

But then he remembered. It wasn't over yet. Spencer.

Groaning, he used the board in his right hand and pulled himself around so that he was floating upward in the water. His eyes slowly opened, as though from a long, deep sleep. It was dark. He could just make out the remains of the two boats.

He felt something on his right side and touched it with his left hand. A jolt of pain shot through him, making his whole body jump. He could feel with his hand a gash on the skin over his ribs, about four inches long. Warm, slippery blood covered his fingers.

Unlike his last experience with boat debris, the damage to these two boats had not been nearly as catastrophic. To his left was the speedboat. It was still right-side up with a gigantic, jagged hole in the starboard side. Farther away and to his right was the old boat he had been in. It was capsized with its nose angled into the water, the motor dangling a good five feet in the air.

The two boats were accounted for, but Spencer wasn't.

Dale looked all around him, scanning the darkness for anything other than boards and nautical corpses. The waves rocked his head around, and the pieces of wood clanked into one another. Nothing resembled a person. Spencer must have still been in the speedboat.

Dale slowly paddled himself over to the speedboat with what strength he had left, slapping at the water on either side of his board. The cut on his side bellowed at him. He inched forward, and as he did, he pictured Spencer popping out from the hole in the side of the boat, his AK-47 in hand, firing at him. There would be little Dale could do to avoid it.

There was a crackling sound to his right, and Dale turned just in time to see the motor on his upturned boat explode. A flash of blinding light. Then a wave of heat. It smacked him across the face, rolling him onto his side. He righted himself, and when he did, he saw that Lady Luck had finally shined upon him in the form of a burning boat. He now had visibility.

In the flickering, yellow-red light, he paddled a couple feet closer to the speedboat and craned his neck to the right to look into the hole. He couldn't see Spencer, but—

Something touched him on the side, and he looked down just in time to see Spencer's hand. Dale swung his elbow, a surge of adrenaline belying his exhaustion.

But he hit only water.

Dale's misplaced swing disoriented him, and he thrashed about. He'd lost hold of his board. He flailed wildly, trying to stay afloat, not knowing from what direction Spencer would be coming. But Dale never touched him.

Then he saw why his first blow hadn't connected. The hand that had touched him was no longer connected to Spencer. It floated upside down in the water, bloody tendrils drifting behind it where the wrist once was. It was already white and bloated, as though Death was eager to claim any part of Spencer Goad.

And just like that, the whole case was done. Some investigations go out like a dimming light. Others go out with a literal bang. Spencer had been blown to bits.

"Spencer..."

Any moment now more pieces would start to appear. It made Dale a little queasy to think that he was swimming in a pool of the man's blood. He pulled the boards to the side, searching the area around the speedboat for other remains.

It would be strange returning to the BEI office in D.C. after this case. Taft would congratulate him and tell him that he was once again the top agent in the Bureau. He'd probably give Dale a medal. But the case had been so close to home that Dale knew he'd always hear its echo.

Now that Spencer was dead.

CHAPTER SIXTY

PAIN HADN'T BEEN a problem for Spencer in years. Not since that fateful night with Darnell and the bullwhip. The *second* time with Darnell and his whip. When Brad abandoned him. Since that night, Spencer had even come to like pain. Controlling it was an addiction. Sometimes he would cut himself on the thigh or upper arms, places people wouldn't see. This helped him to learn to manage his reaction to pain. One had to think of pain as an entity, not something that was hurting you but something that was there. Something that existed. Like warmth. Or noise.

The pain coming out of his left wrist—the bloody, mangled stub that had once housed his hand—was the greatest test of his threshold. He couldn't think of this pain as some sort of warm sensation. This hurt, and it hurt bad.

The wet strip of cloth he'd torn from his tattered shirt dripped brackish water into his mouth. He bit down on it and jerked hard to the right, cinching off the tourniquet he'd tied around the end of his left arm. The bleeding slowed, and the coursing pain eased ever so slightly.

He hid under a chunk of the destroyed speedboat and

watched as Brad searched through the debris for him. A chuckle almost escaped his lips watching Brad panic after the hand touched him. The whole area around him was lit up by the fire on Brad's capsized boat. Flaming debris bounced about on the waves. There were crackling and hissing sounds of fire meeting water.

Brad's back was now turned. He was sifting through a clump of boards. He didn't go about it with any urgency. He must've assumed that Spencer was dead. That's one thing that Spencer never did. Make assumptions. Maintaining constant vigilance was a part of adaptability.

Spencer didn't have much left in his tank. The shock of losing an appendage had left him in a near catatonic state. But Brad too was dragging. His movements were sluggish, like a slow-motion replay. He had a wound on his side, and he was losing a ton of blood. Other than the disparity of hands, they seemed to be in about the same state.

Spencer liked his odds.

He was about twenty feet away from Brad. He lowered himself into the water and swam beneath the piece of rubble he was using as cover. When he slowly resurfaced, there were only five feet separating him and Brad.

Brad pulled boards to the sides, peering under each of them.

A jagged piece of wood floated in front of Spencer. It was about two feet long and six inches wide. The perfect size. He grabbed it.

Brad was so close, he could hear the man breathing, talking to himself. Two feet away.

And then Spencer struck.

He swung the board hard, every muscle in his good arm taut and bulging. The shot was perfectly placed, and the board made a satisfying *crack* as it hit the back of Brad's head.

Brad screamed.

Spencer latched onto Brad's back, put the board in front of his neck, and yanked back hard, gritting his teeth. He loved everything about this. Brad's panic. The closeness, being pressed against his body, hearing his fear, feeling him struggle. This was what he had wanted for so long. If Brad had died back in the explosion, he wouldn't have gotten this satisfaction. He wouldn't have seen it. He wouldn't have felt it.

This was destiny once again. It was meant to happen this way.

Brad coughed and gagged. Spencer could feel it through the board. He loved it. He dug his fingers in tighter.

Spencer could have toyed with Brad like this all night. It was thrilling. But as great as delayed satisfaction can be, it can also create problems. The longer he waited, the greater the chances were that Brad would figure out a way out of his predicament. Brad Walker had a tendency to find a way.

"You always thought you were better than me," Spencer said, "but now who's the one holding the board?"

Spencer pulled back harder. Brad's face turned purple-red, and his eyes were wet and bloodshot. His breath came out in wet gurgles. His tongue bulged between his teeth.

It was time now. Time for his reward. He had deprived himself for so long, planned this thing out so well, all for this moment. Brad's death throes were orgasmic, and the only thing that could bring this thing to a close was his death.

He pressed the board even harder and felt the give of the inner workings of Brad's neck. The esophagus, the muscles, the tendons. They were all being pressed back to his vertebra.

The time had finally come. Finish it.

But then he stopped. He saw something from the corner of his eye.

Beyond the starboard-side hole in the speedboat there

was a light. A tiny green light. The detonator. The collision had thrown it just far enough.

He was within range of Manteo.

And Brad was going to see this before he died.

He gave one final, hard tug of the board to Brad's throat, enough to ensure that he wouldn't follow. Then he swam toward the speedboat.

This was working out beautifully after all.

CHAPTER SIXTY-ONE

DALE'S THROAT WAS ABLAZE. He feebly put his hands to it, willing the pain to cease. His breath came in short, choppy bursts that felt hot and poisonous.

Spencer had left suddenly and with urgency. He was up to something. And whatever it was, it wouldn't be good.

Dale slowly twisted his damaged neck to the left, in the direction Spencer had gone. He spotted him by the speedboat, his shortened arm dangling over the edge of the hole, holding him up. In his remaining hand was the detonator. The one he had shown him earlier. The one that was connected to the explosives at the theatre. Its green plastic button was alight.

A pulsating noise came from above, and both men looked up. An orange and white Coast Guard helicopter was approaching.

Spencer's thumb hovered over the button. "Your government friends have found us. That's okay. We're within range now. Time for the final act."

After years at the BEI, Dale could tell when someone was bluffing. Spencer meant business. If Dale didn't think of something this very moment, all those people at the play would be blown to bits.

He could hardly move. The wound on his side sent out pulses of blinding pain that melded with the fresh pain from his throat. About the only thing he could do in his current state was talk, even if he felt like he'd swallowed a steak knife. But if there was one thing that Dale knew how to do, it was talk.

He threw his right shoulder over and twisted his body around to face Spencer. As he turned his neck, it felt like a piece of old, wet leather that had been left in the sun, all tight and cracked. He began to slowly make his way toward Spencer. His lips barely stayed above the water line. "What do you want, Spencer? Why have you done this?"

"I want you to feel it. To feel what I've gone through all these years since you abandoned me."

"I didn't abandon you. The boat had already taken off. You had already been captured. We both agreed—"

"Agreed to the risks. I remember. But somehow I ended up being the one left behind. If I left one minute earlier I would've been fine, but a guard happened to walk by my cottage the moment I was to go. I couldn't leave until he was gone. It's a funny thing, fate."

The helicopter was louder now. It was right overhead.

There was a board floating beside Spencer. It was about six feet in length. Long and thin. It could work.

"And you hold me responsible for that?" Dale said.

Keep him talking.

"No, I hold you responsible for leaving. You could've come back. Never leave a man behind, isn't that the mantra of your bureaucratic institutions?"

Dale pulled himself closer and closer. He was close enough to see the firelight dancing off Spencer's eyes. "I've thought about that every day since it happened. Whether I should have gone back or not. Maybe I could have. Maybe you're right." He didn't believe that. As much pain as he'd felt since that night years ago, the fact was that Spencer had known the risk and taken it. But right now, Dale's smartest move was to let Spencer think he was right, that he was justified. Whatever it took to get that detonator out of his hand.

A spotlight flashed on them from the helicopter above, and they were bathed in bright, white light. Spencer squinted.

Dale's throat was killing him. Just talking hurt as bad as anything that had happened to him that night. But it was worth it. It was delaying Spencer. And he was drawing closer. The long board was almost within his reach.

"Somehow I don't think that sentiments like that are enough to help you sleep soundly at night," Spencer said. "Are they enough to erase all the rest of your wrongdoings? To silence the deaths of the two people on Old Rag? The two you couldn't save. How about the man who shot himself outside the Sheriff's Office? Or any of the other people you've endangered from your lack of reverence, your nonchalant take on life?"

A voice came from above, a loudspeaker on the helicopter. *Agent Conley?*

The board was inches from him.

Spencer was trying to get into his head, and as much as Dale tried to resist, he couldn't stop him. Somehow Spencer knew him. His darkest worries. Before the BEI, back when he was Brad Walker, Dale had been so very lost. And in that confusion, he'd made mistakes. He often wondered if leaving Spencer had been noble or just another one of his mistakes—even though he'd convinced himself it was not.

He had to stay focused. He couldn't let Spencer get to him. He concentrated instead on the board, which was now right in front of him.

"I've not always been perfect," Dale said, "but I'm damn certain that I never meant to hurt anyone."

Agent Conley, sir? Are you okay?

Spencer was right in front of him. Rage burned in his eyes. "Who the hell are you, Brad? Really. Who is Brad Walker? What are you going to be when you grow up? Do you want to be a reporter or a government man? Do you want to be some protector of the innocent or a childish bully? Even your goddamn car can't decide what it is. Is it a sports car? A muscle car? Italian? American?"

Spencer's words swirled in his head. The kid had broken in and figured him out. He'd seen what no one else had seen in him. The lack of clarity. Confusion.

"*That's* what I want," Spencer said. "I want to know how a worthless, confused sack of shit like you lives with himself. *Who the hell are you, Brad?*"

Dale put his hand on the board.

Calm. Deep breaths. You are what you are, not what you were.

"My name's not Brad," he said. "It's *Dale*."

He smashed his hand down on the end of the board, and the other side went flying up toward Spencer, like a teeter-totter, catching him in the hand. Spencer yelled out, and the detonator flew from his grip.

The small black box twisted around in the air, reached an apex and then headed back down for the water. Spencer reached for it. His finger touched the edge. It slid on his fingertip, dangling, frozen in time.

And then it dropped to the water. The green light disappeared into the darkness.

Spencer roared, and for a moment it looked like he was going to leap out at Dale. He didn't, though. His chest raised and lowered in big gulping breaths. His eyes registered as much confusion as they did anger. He was as exhausted as

Dale. There was nothing left in him. He unhooked his injured arm from the edge of the boat and used his good arm now instead. He slumped down and looked like he might pass out.

A stretcher appeared from the side of the helicopter. The stretcher and a Coast Guardsman descended slowly toward the water on a winch.

It was a good thing that Spencer hadn't made a move because Dale had no more reserves left either. He'd been running on pure adrenaline and hadn't even realized it. He grabbed a large board and flopped down on it, his cheek pressing against the wet wood. He looked at the gash on his side. From the light of the fire, he could see his blood pooling out into the water.

They floated motionless with nothing but the sound of the chopper blades above and their panting below, slow and labored. Spencer's shirt was torn open, and the dancing fire-light threw shadows across the crevices of his scars. His eyes were wide. They darted about. He looked scared, confused. Like someone coming out of sedation. Like a lost, bewildered child.

But when those scared eyes made contact with Dale's, they narrowed, focused. Turned dark. "I could have killed you, you know? Just now."

"Why ... didn't you?" Dale could hardly talk.

"Because," he said and motioned toward the helicopter, "I have one last chance to show the world what you're really made of, Brad Walker. There's only room for one on that stretcher. Neither one of us is going to make it much longer. By the time he comes down the second time, whoever stays behind will be dead. Can you leave me again? Can you leave behind the whipping boy?"

Spencer had thrown more ethical questions at him in the last few days than his soul could handle, and now, as his half-dead body bobbed in the water, he didn't know if he could face another moral dilemma. The man with a severed hand floating next to him had kidnapped 147 people. No one would judge Dale if he took the first stretcher. In fact, everyone he knew would tell him to do just that. But what would *he* think? How would he judge himself another few years down the line?

The light above Dale shifted, and he looked up. The Coast Guardsman was ten feet above with the stretcher next to him. Time came to Dale in short bursts, like a timing light. The man was several feet above him. Then he was beside him. Then he was talking, but Dale couldn't hear him.

Dale squinted and looked the man right in the eye. His lips continued to move, and sound finally came out. "Agent Conley?"

"Here..." Dale heard himself say.

"Sir, we need to get you up."

The Coast Guardsman had asked for Dale by name, which meant that the man had made his decision on whom to save first—the federal agent or the murderous lunatic the agent had been tracking.

Dale had determined some time ago that life was simple. Life was nothing more than decisions. A man was determined by the decisions he made. And Dale didn't want to live another day with regretted decisions.

"No," Dale whispered. "Take him first..."

The Coast Guardsman turned and looked at Spencer, then back to Dale. "Sir?"

"Do it."

"Um ... yes, sir."

Dale blinked, and the man was no longer there. A hoarse breath left Dale's lips, and his head slowly slid to the side.

The Coast Guardsman put Spencer onto the stretcher. As he moved him from the boat, Dale saw that Spencer's eyes were closed. He had passed out sometime during Dale's decision.

Dale blinked again, and the Coast Guardsman and the stretcher were above him, ascending toward the bright light beaming down upon him. Up and up and up. Dale saw Spencer's face. Unconscious.

He disappeared into the light.

Dale's eyes closed.

CHAPTER SIXTY-TWO

THERE WAS A NOISE. Something echoing. It rattled in his brain. Although the brightness was all around him, something was trying to come through. A thumping noise and something higher pitched. *Lee. Thump, thump. Lee. Lee.*

A beam of blackness broke through the light. And disappeared. And returned.

Thump, thump. Lee! Thump, thump.

The darkness pierced the light and spread out to the sides, stretching to the periphery of his vision. A black sky above him. And something else. A round shape. He recognized it. A helicopter. Its rotor was thumping. The sound brought pain to his temples.

A face came into his vision. A man. He wore a helmet.

"Agent Conley, sir? Agent Conley?"

He felt something on his side, and his head rattled back and forth, disorienting him, throwing the images around. The man, the helicopter.

His eyes closed.

He was flying. No, he was floating. Rising. There was light above him, and as he continued to rise, it pushed the darkness away again.

All was white.

———

He was in a square space. There were two people near him. Coast Guardsmen. He was in the back of the helicopter.

There was a flat metal ceiling above him. His eyes began to close again, but something told him to stop.

His head turned, almost as if by its own accord. Next to him was Spencer. On a stretcher. His eyes were closed. They'd been like this before. Two men, tied to beds, beaten.

Spencer looked like a good kid. He'd always looked like a good kid to Dale.

A surge of pain came to Dale's stomach, and his mouth opened wide. The faces of the Coast Guardsmen appeared above. They spoke, but he didn't hear. One of them put a hand to his shoulder.

And all was white again.

CHAPTER SIXTY-THREE

HE WASN'T sure how long he had been there, but as the fog began to lift, Dale realized that he was in a hospital room. He felt dull all over. They'd drugged him up. There was something on his arm. An IV.

Someone sat at the chair at the end of his bed. It was Special Agent in Charge Walter Taft. He stood up and walked over to Dale.

"I always like waking up to a beautiful face," Dale said. He regretted speaking. It felt like he'd swallowed a pack of razor blades and they got stuck halfway down.

"You did good, Conley. Real good," Taft said with a smile. The last time Dale remembered him smiling was when he found an unopened pack of smokes on the sidewalk. "We got all the Marshall folks out of there. Not a single fatality. I'm going to put you up for a medal for this."

"Thank you, sir. And Spencer?"

Taft waved it off. "Bastard didn't even make it to the hospital."

Dale expected as much. In his last fuzzy memory of Spencer, there was little, if any, life remaining.

Dale was blank. He couldn't react. As much as he had been through with Spencer, as unfair as it had been that Glenn Downey and the CAE had short-circuited his brain, the undeniable truth was that Spencer had become a monster. The BEI operating instructions requested that agents remain emotionally impartial to all cases, even those in which an agent had a personal connection.

So all Dale did was nod.

"I need you to sign," Taft said. He held out a pen and an open manila folder.

Paperwork is like a really tough flu bug. It keeps fighting to the very end.

Dale took the pen. His hand was still weak.

Form BEI32A9: Case Finalization. At the end of each BEI case, the agent signs over all accountability and is expunged from the record. Officially, the liaison agent is given credit. The press would know FBI Special Agent Cody Wilson as the man who took down Spencer Goad.

Dale signed the form.

CHAPTER SIXTY-FOUR

DALE WAS happy to be in his street clothes again—that is, what remained of his street clothes. His T-shirt had been properly destroyed during all his misadventures, and the hospital saw it prudent to dispose of it. Thankfully they saved his jeans. If they'd tossed out his 501s, there would have been hell to pay.

He asked Taft to buy him a new T-shirt from the gift shop. Taft returned with the only shirt left in the store. Fortunately, it fit Dale well and was a nice shade of brown. The downside was that it read, *Get well, Grandma.*

But it was a good conversation starter. Dale had been flirting up the hospital's front desk receptionist for the past ten minutes. Karen was twenty-three, worked nearly full-time, took classes at the local community college, and had gorgeous hair. She thought the shirt was a riot.

Dale was now planning on working the Grandma shirt into his regular rotation. He loved happy accidents. Before Karen could get too attached, though, there was a tapping on Dale's shoulder. He turned around.

It was Susan.

Her eyes were tired, her face puffy and covered in painful-looking red scratches. Her good looks were so natural that even now they blew Karen's out of the water. *This* was a woman.

She motioned for Dale to follow her, and they stepped away from the desk. Dale gave a little goodbye wave to Karen, who scowled at Susan before returning to her work.

There was a quality to Susan's eyes, something that hadn't been there before. When two people had been through what they had, there would be a strange connection between them forever. Like there had been between Dale and Spencer.

"I want to thank you for last night," Susan said.

"I knew you'd end up telling me that someday."

She laughed. "Never a reverent moment for you, is there?"

"Rarely. You headed back to Virginia?" He affected a tone of disappointment, just so she'd know he was still interested.

She nodded. "Yeah."

"Give your brother a knee to the stomach for me."

Susan scoffed. "After everything that happened last night, do you think I'll let a person like Brian push me around again?" She gazed into him for a long moment with that new look in her eyes. "I have to admit, I was wrong about you. You proved your true mettle."

"So does that mean I can buy you dinner?" His asking her out was partly his natural inclination. After all, he'd had salacious thoughts since he first saw her. But after the previous night and the bond they now shared, Dale wondered if maybe, for once, he might be able to make something real out of a date.

Susan smiled. She put her hand on his chest and gazed up at him. Those eyes again. Hazel. Her hair was down. Dale touched it, putting his hand next to her face.

He leaned in, and she did too. Their lips met.

This kiss was unlike the one in the motel. It was long and

strong, and Dale knew there was something to it. Like the look in her eyes. This could be something that could fill the void in him. Something more for Dale Conley. Something other than tacky smiles and hollow pickup lines. Something to replace the memories and Brad Walker.

Susan finally pulled away. "No. You can't take me to dinner." She paused, and her face was surprisingly blank. She either didn't realize or didn't care that she just killed a small piece of his hope. "But I do want you to know that you're someone I'll never forget."

She turned and went toward the front entrance. Dale watched her walk away, shoes tapping on the floor.

There was a voice behind him.

"Hey there, All-Star." It was Wilson. He leaned past Dale and looked at the entrance where Susan was leaving. "Crash and burn, huh?"

Dale looked down the hallway too. Susan was just getting in the revolving door. She stepped through, took a turn, and was gone.

"Yeah," Dale said. "I suppose so."

————

Wilson took Dale to the parking lot with the promise of a "surprise." Dale was sore and stiff as could be, even with the pain meds they'd put him on, but Wilson helped with his walking, even kept a hand on his shoulder. Deep down, Wilson was a softy.

And, Dale finally realized, he wasn't a half-bad guy after all.

It was a clear day outside, mild and comfortable. When they rounded a corner, Dale saw the surprise.

It was Arancia, glistening in the sun like a piece of pure steel sex.

"Snatched your keys. Went all the way back to Virginia and drove her here myself," Wilson said, beaming.

Dale nodded and gave him a pat on the shoulder.

"Damn decent of you, Wilson." He looked at Wilson and smiled. Wilson's Custom Cruiser was parked right next to Arancia. "But why'd you have to park so close?"

He checked for door dings.

"Maybe if you treated a real woman as well as you treated 'her,' you might land yourself a keeper someday."

There went Wilson's brutal objectivity again.

"Look on the passenger seat," Wilson said. "There's another surprise for you."

Dale looked through the window. Sitting on the seat was his Model 36. He was pleased.

"They found it in the warehouse, stuffed in an apple crate."

"Was your latest BEI adventure everything you thought it would be?" Dale said.

Wilson loosened his tie. "I need to remind Taft of my request to stop getting these assignments."

"BEI assignments in general or those with me as a partner?" Dale was testing the waters. He didn't have many friends, and a guy like Wilson was the kind you wanted on your side.

Wilson grinned. "Hey, you're the Bureau's golden boy again. If I gotta have a BEI case, I might as well work with the best."

"Flattery will get you nowhere."

Wilson got in his station wagon, gave Dale a half-wave-half-salute, and took off.

CHAPTER SIXTY-FIVE

DALE SAT at a booth in Rich's Diner.

A coffee was on the table in front of him. He aimlessly twirled a spoon in his mug and watched as it clinked against the sides. The assignment had wiped his brain clean, and Taft had been gracious enough to give him some time off.

Julia walked up to his table and set down a piece of apple pie.

"How's it going, secret agent man?"

He glanced up from his coffee.

She looked really good today. Her hair was in big waves, a style more classic and less trendy than the one she had been wearing the last time he saw her. There was a relaxed smile on her face. Her eyes were bright. She looked like she was having a good day.

"It's going okay," Dale said.

"You don't look okay. Your latest mission not treat you well?"

Dale grinned. By the way she said *mission*, he knew she was once again joshing him. She was coy, that Julia. This girl was dangerous. In the best possible way. After what he'd just been through, it would be fun to play this game again.

"Well, I stopped the bad guy, and he sure as hell isn't coming back," Dale said. "But I didn't end up getting the girl in the end. In fact, she completely rejected me."

Julia looked at him for a moment, and her lips parted. Her expression changed. She believed him finally. At least about losing the girl.

"Sounds like a pretty crappy mission, if you ask me." Her tone imparted a level of concern. "You know what always brightens my day?"

"What's that?"

Julia pointed at the plate in front of Dale. "Apple pie."

This girl was great. And Dale wasn't going to waste any more time. He intended to make up for his romantic short-comings yesterday at the hospital.

"That's all well and good," he said, "but you know what makes me feel even better?"

"What?"

"A meal with a beautiful woman. How about we have dinner tonight?"

"I don't think so."

Dale nodded and twirled the spoon in his mug again. "You're the second lady in as many days who's rejected me."

"I didn't say I wouldn't have a meal with you. I just turned down your dinner offer."

Up and down. Julia's spunk was never-ending. Dale liked that. He liked it a lot. And her constant propagating and subsequent dashing of his hopes only served to further pique his interest.

"So what do you have in mind?" Dale said.

"This." She reached into the nearby cooler and pulled out another slice of apple pie. She sat down across from him.

"My shift just ended. Tell me about yourself, Dale Conley."

Everything works out if you give it time.

"Well," Dale said, "where do I begin?"

ALSO BY ERIK CARTER

ACKNOWLEDGMENTS

For their involvement with *Stone Groove*, I would like to give a sincere thank you to:

My beta readers, for giving me such fantastic feedback: Mom, Dad, Jim, Aunt Amy, April, and JMM.

The wonderful April Snellings, for amazing editing and being the type of friend who is always willing to evaluate sentences or website graphics or cover design or ...

Dad, for copious police procedure, automotive, firearm, and 1970s period information.

Jim, for being my go-to '70s guy.

Mom, for further '70s insight and a lady's perspective.

JMM, for various assistance.

Micah, my friend and brother, for aeronautical technical information.

Aunt Amy, for medical advice and being my #1 fan.

Dave King, for astute editorial assistance.